KRIMSON FLARE

KRIMSON EMPIRE BOOK 4

JULIA HUNI

KRIMSON FLARE
KRIMSON EMPIRE
BOOK 4

JULIA HUNI

Krimson Flare Copyright © 2020 by Julia Huni

All rights reserved

All names, settings, characters, and incidents in this book are fictional. Any resemblance to someone or something you know or have read about, living or dead, is purely coincidental. This is fiction. They're all made up.

The distribution of this book without permission is a theft of the author's intellectual property. If you would like permission to use material from the book (other than a short excerpt for review purposes), please contact info@juliahuni.com. Thank you for your support of the author's rights.

Cover by Deranged Doctor Designs

Originally published by Craig Martelle, Inc.

Published by
IPH Media, LLC
PO Box 62
Sisters, Oregon 97759

Second US edition, August, 2023

In loving memory of:
Kathleen Kukowski
Jerome Kukowski
Margaret Huni
Robert Huni
Tom Huni
Shawn Ryan
Micky Cocker

CHAPTER 1

"WHAT ARE THESE THINGS?" Quinn Templeton asked Liz Marconi.

Twenty-six cubes, each a meter high, lay along the cargo bay wall of the *Swan of the Night*. The metal cases bore no markings, which struck Quinn as suspicious. That and the fact that the *Swan* had received them from an unmarked shuttle while parked in orbit around a moon far from an inhabited planet. She walked along the line, checking the straps holding them to the deck.

The other woman pushed her hand through her short, dishwater blonde hair. "The communication satellites." She returned to swiping through screens on her comtab. "They're going to replace Federation equipment at the jump points on the Russosken planets. There have been some unusual outages."

"*Formerly* Russosken planets," Quinn corrected with a smile. Lunesco was the first planet they had helped break free from the Russosken. Others had followed. "Why aren't they labeled? It's not often you find a completely blank crate."

"They're Commonwealth equipment." Liz put a finger to her lips in mock warning. "Something Tony arranged. But the Commonwealth is trying to be low key about it. They probably don't want to jeopardize diplomatic relations with the Federation."

"Relations aren't very good, so what difference does it make?"

"Actually, relations are much better than anyone in the Federation is allowed to know. Your premier calls us the Krimson Empire, but that's internal rhetoric. Outside the Federation, he's always trying to buddy up to President Verdrahn."

"Us?" Quinn repeated. "I thought you Marconis were neutral."

"Don't you believe it," Liz said. "We're one hundred percent Commonwealth citizens, and proud of it."

"Except when it's inconvenient for work." Maerk Whiting, Liz's partner and ex-husband, walked into the cargo bay. "That's the key word. Convenient."

"Hey!" Liz slapped his arm. "You say that like it's a bad thing! We're always loyal to the Commonwealth; we just don't advertise it when we're dealing with Federation citizens."

"Or thugs."

Liz glowered.

"Oh, come on," Maerk said. "You know Lou's best clients are thugs. Heck, she likes to pretend she's one herself. The fabled Marconi family."

"The Marconis are not thugs." Liz lifted her nose in the air.

"Sorry, my mistake." Maerk winked at Quinn. "Not thugs. How about gang? Clan? Syndicate? Cartel?"

"Family," Liz said firmly. "If others choose to see us as those other things, that's on them, not us. We're a family business. A business that sometimes takes on less-than-savory jobs, in the service of the Commonwealth."

"And for the credits," Maerk said.

"We have to make a living," Liz said. "And we only work for the bad guys if it will help the good guys."

"I guess it all depends on how you define 'good' guys." Quinn chuckled. "And since we just helped a bunch of planets escape the iron hand of the Russosken, I guess that makes us good guys."

"Exactly." Liz pushed past Maerk toward the internal hatch. "Let's get these things deployed."

THE *SWAN* ARRIVED in the Lunesco System right on schedule. Quinn watched from the jump seat as Maerk and Liz worked through the post-jump checklist and set in a course. It was the middle of the night shift according to the ship's clock, and the kids were asleep in their bunks on the deck above the crew lounge.

"Checklist complete," Maerk said over his shoulder. "You can get the node set up. End showed you how to complete the launch, right? We'll be in the release location in about twenty minutes."

"On it," Quinn said through a yawn. She unlatched her harness and headed to the cargo bay. Undogging the hatches slowed her and stopping for a cup of coffee didn't help. Fortunately, she and End had done the pre-deployment setup earlier in the evening.

She drained her coffee, mag-locked the cup to a shelf, and moved to the open crate set away from the wall for easy access. She plugged her comtab into the first one and ran a system check. "Ready to deploy."

"Roger," Maerk replied. "Lowering the gravity in the cargo bay so you can move it into the airlock."

The kinks in her spine unfolded as gravity lightened. When her feet drifted off the floor, she activated her magnetic soles and squatted to lift the device out of the crate. It rose smoothly, twisting slightly as one corner caught on the side of the box. She stopped the spin and pressed it toward the airlock.

When she reached the hatch, it popped open ahead of her. "Thanks for the assist!"

"No problem," Maerk said. "I'll tell you when we're ready. We'll be on target in three minutes."

"It'll take me that long to get through the security settings." She latched the device to the airlock deck so it wouldn't float away as she tapped the buttons, then started through the security setup. She and Tony had worked hard to free these worlds from the Russosken, but that left them in a no-man's-land between nations. Providing a comm gateway to the Commonwealth—with access to trade and protection—was the least she could do. Then she could consider it a job well done and get on with her new life. "I'm ready," she said a few minutes later.

"Roger, we're in position," Liz replied. "Release when ready."

With a tap on the panel, a robotic arm swung out from the wall and grasped the device. Quinn pushed off the deck at an angle that took her through the hatch. She closed the lock and set the controls to cycle. "System is connected to the net. Registering location correctly. All functions green. Releasing now."

The airlock pressure lowered, bars turning from green to red on the access panel. When the airlock reached vacuum, the outer hatch popped open. The arm swung out into space and released its grip. Once it had exited the craft, tiny attitude adjusters on the comm box fired, rotating the blocky thing into the proper alignment and easing it away from the ship.

"Green across the board." Quinn tapped at her comtab. "I'm going to call Doug." She placed a call through the new system to the planet.

"Doug, it's Quinn!"

"Quinn!" Doug's voice came through loud and clear. After a moment, his face appeared onscreen. "Did you bring the new comm box?"

"Up and running." She headed back to the cargo bay. "I'm using it now. I sent a checklist—run those tests. If anything is less than optimal, let me know and I can tweak it."

"That thing has protection, right?"

"Of course," Quinn said. "We aren't going to leave a comm relay laying around for the Federation to burn out. It's got the full suite of laser shields and we'll launch the backup next."

"Sweet. You and Tony coming down to Lunesco?"

"Tony's not here. And we have a half-dozen more systems to get to, so I'll have to visit another time. Everything good for you?"

"I've been in touch with the new *nachal'nik*." Doug's lips twisted. "Fyo seems like a good guy. Of course, it's pretty clear Francine is steering the ship." He grinned. "I knew that girl was in line for bigger things than bumming around the galaxy with the Marconis." He grimaced. "Not that there's anything wrong with that!"

Quinn laughed. "Bumming around the galaxy with the Marconis suits me fine. I don't need 'bigger things.' They usually lead to bigger problems."

"True enough." Doug glanced down. "I'm reading all green. Looks like I could send a personal memo to the premier if I wanted."

"I think I'd stay away from that if I were you. He might not be too happy with what you've been up to."

Doug laughed. "Good advice. Stay safe out there, Quinn."

"I will. Talk to you later." She shut down the connection and turned to focus on the backup relay. This one would stay turned off and hidden, passively logging pings from the primary. If it didn't receive a signal from the primary for more than three cycles, it would turn on and send a message to the planet. Then it could be activated to replace the primary or sent back into hibernation. More populous planets kept multiple backups, but a low-income place like Lunesco would have to make do with one.

TONY BERGEN PULLED his hat down his forehead. After years of working as an operative, it was an easy, almost instinctive action that both shaded his eyes and lowered the chances of a surveillance system matching his face. Not that he needed to hide from the cameras here in the heart of the Commonwealth. He smirked at the thought but left the hat in place.

He entered a broad courtyard, approaching a fountain and a few statues. Ornamental trees stood guard along two sides of Independence Plaza with government buildings lining the other two. Carefully-trimmed plots of grass broke up the vast stretch of stone, with benches, flowerbeds, and shrubs laid out in attractive patterns. The scent of recently-trimmed lawn tickled his nose. Tourists strolled about, while others—likely office drones from the two buildings—strode purposefully across the paving.

Tony slowed to watch a juggler perform, both because he enjoyed the spectacle and because he liked to mess with the surveillance algorithm as often as possible. Then he picked up the pace and marched to the closest building.

He pushed through the large double-doors and crossed a wide marble lobby. Ignoring the chairs ringing the room, he went directly to the desk at the back. He flashed the VIP visitor badge at the guard, then slapped his hand down on the ID panel. The screen went green, and a door to the right opened. Tony smiled at the guard and went through.

Another, smaller lobby waited for him. A bank of elevators filled the far wall, and wide stairs led upward on the right. He started that direction but switched course when one of the elevators dinged. A young woman stepped out, holding the door when she saw him approaching.

"Thanks!" He touched the brim of his hat with a smile as he stepped into the car.

The woman nodded, and the doors shut.

On the fifth floor, he stepped out. Following the map that had automatically appeared on his comtab, he wound through a maze of corridors, nodding to other government employees as he went. When he reached room 568, he went in.

The room was small, with a single door in each wall and a chair on either side of each door. He turned to look at the entry he'd used—it looked identical to the other three, except for a small green sign that said "exit" above it. The room screamed efficiency and order.

With a shrug, he took a seat.

A few minutes later, the door directly across from the exit opened. An older woman smiled at him, then beckoned with a crooked finger. Tony stood and followed her into the office.

This room was much wider than the waiting room, with four tall windows stretching from the high ceiling to knee height. Heavy blue curtains framed each window. A large desk sat at the left end of the room, and a small seating area with a plush couch and two well-upholstered chairs took up the right side. A closed door presumably led to the room to the left of the waiting room, and another door might lead to the room on the right. Assistants' offices or a bathroom? Tony made note of the exits and followed the woman to the seating area.

"Antonin Marconi." A woman rose from the couch. Fine lines crinkled at the corners of her blue eyes, behind half-moon glasses. Her white teeth nearly blinded. She wore the conservative clothing typical of a career public servant. Her short hair curled in a salt-and-cinnamon helmet. "It is such a pleasure to finally meet you!"

"Dr. Fallstaff." He nodded respectfully and removed his hat. "Why is it such a pleasure?"

She laughed—a practiced, polite laugh—and gestured to the couch. After taking one of the side chairs, she looked him over for a moment. "I've read your file. You've been undercover for longer than any other Commonwealth operative."

"Had been," Tony said.

"I beg your pardon?"

"I *had been* undercover longer than any other operative," Tony repeated. "I'm retired now. Have been for months."

"Yes. Of course." Her eyes narrowed for a moment, then she shook it off. "Can I offer you refreshments? Tea, coffee, water? These Tornell butter biscuits are excellent. I have them imported from Romara. I'm afraid I got addicted when I was stationed there. But I'm always happy to share with someone who appreciates them."

"Not really my thing," Tony said. Tornell butter biscuits were high-end confections. The woman was obviously trying to establish her bona fides as a VIP. He wasn't sure why, but he took note. Selecting a bottle of water, he surreptitiously checked the seal before opening it. He had no doubt Dr. Fallstaff could find a way to introduce a contaminant to a sealed bottle, but why bother? They were on the same side. And it would be easier to have someone tag him in the halls. He gave himself a mental shake. Old habits died hard. "I'm more of a Choco-roll man, myself. Sugar, fat, and empty calories."

She set the plate back on the low table, carefully aligning it to the edge. "Being in the diplomatic corps can spoil one."

Tony decided to come to the point. "Why did you invite me here, Dr. Fallstaff? I'm a busy man. Lots of puttering and tinkering to do when you're retired."

"I'm sure there is. I need your report on the current state of the Federation."

"As I mentioned, I'm retired." Tony sipped the water.

"Perhaps," Fallstaff said. "I'd hate to have to reactivate you, but it is within the government's purview to do so. That requires so much paperwork, and it means we'd have to buy you another cake when you retire again."

"You didn't buy me one the first time," Tony said. "I would prefer to remain retired. And I filed a report with my *former* handler when I arrived yesterday. As a courtesy. I'm not required to do that."

"Yes, I know. That's why I called you here. Your report was quite vague. I need specifics." She sat forward in her chair, pulling a comtab out of a pocket. "I want troop strength, general impressions of the government, attitudes of any civilians you might have encountered, the works. Names, locations, everything."

"Why?" Tony crossed his arms over his chest. "You have any number of active operators within the Federation. Why do you need my report?"

Fallstaff looked away, her confidence fading for the first time. She took a deep breath, seeming to come to a decision. "We don't."

"Don't what?" Tony asked.

"Don't have any operatives." Her lips pursed. "Every Commonwealth operative, even the deep-plants like you, has stopped communicating. Three weeks ago, it all stopped, like a switch being flipped. We're getting nothing."

CHAPTER 2

"YOU'RE GETTING NOTHING," Tony repeated. "What does that mean? I listened to the Federation news on my way here, so obviously regular communication channels are open. I know for a fact there are dozens of operatives who communicate via open channels. Hell, Harvard is one of ours, and he was on today." The Federation had no idea the famous newscaster Sven Harvard sent coded messages to his handlers in almost every newscast. Tony knew because he had helped Sven develop the code.

"Obviously, I didn't mean him," Fallstaff snapped.

"Then what did you mean?" Tony asked. "If it's just covert comms, that sounds like a technical issue. Have you checked the equipment? Maybe try turning it off and on?"

Fallstaff glared. "Of course we've checked it. Well, I haven't, but my people have."

"And?"

"And the comms are down." Fallstaff stood and stalked across the room.

Tony stared after her. "So, you've got a technical glitch, but you're still getting information from inside the Federation?"

"Some." Her jaw tightened.

"Then what's with all the drama? Get your comm guys to fix it. I'll give you a detailed report of my last visit. You don't need to try to guilt me into it with a manufactured crisis."

"It wasn't manufactured," Fallstaff sulked. "I might have exaggerated slightly to get your attention. But we've lost access to several top undercover operatives."

"Who? Anyone I know?"

Fallstaff reeled off a list of codenames.

"*Futz.*" Tony rubbed the back of his neck. He really didn't want to get back into that world, but he couldn't leave his compatriots—some of them friends—in the lurch. "What do you want from me?"

"You're going back." It wasn't a question.

After a long pause, Tony nodded.

"Can you check in with a couple of those agents? In-person, just to make sure they're still alive and well?" She grimaced. "You can report back however you want. Maybe get word to Harvard—I know the two of you worked together."

Tony leveled a look at her. "I'm not going to Romara. It's too hot. I'm a wanted man."

"Harvard isn't in Romara anymore," Fallstaff said. "His studio moved him to Robinson's World. Apparently, it's where all the budget-conscious broadcasters are working."

Tony looked away. He could get to Robinson's. In fact, that was where he intended to rejoin the family. "Fine. I have to go there anyway. I'll have Harvard send word."

⸺

QUINN PULLED out a chair and joined Liz, Maerk, Ellianne, and Lucas at the table in the *Swan's* lounge. End, Liz and Maerk's son, placed a bowl on the table with a flourish. "Ta-dah! My specialty, Torworld casserole."

"Cool!" Lucas pushed his plate forward. "Torworld is an awesome game."

"What's in it?" Ellianne wrinkled her nose. She had been unimpressed with End's orc noodle soup.

To be fair, so had Quinn. The broth had been tasteless. Ferben globes, a vegetable native to Ferben with the appearance and consistency of large eyeballs, had added a creepy appearance and slimy texture. The noodles had been overcooked.

"Nothing like orc soup," End said. "This has sautéed veggies, noodles, cheese, ground meat. Try it, you'll like it."

Lucas scooped a huge portion and dug into it. "Tastes like chili mac." He sounded the tiniest bit disappointed.

"Close," End said, "but I added a secret ingredient."

"Not more Ferben globes." Ellianne paused with a half-full spoon over her plate.

"Nope," End said smugly.

She stuck out her tongue and touched it to the drip of sauce in her spoon. "Barbeque sauce?"

End winked.

Maerk took a bite. "Definitely better than the orc stuff,. But why Torworld?"

End shrugged. "Sounded good. Plus, it totally looks like the stuff they eat in the game."

Lucas nodded enthusiastically, his mouth too full to answer.

"We're scheduled to drop units at Daravoo and Iraca, then on to Robinson's." Liz speared a noodle on her fork. "Tony should meet us there."

A spark of happiness flickered in Quinn's chest, but she played it cool. "It will be nice to see him again."

Liz's eyes flicked to her, appraising. "Yes, it will be. When he retired, I thought he'd spend more time with us. Of course, I thought we'd still be on the *Peregrine*, so things change."

"What's Tony doing on Robinson's?" Maerk asked. "I thought he was focusing on the Federation strongholds."

"I dunno," Liz said. "It's not safe for him in the central planets—

too much surveillance. Amanda and Pete are still working those. And that Maarteen fellow, I guess."

"As far as I know, Maarteen is still running courier routes," Quinn said. "But his travel has been curtailed by our recent activities. They don't send census workers to dangerous places. And all those planets we took back from the Russosken are considered lawless now."

"Do you think the Federation will send troops and impose martial law?" Maerk added another serving to his plate.

"They could try, I suppose," Quinn said. "But I don't think their troop strength is up to that. That's why they let the Russosken do the enforcing for all these years—covering all those planets would have them spread too thin. Plus, we've armed the civilians, which makes it a lot harder to retake those worlds."

"Maybe we can visit Daddy," Ellianne said.

"What?" Lucas and Quinn asked in concert.

"Where?" Quinn continued.

"Why?" Lucas added in disgust.

"I miss him." Ellianne stirred her casserole with her fork. "Maybe we can call his pirate friend and meet him somewhere."

Everyone looked at the girl. "We can't call pirates," End said kindly. "How would we even get their contact number?"

Ellianne shrugged. "I dunno." She stirred the food again. "I'm not hungry."

"But I made chocolate cake for dessert." End said, looking distressed.

"Cool!" Lucas spit breadcrumbs across the table with the word. "You have to eat dinner first, though."

"Lucas." Quinn gave her son the stink-eye.

"She doesn't have to eat dinner? That's not fair!"

"I thought you liked my Torworld casserole," End said.

Liz held up both hands. "Enough! Eat what you want." She glanced at Quinn. "Sorry, but—" She got up and stomped to the cockpit.

"Lucas, Ellianne, eat your casserole." Quinn exchanged a look with Maerk and stood. "No cake until that's all gone. And I mean in your stomach, not Sashelle's bowl." She glanced at the caat.

Sashelle, Mighty Huntress and Eliminator of Vermin, ignored her.

Quinn glared at the kids for a second, then followed the captain to the cockpit. Liz sat in the pilot's seat, swiping through screen after screen, not stopping long enough to look at any of the data. "What?" she barked when Quinn stepped in.

"What's up? I know the kids can be bothersome—there are days I almost feel like spacing them myself—but they don't usually bother you. Is there something you'd like to talk about?"

"No."

Quinn waited for a second, then turned to leave.

"It's Lou," Liz said. "I don't know where she is or what she's doing."

"I thought your mother took Tony to Athenos." Quinn slid into the co-pilot's seat, turning so she could look at the older woman.

"She did. But then what? We haven't spoken to her in three weeks. They've all been silent."

"Is that unusual?" Quinn asked. "You were on N'Avon for months—"

"That was different. I told her we were leaving. That she wouldn't hear from us again. And Dareen and End stayed in touch. But this is like they disappeared. How would you feel if your family—your mom, brothers, daughter—all stopped communicating like that?" She snapped her fingers.

Quinn sucked in a breath then blew out a heavy sigh. "Is this about Reggie? Are you mad because I cut off communications between him and our kids?"

"What?" Liz's head snapped around. "Hell no. That bastard had it coming. No, this is nothing about you. Well, it is, because you brought it up. Mom hasn't been herself lately, remember? So now I'm worried something is really wrong."

"It's probably not very comforting, but if you haven't heard from any of them, she's fine," Quinn said. "Someone would have called if there was a problem."

"You're assuming she hasn't done something crazy and gotten them all into trouble," Liz muttered.

"How much trouble could they get into? They're in the center of the Commonwealth."

Liz grunted. "Good point." She flipped through a few more screens. Then she jumped up. "I need cake."

QUINN TUCKED Ellianne into her bunk. She shared one of the cabins with the girl, while End and Lucas shared the other. The common bathroom—or "head," as Maerk insisted it be called—had been a bone of contention, until End re-engineered a cleaning bot to keep the place sparkling.

"Have you talked to Sashelle lately?" Quinn asked her daughter as casually as possible. The Hadriana caat, who had recently revealed her ability to communicate telepathically to humans, hadn't spoken to Quinn since they'd left Dusica's estate on Taniz Beta, despite living on the same small ship.

"I talk to her all the time," Ellianne said.

Quinn unfolded and re-folded a shirt, not looking at the girl. "Does she talk back?" She wasn't sure if the caat spoke to the little girl, and eight was old enough to start questioning that kind of thing.

Ellianne shrugged. "Sometimes she does. In my head. She's been kinda quiet since we left Dusi's house." She lowered her lashes and peeked up from under them. "Does she talk to you?"

"She did, a little."

Ellianne smiled. "Good. I wasn't sure you'd believe me if I told you."

"I probably wouldn't have," Quinn muttered under her breath.

When Ellianne frowned, she smiled again. "I do believe you. She talked to me and Tony. And Francine."

The girl nodded. "I think she misses Francine. Just like I miss Daddy."

Quinn looked away. "Not quite the same." She ruffled the girl's hair. "I'm sorry you can't talk to Daddy, but if he knows where I am, that would get me in big trouble." Understatement of the year. If he found out where she was, it would be a matter of seconds before his bosses in the Federation knew. And then she'd be back on death row —if she was lucky. More likely, she'd be dead.

"I know." Ellianne sighed. "But I miss him. Maybe Dareen can take me to visit. Or Francine?"

"If anyone could do it, it would be Francine," she agreed. "But she's busy. Maybe later, after things..." She trailed off. After what? After they won the revolution? Then she could visit Reggie in prison instead of the other way around. Not a great place for an eight-year-old, though. But while Reggie didn't deserve any consideration from her, Ellianne did. Quinn smiled sadly. "Go to sleep. We'll try to figure out something. Someday."

CHAPTER 3

DAREEN WHITING, Liz and Maerk's daughter, guided her shuttle—newly renamed the *Romantic Wizard*—to a parking spot on the Athenos landing field. She ran the shutdown checklist and smiled when she reached the end. Tony wasn't due to meet her for three more hours. Time to sightsee!

She jumped out of the pilot's seat, slung a bag over her shoulder, and stepped into the airlock. No need to run the cycle—on a friendly, planet-based shuttle field, she could safely pop both hatches.

She pulled the inner hatch shut by habit anyway. No point in making it easy for someone other than her to enter the craft. She stepped onto the retractable platform and pulled the outer hatch into place. After sealing it with a handprint, she jumped the three steps to the ground.

The sun shone down, warming the tarmac and making her jacket superfluous. She slid it off as she strode across the lot, knotting the arms around her waist. A commercial shuttle roared over her head, coming to land on the flight line.

A panel lit up as she approached the pedestrian opening in the force fence. A message scrolled across, and a voice repeated the words. "Identification will be required to return to this field. Please scan your ID before leaving to register for easy access."

Dareen pulled up the ID screen on her comtab and flashed it at the screen. Then she pressed her palm against the panel.

"Thank you for visiting Athenos Shuttle Field. Your location has been noted on your map. Our underground subway system is also noted. When returning to the field, take the green tube and exit at the shuttle field station. This field is for small shuttles only. There is no access to this field from the interstellar passenger concourse. That facility is on the red line."

She glanced across the broad runway to the huge terminal building on the far side. Large commercial shuttles landed there to deliver passengers from the enormous interstellar transports at the Athenos Prime and Second stations. The field was big enough for the *Peregrine* to land, if Lou had a reason to do that. But as long as Dareen was around to fly the *Wizard*, Lou didn't like to land the whole ship. Cheaper and safer to stay in space.

With a little skip in her step, Dareen exited the field. A wide sidewalk wound through a broad grassy area, with trees, bushes, and flowers planted in geometric patterns. A haze of sweet fragrance wafted over the walk. Athenos, capital of the Commonwealth, was known for its carefully-cultivated gardens and pedestrian-friendly weather.

A few meters on, the walkway rounded a hedge and stopped at the tube station. A ramp curved down into the brightly lit underground. Dareen used her comtab to purchase a ticket and hurried into the station. Gleaming white tiles, punctuated by colorful mosaics, lined the walls. The art depicted meadows, forests, waterfalls, and an idealized shuttle field. Probably to reassure the passengers they'd gotten the right station, Dareen thought. The lighting mimicked the gentle sunlight outside.

At the bottom of the ramp, she joined a queue waiting before the City Center sign. The line moved swiftly, and within moments, she reached the front.

She flashed her comtab again, verifying payment. The double-doors before her swished open, revealing a pair of chairs and a small table. Dareen sat in one, and the person in line behind her took the other. The doors swished closed, and the pod smoothly accelerated out of the station.

The clear pod revealed featureless walls outside, so Dareen turned to study her companion instead. He was thin and kind of gawky, with thick, dirty blond hair that fell over his forehead. And a killer smile.

She suppressed a gasp. "Hey, you're that kid!"

"I'm not a kid. I'm almost twenty."

She shook her head. "But you're the guy from Hadriana! What are you doing here?"

"I'm Autin." He extended a fist to bump. "I'm not from Hadriana; I just happened to be there. Like you."

She tapped her knuckles against his, watching his face. His totally cute face. She didn't remember him being this good-looking. She glanced at his arms and shoulders. Or this built. "And you just happened to get in the same tube pod as me, in a totally different star system?"

"Don't be silly, Dareen. I'm here to talk to you."

"Who are you?" As he opened his mouth, she cut him off. "And I don't mean your name. Who do you work for and why were you looking for me? And how did you know I'd be here?"

"Lou told us."

"Lou?" Dareen's voice cracked. "My gramma told you I'd be here?"

"Like last time," he said with a warm smile. "You look good today."

"Wait a second, Mr. Smooth." Dareen ignored the little tickle of warmth that zipped up her spine. "Cut the flirting and tell me what the hell is going on."

He nodded. "Right. I work for the government."

"*You* work for the Commonwealth?" Dareen repeated flatly. "I don't think so. For one thing, you said you're only nineteen. If that's true, you'd be at the academy, not working yet. And what were you doing on Hadriana? That was *family* work."

"I *am* at the academy," Autin said. "The trip to Hadriana was an internship. I was there, under cover, for six months, working with an experienced agent. He wanted to get that device off the planet, so he called for a retrieval. That's what you Marconis do, right? Lou sent you to pick it up. Standard stuff, really."

"And this?"

"This is a recruiting visit."

Again, his smile transformed him. He was already good-looking—strangely better looking than before—but the smile? Dareen's breath caught in her throat. "Recruiting?"

He gazed at her as if she was the only woman in the world. "The academy wants you."

"Really?" Dareen gulped. "How do they even know about me?"

"I put you in my report. But I don't think that made any difference. I think someone else must have recommended you. You Marconis work with a lot of Commonwealth agents, right?"

The pod eased to a stop, and the doors opened. "Welcome to City Center Station," an androgynous voice said.

They stood and walked into the busy station. It looked much like the station at the shuttle field, except the mosaics showed urban views instead of pastoral. Green tiles around the pod door and along the walkway reminded them which line they'd ridden.

Dareen spotted an exit sign and cut through the throngs of people to follow the ramp to the surface. Autin hurried behind, staying within an arm's length, but not touching her. When they emerged into the sunshine, Dareen spun around. "Are you going to follow me all day?"

Autin scratched his neck. "Well, I have all day for this assignment. If I go back to the academy, I'll have to go to class. I'd rather hang around with you. I could be your tour guide?"

"Do you know Athenos City? I've never been here before, but

I've read about the market, and the waterfront, and the Pythian Tower."

"I grew up here," Autin said. "I know where all those things are, plus the best places to eat along the way. Are you hungry? They gave me a food allowance for the job, and it would be a shame to have to turn that back in."

Dareen laughed. "You obviously don't know me. I'm always ready to eat. Can we go to Ferati Gelato?"

"Of course." He swept out his hand. "This way, please!"

TONY LOOKED at his comtab in surprise. It had pinged, indicating a family member nearby. He squinted into the lowering sun, assessing the crowd near the Pythian Tower.

"Uncle Tony!" Dareen rushed across the smooth tiles toward him. Behind her, a tall young man hung back.

"What are you doing here?" Tony asked. "I thought we were meeting at the shuttle?"

"I arrived early and wanted to see the sights. Gramma didn't say I had to wait at the field."

"No, of course not," Tony said. "Who's your friend?"

"Oh, this is Autin." She swung around and grabbed the boy's arm, dragging him forward. "Autin, this is my cousin Tony."

"I thought you said uncle?" Autin's brows drew down in confusion.

"He's my cousin." Dareen giggled. "But he's old, so End and I always called him 'uncle' when we were little."

"You aren't little anymore." Tony smirked. Clearly, this boy had her flustered. "And I'm not old. Where'd you meet Autin?"

"You won't believe this. He's from the academy. He wants to recruit me!"

"Oh, I believe it," Tony said. "They always send a good-looking cadet after the bright ones."

Autin turned bright red.

"Is that how you got recruited?" Dareen asked.

The young man straightened up in surprise. "Are you a grad?" He slapped his right hand to the front of his left shoulder. "*While we breathe...*"

"*We shall defend.*" Tony mirrored the boy's movement. "Long time ago. Glad to see the motto hasn't changed. How'd you know where to find her?"

"The recruiting office told me to wait for her at the shuttle station today," Autin said with a shrug. "We were told she'd be coming down."

Tony's brow drew down. The *Peregrine* had been docked at the Athenos Secundos retrofit dock for a couple of weeks. While they were in the Commonwealth, Lou had decided to get a full overhaul and a few upgrades. Their whereabouts weren't a secret, and Tony's visit to Dr. Fallstaff had not been covert. Even so, it made Tony nervous when people predicted his movements.

"Hm." Tony gave a sharp nod. "Are you two done with your *nominee enticement opportunity?*"

Autin looked confused, but Dareen laughed. "We just came down from the tower." She glanced over her shoulder at the imposing edifice. "And we had gelato!"

"From Zaretto's?" Tony pointed at a cafe across the square.

"No, Ferati." Dareen turned to look. "Is Zaretto's better? Can we stop on the way to the shuttle?" Without waiting for an answer, she started across the tiles toward the shop.

Tony laughed and glanced at Autin. "You got room for more gelato?"

"There's always room for ice cream, sir. It melts and fills in the cracks." Autin turned to follow the girl. "Gelato doubly so."

"Grab a tiramisu for me, will you?" Tony called after him. "I need to make a call."

Autin gave him a thumbs-up and trotted across the plaza.

Tony pulled out his comtab and tapped the screen. "How did the academy know Dareen would be here?" he asked when it connected, not bothering to say hello.

"Tony, how nice to hear from you." On the screen, Lou looked smug. "I expect you'll be aboard soon, right?"

"Did you tell someone at the academy that Dareen would be coming to get me today?"

"Why would I do that?" Lou asked. "So they could send a handsome recruiter to steal her away? They didn't, did they? I need her on the *Peregrine*. Not running off to play girl scout at the academy."

"So you say." Tony glanced at the two youngsters tasting the large selection of frozen treats. "But twenty years ago, something very similar happened to me. Never did figure out how they knew I was coming."

Lou glowered from the screen, but she didn't say a word.

Tony waved his hand. "Whatever. We'll be up in a bit. Are you still in drydock?"

"No, we moved to the cargo docks on Prime after Dareen headed down."

"Great, we'll see you soon." Tony started across the plaza toward his cousin and her escort. "Getting one last ice cream for the road."

Kert leaned over Lou's shoulder. "I hope you're bringing gelato back with you. Get Astrella's. It's the best."

CHAPTER 4

FRANCINE ZIELINSKY PRESSED a finger to the corner of her eye to stop the twitching. Her brother—Fyotor Nartalov, the new *nachal'nik*—was missing.

Again.

"We'll send a food shipment this week," her sister Dusica said from a desk behind her. Francine turned away from the window to see her sister gesturing for her to come closer. "Yes, Faina told me. *Spaseeba*." She swiped an icon on her screen and glared at her sister. "Did you tell Markhil I would send him weapons?"

"Markhil?" Francine repeated. "The guy on Sendarine? Please. I'm not an idiot. He was bluffing."

Dusica blew out an exasperated breath. "I wish they'd stop trying to game the system! We're providing enough support to keep their clans alive while they figure out how to navigate this new situation, but I'm not arming anyone! He said the locals are attacking them."

"Maybe they are." Francine turned away. "Have you ever been to Sendarine? I have. The Russosken were not nice there. Markhil is getting exactly what he deserves. In fact, he's probably lucky someone hasn't taken him out by now."

"He's the youngest of a family of eight," Dusica said in outrage.

"Everyone over the age of twenty-five was wiped out! How is that lucky?"

"I'd say the Sendarines showed a great deal of restraint in limiting their purge to full adults." Francine crossed her arms over her chest. "You've been here in your protected cocoon all these years. You haven't seen—War sucks, but life under his family sucked more. Trust me, he's lucky to be alive. Has he applied for asylum?"

After the recent multi-system coup had destroyed the Russosken's hold on this sector, most had gone underground. The locals on every planet had killed *soldaty* and leaders indiscriminately, and in a few cases, they massacred family members, too. Many Russosken had begged Fyo for sanctuary.

"He seems to have engineered a truce or amnesty for his family." Dusica sighed. "I guess he had to. He's taken responsibility for dozens of orphans."

"You think he shouldn't have?" Francine asked in disbelief. "You should be singing his praises. Holding him up as an example. Building friendship and trust is the only way most of our people will survive."

Dusica rolled her eyes. "Russosken weren't built for trust and friendship. We're bred to rule."

"That's the kind of thinking that got us into this mess in the first place," Francine snarled. "We aren't any better than anyone else. The sooner we forget about our 'breeding,' the better off we'll be."

She paced across the room, swinging around at the far side. "We could be the catalyst to free the Federation if we were willing to work with the other citizens. We have the military might and understanding of tactics to kick the Feds off all our worlds, if we can build trust with the rest of them. We'll have to convince them that we won't go back to business as usual when we're done."

Dusica gave her a sly look from the corner of her eyes.

"I mean it, Dusi." Francine stabbed a finger at her sister. "We are not going to kick out the Feds so the Russosken can take control. You think a lot of our people were slaughtered in this rebellion? It will be nothing to what happens if we try to—" She broke off as the door opened.

Fyotor poked his head into the office, then ducked back out.

"No way, Fyo." Francine lunged through the door and grabbed his shirt collar. He put up a brief struggle, but she had him in a headlock within seconds. "Get your butt back in here and deal with this mess."

"I didn't cause the mess," Fyo grumbled. "Why do I have to fix it?"

"The joy of being the *nachal'nik*," Dusica said. "You were born to this role."

"That's what you keep saying." Fyo glowered at her. "But Francine keeps talking about democracy. I didn't run for office. I don't want to be *nachal'nik*. I'm not even sure I believe I'm actually *her* grandson." He glared at an oil painting on the wall. A young blonde glared back at him: Ludmilla Nartalova. The painting was old —painted decades before any of them had been born—and now that she was dead, Fyo had become the *nachal'nik*.

"Sucks to be you," Francine muttered. "You've benefited from your position for twenty-one years. Now it's time to pay up. Until we get the political situation settled, it's our responsibility to care for our remaining people."

"I've benefited for twenty-one years?" Fyo repeated in outrage. "I've been a virtual prisoner for the last four of those!"

"Wah, poor you," Francine retorted. "Forced to live in luxury on your sister's estate. Grow up, Fyo. Take responsibility. You've got your whole life to be free."

"Democracy is overrated." Dusica held up her hands to fend off Francine's furious expression. "I'm not standing in your way. If you think the people of the Federation can govern themselves, then fine. As long as I keep my home, I'm staying out of the way. But until then, let's take care of our own. Fyo, get to work."

Fyo slunk across the room to his desk, pulling up messages as he sat. Francine sighed. She hoped Dusica and Fyo would be able to keep their home, but revolutions were tricky things. She would keep an ace up her sleeve.

———

THE AIRLOCK POPPED, and Tony and Dareen climbed out of the *Wizard*. While the girl finished her post-flight, Tony headed to the crew mess. He put the gelato in the freezer and grabbed a bottle of water. Lou had scheduled an all-hands meeting so he slouched into a chair and closed his eyes.

Stene, Kert, and Lou showed up a few minutes later. He heard them coming; the men argued in muted voices. Conversation stopped when they reached the hatch to the mess.

"Hey, Tony," the brothers said together. Although Stene was Tony's father, he'd been raised by the whole family. In different ways, both men had been a father to him.

"Welcome back," Lou said. "How long are you with us?"

"Depends on where you're going," Tony said. "I need to check in with a few people scattered around the edge of the Federation."

"Things are getting hot there." Lou took a seat. She glared at Tony. "Stirring up rebellion is bad for business. I don't want to get close to the inner worlds."

"Ha, revolution is good for lots of businesses. Yours is one of them," Tony said. "I need to hit some of the places we've already been. They should be safe enough. But war usually offers great fiscal returns if you're in a position to exploit the situation. The Commonwealth seems to be extending their reach. I'm sure there are plenty of fat and juicy contracts to scoop up."

Lou tried to grumble, but she couldn't keep the tiny grin off her face. "We've got a few things set up. Liz is a genius at that stuff."

"You just like to bitch." Tony shook his head.

Dareen hurried in. "Sorry, had a little trouble with my shutdown. I started a diagnostic scan, so if anyone has to go dirtside, they'll have to take the other shuttle." She gave an artistic shudder. Her brother

End usually flew the second shuttle, and he was known for leaving it less than sparkling.

"Should be fine." Kert snickered. "End's been gone long enough for the funk to dissipate."

Dareen smirked. "I sprayed it with SwifKlens after I took him to the *Swan*."

"Now that we're all here—" Lou began.

"I told you—" Dareen interrupted, only to be cut off herself.

"Calm your jets, I wasn't poking you." Lou tossed a file from her comtab to the table projection. A three-dimensional star chart annotated with colorful lines and arrows hovered over the surface. "Here's the route I've plotted. Blue is us; red is the *Swan*. We're picking up cargo in the morning, then going to Varitas and Taniz Alpha. We'll meet the rest of the family at Robinson's in ten days, unless one of us gets delayed. Tony, where do you want to be dropped?"

Tony leaned forward, rotating the view a few degrees. He pointed. "I'll leave you at Varitas, then meet you at Robinson's."

Lou gave him a narrow-eyed look. "You sure?"

"I have a couple things to check on and one of them is on Varitas. If I'm quick, I'll catch a ride to Taniz, but no guarantees. Keep an eye on the drop box. I'll send you updates as usual."

"Right." Lou flicked a document to the table screen and looked at her sons. "Are you two able to handle all the cargo, or do we need to hire temps?"

Stene opened the manifest. "We can handle this."

"I'll be here to help load," Tony said. "And you've got Dareen."

The girl nodded. "I can run the lifters as well as anyone."

"What about delivery?" Kert swiped a copy of the document to his side of the table. "Doesn't look too bad. I think the two of us can take care of it."

"That's what I said." Stene got up and started preparing dinner.

"Supplies are being delivered first, then cargo." Lou pointed at another list.

Dareen groaned. "Oh-six-hundred? Why so early?"

Tony laughed. "It only sounds early. You're still on Athenos City time, so that's eleven in the morning for you."

"Some teens get to sleep until noon," Dareen grumbled.

"Not at the academy," Tony said. "I'll bet young Autin will be up at five."

"Good for him," Dareen said. "I'm not a cadet."

"No, you're a shuttle pilot," Lou said. "They fly—or load cargo—when they're told."

"Maybe I should be a cadet." Dareen put her fists on her hips. "Autin doesn't have to load cargo."

"You might want to ask him about that." Stene pulled dishes from a cupboard. "I remember Tony complaining about a lot worse than loading cargo before lunch."

"Yeah, remember when he had to do a tour in the stables?" Kert chuckled. "Why does a space academy have horses anyway?"

"We all learned to ride," Tony said. "You never know when you might need to use less conventional transportation."

"Have you ever ridden on a mission?" Dareen asked.

"A couple times. I had to meet an asset at a dude ranch once." While they ate dinner, Tony told a convoluted story about a horse trainer turned secret agent, and the jockey who tried to sell them out.

When he finished, Kert pulled the gelato out of the freezer. "Zaretto's? I thought you were getting Astrella's?"

"Zaretto's is the best," Stene and Tony said together.

"I kind of liked Ferati's," Dareen said.

They spent the rest of the evening arguing the merits of gelato on Athenos.

CHAPTER 5

SOMETHING SOFT TAPPED Quinn's cheek. She batted it away and rolled over. Sharp needles spiked into her right shoulder. She sat up with a yelp.

Sorry. Sashelle sat on the edge of Quinn's bunk, blinking her big orange eyes at the woman. *They're golden, not orange.*

"You don't sound sorry," Quinn whispered, glancing at the bunk above her. "And stay out of my head."

That's why I pricked you. Sashelle lifted one of her front paws and popped the claws out then back in. *I didn't want to intrude.*

Quinn glared. "You intruded anyway. How else would you know what color I think your eyes are?"

You were thinking quite loudly. And they are definitely gold.

"Did you wake me up to tell me I was thinking too loud?"

No, but thinking loudly and clearly is a good thing. If anything, you need more practice.

"Then what do you want?" Quinn rubbed her shoulder, but it didn't hurt, and the caat's claws hadn't drawn blood.

The pirates are nearby. The caat stood and paced to the foot of the bunk, then back to Quinn's pillow. Her tail twitched in agitation.

"What pirates? We're docked at Daravoo Station. Are you saying the station personnel are pirates? They *did* charge us a fortune to dock."

The pirates who attempted to remove our kittens. The one who called himself Dean.

"Reggie's friend?" Quinn rolled out of the bunk and onto her feet. "They're here, trying again?"

I don't know what they're planning. But the man 'Dean' is nearby.

"You weren't with the kids when they encountered that ship." Quinn pulled a sweatshirt over her tank top and stumbled toward the door. "How could you recognize this Dean fellow?"

I heard the Whiny Tom talking to him. The caat leapt down the stairs to the lounge.

"The Whiny Tom?" Quinn asked. An image of Reggie appeared in her head. She growled and she raced to the airlock. "Is he here too? Why didn't you lead with that?" She grabbed one of the ArmorCoats and flung it over her pajamas. After slinging a blaster over her shoulder, she cycled through the airlock.

What are you going to do? Sashelle sat by her feet, washing a paw.

"I'm going to—" What was she going to do? She grimaced at her bare feet. She really hadn't thought this through. She should probably go back into the ship and consult with Liz or Maerk. Still, it wouldn't hurt to take a look. And her feet would be fine in the station corridors. She crossed the access bridge to the station lock. "You're sure it's them? Just the two of them? And they're close?"

Positive, Sashelle said. *My range is not enormous, so they must be nearby. Perhaps the next ship, or—* She broke off as the hatch to the station popped open.

Quinn slowly pushed the hatch with her shoulder, her hands holding the weapon ready. She squinted into the brightly lit terminal. Two men stood a couple of meters away arguing. Quinn immediately recognized her ex-husband. The other wore an eyepatch. She glanced up and down the long docking arm. It was the middle of night shift, leaving this part of the station deserted. Anger swirled through

Quinn's chest. How dare they stand there and plot in the middle of the night? Right there in plain sight!

"You got my back, caat?" Quinn whispered.

Sashelle didn't answer in words, but a feeling of security and power washed over Quinn. Good enough. She stomped across the terminal and pointed the weapon at her ex. "What do you want?"

Both men jumped, swinging around to confront her. The second man—Dean—flung his hands into the air when he saw the blaster.

"Told you she was here!" Reggie gave his friend a triumphant grin.

"What are you doing here?" Quinn growled again. "And how did you find us?"

"That's my little secret," Reggie replied smugly. He took a step forward.

Quinn raised the muzzle of the blaster to point at his chest. "Don't get any closer."

"You won't shoot me with that." Reggie laughed loudly. "Killing people isn't your style."

"Good point." She let the blaster dangle from her shoulder and pulled a stunner out of the coat. "I wouldn't mind zapping you with this, though."

Reggie stopped, mid-stride. He rubbed his chin, as if remembering the punch Quinn had landed when they'd last met on Hadriana. "I want to see the kids."

"Tell me how you found us." Quinn darted a glance at the other guy as he started to edge away. "Don't move, Dean."

"How'd you know my name?" Dean's eyes were wide.

Quinn smiled without humor. "That's *my* little secret."

"You told the kids your name, you idiot. When you lost them near Robinson's." Reggie turned to Quinn. "If you know that, then you know it's more than just Dean and me. We have enough men and ships to take all of you down."

Untrue, Sashelle said.

Quinn glanced around the area, but the caat had disappeared.

"Right." Quinn sneered. "You appear to be alone. Tell me how you found us."

Dean eased away. "I'll leave you two—" He broke off with a yelp. "Hey, she shot me!" He shook his hand then stuck his fingers in his mouth.

"Lowest power." Quinn twisted a dial on the stunner with a flourish. "Last warning. How did you find us?"

"We got lucky," Dean said sulkily.

"Dean!" Reggie growled.

"You got lucky?" Quinn stepped back to cover both men. "I don't believe in coincidences."

Dean glanced at Reggie, then back at Quinn.

She made a show of targeting Dean's crotch. "That's gonna sting."

Dean whimpered. "Really. We got lucky! We lost the shuttle at Xury, when that girl zapped us with the em-cannon. Our partners dumped us." His face twisted with scorn, anger almost overcoming his fear of Quinn's stunner. "So we decided to come here instead of heading straight to Hadriana. Figured I could pick up some work or cargo under the table. You know, with the rebellion going on and all. We checked with the station manager, flashed your picture around. A guy in fueling recognized you. So we came over here to, ah…" He glanced at Reggie.

Quinn swung the weapon to her ex. "You came over here to do what, exactly?"

"I wanted to talk to the kids," Reggie whined. "It's my right. According to the Federation, I have full custody—" Reggie broke off with a scream and fell to the deck, clutching his groin.

"You have no rights, you son of a bitch," Quinn whispered. "You're lucky I don't fry you and toss you out an airlock."

"Holy hell!" Dean clasped both hands over the front of his pants. "You can't stun a man's junk on the high setting! That's inhumane!"

"It was only medium," Quinn snarled. "You wanna try high?"

"No, ma'am!" Dean cried.

Something flickered on the edge of Quinn's vision. She swung around as Ellianne flew past her and flung herself down on Reggie. "Daddy!"

The second Quinn turned, Dean darted out the door. Sashelle streaked after him.

"Let him go, Sashelle!" Quinn cried.

After I catch him, Sashelle purred. *I am the Mighty Huntress.*

Quinn left Dean to his fate, rushing toward Ellianne.

"Stop," Reggie croaked. He held Ellianne against his chest, her face pressed to his shoulder. He looked like a father embracing his child after a long separation.

Until she noticed the mini blaster pointed at the girl's head.

Quinn froze. "She's your daughter!"

"And she's coming with me." Reggie rolled to a sitting position, Ellianne still held tight against him. The little girl started squirming, and Reggie's arm tightened.

"Daddy?" Ellianne whispered as her eyes focused on the weapon. "Why is your gun pointed at me?"

"Reggie, let her go," Quinn said. "You don't want to hurt her."

The muzzle of the weapon swung around to point at Quinn. "You're right. But I don't care about hurting you. We are going to get up and walk out of here. After you send Lucas out."

"Daddy, I don't want to go with you," Ellianne said, her face pale. "I wanted to see you, but I want to stay with Mommy and Tony and Dar—"

"Mommy and Tony?" Reggie's face turned red. "You're with *him*?"

"Don't be silly." Quinn edged closer, a centimeter at a time. "I'm not *with* Tony. We're just friends."

"Just friends," Reggie repeated. "I can't believe I fell for that all these years."

"You didn't *fall* for it," Quinn said, "because it's true. We're friends." Even as she said it, she knew it wasn't true anymore. She felt more for Tony than she'd ever felt for this whiny— *Focus, Quinn,* she thought with a mental shake. *Take him out.*

"Get Lucas!" Reggie demanded.

"Never!" Quinn yelled.

A ferocious roar rang through the station, seconding her response. Reggie's eyes bugged out as he swung around to face the door.

Time seemed to stretch for an instant that lasted a lifetime. Quinn flung herself at Reggie, legs whirling almost without thought. She whipped into the air, swinging—dancing—in a perfect spinning roundhouse kick. The top of her right foot connected with the back of his head with a satisfying thunk, the impact stinging her bare toes. Reggie stumbled forward, releasing Ellianne.

The girl darted away to hide behind Quinn.

Reggie caught himself before he hit the ground, swinging around to face Quinn. At that moment, Sashelle burst through the doors. She flew at Reggie, all four feet impacting the center of his chest. Reggie slammed to the ground.

The caat flexed her claws in and out of Reggie's shirt, drawing blood. Her tail whipped back and forth in agitation. *Is the kitten safe?*

"I'm okay," Ellianne said. "Are you okay, Mommy?"

Quinn swept the girl into her arms. "I'm fine. Thanks to Sashelle."

They looked at the caat, who now sat on Reggie's face, calmly grooming herself. *My pleasure. It's not every day I get to take down vermin.*

"Is...is he still alive?" Quinn asked.

Reggie groaned before Sashelle could answer. *Get the kitten inside. I'll finish this one.*

"How about we all go inside," Quinn suggested. "We probably shouldn't 'finish' Reggie. Or anyone else. What happened to Dean?"

Sashelle's ears twitched as she stalked across Reggie's chest, deliberately stepping on his groin before jumping to the ground. *I let him go,* she finally replied. *After I played with him for a while.*

Quinn bit her lip, trying to hide her smile. "Works for me."

CHAPTER 6

MAERK MET Quinn and Ellianne at the inner hatch, his hair rumpled. After she got her daughter settled in her bunk, she returned to the lounge where he waited.

"Why does he want your kids so badly?" Maerk poured her a glass of water. "He doesn't seem to be the paternal type."

"I think it's Gretmar. She can't stand the neighbors knowing she lost them. Especially since I'm a traitor." She snickered and lowered her voice to a gossiping tone. "The heirs to the LaRaine Estate are being raised by a Krimson agent! I've heard she's teaching them to enjoy human flesh." She rolled her eyes. "It's bad for her image."

"He probably doesn't want to 'lose' to you, either." Maerk dropped into a chair. "He seems pretty competitive."

Quinn nodded. "I guess it doesn't matter why. But I suspect he'll keep trying. I wish I knew how they found us. I don't believe in coincidence."

"Me, neither. What do you want to do about him?"

"I'm not going to take him prisoner." Quinn grimaced. "I'm certainly not going to kill him. And we can't turn him in—I'm not sure I trust the good folks of Daravoo to take my side against his. Dean said they were out of credits—I say we leave him."

Maerk pondered for a moment. "I'll run a scan of all our surveillance. We usually take vid of all the other ships before we dock at a station. One of Lou's semi-paranoid procedures that Liz can't let go of. I'll admit it has been useful. I might be able to pull other data from the station. Then we can see if their ship has been to the other stations we have. Of course, if they docked after us, and departed before, we'd miss them."

"It's a start." Quinn yawned.

"Go back to bed," Maerk said. "The hatches are locked down with biometric access enabled. They can't get in."

"They can't do anything to the hull, can they?"

"Do you think either of them are capable of full-vacuum spacewalk?"

"Reggie had to do it as a cadet, but I don't think he's been out since." Quinn snorted. "Public relations guy. They aren't required to be vacuum-certified unless they're assigned to a ship."

"He was at Fort Sumpter," Maerk said in surprise. "That's almost front line."

"Not really. They don't allow family members to live on the front line. The media played up the 'asteroid outpost' story. They had to make it sound like a dangerous place to justify the emergency evacuation."

"I wondered about that," Maerk said. "It's not any closer to hostile areas than any other fringe world, but they made a big deal about relations with the Commonwealth."

Quinn nodded. "The Krimson Empire is the premier's favorite bogeyman. Anyway, unless he's retrained recently, Reggie's zero-vacuum cert isn't up to date. That doesn't mean he won't try something stupid."

"True enough." Maerk swiped at his comtab. "I've set the proximity alerts to notify us if anyone comes within two meters of the ship, and I've tightened the tolerances. It'll eat up some computing power, but since we're sitting idle, that's not a problem. We might get some false positives, but we're only here for a few more hours. Get some sleep."

SOMETHING BOUNCED against Francine's hair. She glared at Fyo through narrowed eyes and reached down to retrieve the crumpled paper. "Are you so bored you're reduced to throwing things at me?"

"I wasn't throwing things, I was delivering a report." Fyo grinned. "Open it."

Francine spread the paper out, smoothing the wrinkles. A note scrawled across one side in thick, dark ink read, "Is it lunchtime yet?"

"This is an inquiry, not a report, Fyo. You're an adult. You can take lunch whenever you want. But it's only ten a.m."

"I know." Fyo groaned. "I'm so bored. I hate this stuff. Why do I have to be the *nachal'nik*? What if I abdicate and you take over?"

She put her index finger on her nose. "Not me. Get Dusi to do it. Maybe once the Federation dies, we can escape."

"I could walk away right now," Fyo suggested. "The only thing that kept me here all these years was fear of getting vaporized. With the Russosken falling apart, they're going to be way too busy to worry about offing me."

"True." Francine drew the word out. "But that's not very altruistic of you."

"There's no percentage in altruism."

Francine scowled. "That's a very Russosken way of thinking."

"What do you expect?" Fyo gestured to the opulent office furnishings around them. "I grew up in the Russosken, like you. We take care of ourselves."

"What about Dusica?" Francine said. "She didn't have to hide you all this time. What has she ever asked in return?"

Fyo wrinkled his nose. "She's always on me to do something productive."

"Probably to keep you out of her hair." Francine stood and crossed the room to drop the crumpled paper on Fyo's desk. "Try helping others. It really is a great way to see how fortunate you are. But if that doesn't work for you, consider this payback for all those years she kept you safe." She gave him a hard stare. "I've only been helping you a couple weeks, and I'm already feeling you owe me. Dusi did it for years."

Fyo's face drooped. "You're right. I owe her."

"Come on, let's go get coffee."

"And pastries."

The door burst open before they reached it and Dusica burst in. "Get to the saferoom! We're under attack!" She ran to the wall behind her desk and opened a hidden compartment. Bright blue sparks danced across the windows, then disappeared behind heavy blast shields. A bookshelf rotated away from the wall, revealing a narrow staircase.

"Really?" Francine asked. "A hidden passage behind a bookcase?"

"Down!" Dusica shoved a hand at the dark doorway.

Francine pushed Fyo ahead of her into the gloom. Lights flickered on as they broke the plane of the doorway. The narrow steps descended between rough stone walls. They reached a small landing, and the steps doubled back, descending further.

The temperature dropped as they went lower. Francine lost count of the number of switchbacks before the steps finally stopped at a large, metal door. It looked like the hatch on a ship's airlock.

"Probably because that's what it was made for," Fyo said when she mentioned this. He placed his hand on the scan plate, wincing when it took a blood sample.

Francine swung around to face Dusica. "Where are Marielle and Aleksei?"

"They're guarding our backs, as they pledged to do," Dusica said.

"You left them up there?"

"I didn't leave them. Marielle is your chief of security. She knows how to keep you safe, and if she feels she needs to be up there to do it, you trust her judgement. Once we're inside, we can use the surveillance to see what's going on."

"You don't seem very worried." Francine's eyes narrowed. "Why not?"

Behind her, the panel beeped. She spun. Words appeared on the screen. "Welcome, Fyotor Nartalov. Password?"

Fyo typed on the screen. It blinked, then, "Duress code?"

Fyo glanced back at Dusica and said, "Warhawk 4.9."

A mechanism inside the door clicked loudly and gears turned. When the noise stopped, Fyo pushed the huge hatch inward. The three siblings stepped inside, and Dusica pushed it shut behind them.

They stood in an airlock identical to many Francine had seen on Russosken spacecraft. Fyo worked the controls, cycling the air, and the inner hatch unlocked. "Kind of overkill for a terrestrial saferoom," Francine muttered.

"Not really." Dusica nudged her forward. "This keeps us safe from gas attacks as well as armed."

"Don't your air handlers counter gas attacks?" Francine waved at the ceiling to indicate the house above them.

Dusica pushed past her, shaking her head as she went. "Redundancy keeps us alive."

Francine followed her sister into an opulent room. Thick carpet covered the floors. Expensive-looking chairs and couches provided seating areas for a dozen or more people. Through an open doorway, she caught a glimpse of vast stainless-steel counters and high-end appliances. A hallway in the far corner undoubtedly led to plush bedrooms with en suite baths.

"Fancy." She dropped into a massage chair.

"Close the hatch!" Dusica snapped. She stood before a highly-polished cabinet. The open doors revealed a state-of-the-art surveillance pod.

"If that is a real airlock, it's safer to leave the inner hatch open," Francine said as Fyo headed toward it.

"Really?" Fyo pivoted to look at her.

She nodded. "The outer door won't open if this one is. Of course, if they can't get it open, then they'll try to break through, so..." She shrugged. "Where's your armory?"

"Through here." Fyo changed directions, leaving the hatch open.

Francine stood and followed him into the vast kitchen. "Who's going to use all this stuff?"

Fyo opened a door at the far end, revealing a small room full of neatly-racked weapons. "If we have enough notice, Dusi brings the staff down. If not, we eat whatever we can cobble together. I make a pretty good casserole." He stopped in the doorway, blocking Francine's access to the armory. "You can take a look, but we won't need any of these."

She pushed past. "You're that confident in Marielle and Aleksei?" Marielle knew her stuff, for sure. She'd been a Federation Secret Service agent before she'd married an admiral's aide. But she was new to Dusica's estate.

"It's just a drill." Fyo lounged against the doorjamb.

"What?" She swung around, a mini blaster in hand, carefully aimed downward. "This is a drill?" Anger burned in her chest. "How do you know? She didn't— Get out of the way." She tried to push past her brother.

"I know because she does these regularly. Not on a schedule, but every few weeks when we're home. I actually expected one last week, but I guess she was busy."

"You could have warned me!" Francine shoved him out of the way and stomped across the kitchen. "Dusi! Is this a drill?"

Dusica looked up from the surveillance system. The screen showed a diagnostic being run. "Yes, didn't you get the memo?"

"What memo?"

"I sent you a message." Dusica waved her comtab.

Francine whipped out her device. It got a surprisingly good signal in this bunker; she wondered what would happen if the house net went down. She swiped open her messages. "Ten minutes ago!" She glared at her sister. "That was...what, thirty seconds before you burst in?"

"Forty-five," Dusica said. "System is up to date. We can go back up."

"You ran us through a drill so you could update the computer?" Francine spluttered. "Don't you have tech guys for that?"

"Of course I do," Dusica snapped as she stepped into the airlock. "But I always check their work. Besides, the discipline is good for us."

Francine glanced back at Fyo. He lifted his hands. "My plan is looking better, isn't it?"

"Getting lunch?" Francine asked. "Or walking away?"

"Both."

CHAPTER 7

VARITAS WAS NOT one of Tony's favorite places. The Russosken had a heavy presence here, and only the fact that most of the *soldaty* had been deployed to other planets had allowed this piece of the rebellion to succeed. They'd removed the local ruling family, but Tony wasn't optimistic about the new regime.

He strolled out of the nearly deserted commercial shuttle terminal into warm sunlight. A light breeze ruffled his hair, and a heavy floral scent assaulted his nose. He sneezed.

"I hope you aren't allergic to the patonia flowers," an oily voice said behind him.

Tony swung around. "May I help you?"

A thin young man with dark hair lounged against the door frame. The automatic door tried to close, jostling the guy, and he fought to maintain his balance. He waited a moment, then pushed off, as if proving no moving door was going to displace him. He swaggered forward. "Maybe *I* can help *you*."

The door slid halfway shut, then opened again, and another man approached. This one was huge, with the blond hair and blue eyes typical of Russosken. He stepped up behind the younger man, his hand hovering near a bulge in his jacket.

"I don't need anything," Tony replied.

"I've heard you're here to talk to the new leaders."

"Where did you hear that?" Tony asked, as if only mildly interested. He glanced around the area, stepping back a few paces to keep the two men in view while giving himself a more defensible position. Had the local rebels double-crossed him?

"I have my ways."

Tony shrugged. "I'd say your 'ways' need some refining." He glanced across the road where a familiar figure slid through the gap in a fence. "I'm here to meet a friend. Perhaps you have me confused with someone else. Good day." He angled across the street, keeping the two men in his peripheral vision. "Sebi Maarteen!" He thrust out an elbow. "Good to see you! I thought you were stuck on the inner planets."

Sebi knocked his elbow against Tony's then shrugged. "I retired. I wasn't able to continue my courier service once you disrupted things out here, so I filed my papers and cashed in my retirement account."

"I hope you put the credits somewhere safe," Tony said. "I wouldn't trust the Federation savings banks these days."

Maarteen smiled. "I bought property on Lunesco. Auntie B helped me find a nice little place on the Far Wall." He gestured for Tony to walk with him and started toward the parking area. "Who are your friends?"

Tony glanced over his shoulder. The two men had disappeared. "I'm not sure. Russosken, at a guess. They knew why I'm here."

"That's troubling," Maarteen said vaguely. "We'll have to look into that."

"I'm glad you're here," Tony said. "It might have gotten messy if I'd been on my own."

"My pleasure. Although I'm sure you would have been fine."

"*I* would have been fine." They walked through the break in the fence and into a parking lot. Tony stopped in the middle of the half-empty lot and glanced around. He pulled out his comtab and fired up his jammer. "Say, since you're here, I have a question I've been wanting to ask you."

"If it pertains to our previous encounters, this might not be the optimum place for that conversation." Maarteen glanced up at the closest light pole.

"I think we're good." Tony held up his comtab, displaying his jamming program. "When we left the *Solar Wind* on Lunesco, you passed a memory card to Quinn."

Maarteen nodded, waiting.

"Where did you get it?" Tony crossed his arms. He could play the waiting game, too.

"From one of my usual drops." Maarteen shrugged negligently. "I can't tell you more than that. Not knowing the sources kept me safe."

"I was afraid of that." Tony drummed his fingers against his leg. "We've been trying to figure out how that particular asset managed to get a message into your system. I guess it doesn't matter anymore." Dusica had told them she had an extensive network outside the Russosken sphere. He wondered if other Russosken had infiltrated the rebellion's communication lines. Today's encounter would imply they had.

They continued to a small, green hovercar. "This looks a bit more substantial than the little cart you drove on Lunesco." Tony chuckled as he climbed into the passenger seat.

"And fewer switchbacks to negotiate. This is a rental. I swept it, but a second pass with superior tech is welcome." He nodded at Tony's comtab.

"I'm on it." Tony flicked the icons and held up the device. He scanned the car, spending a few extra minutes on the power equipment. "Looks clean." He settled into his seat and pulled the safety straps tight. "What are you doing on Varitas?"

"Amanda asked me to take them under my wing," Maarteen said. "They wouldn't listen to her or Pete—some nonsense about tax agents."

"Yeah, I ran into that when I was here before."

Maarteen swiped through the hovercar's passenger interface and input a destination. "You'll need to turn off your jammer. The cheap rentals don't allow human drivers, and they won't operate unless they're connected to the net."

"Done." Tony flicked his small screen, then slid the device into his pocket. "How's the climate?"

"Not too hot, not too cold."

Vague answer—not safe to talk then. Tony's mind raced as they pulled out of the parking lot and slid away from the shuttle field. While the Federation was officially still in charge here on Varitas, their control was tenuous at best. The Russosken had provided enforcement. The rebellion on Varitas had not been as smooth as other fringe worlds, but with the resources Maarteen brought to the table, they'd eventually succeeded. If Maarteen was unwilling to speak about the political climate, that meant the Federation still had ears and possibly teeth.

The hovercar brought them to a large hotel near the center of town. When Tony tried to open the door, it remained locked.

"Please rate this service before departure," flashed across the front window in large magenta letters.

"It won't let you out until you give it a review." Shaking his head, Maarteen swiped through five stars and the locks popped. He climbed out and waited until Tony joined him on the sidewalk. "I'm afraid to give less than full points for fear it won't let me out."

They walked into the hotel. Tony used the kiosk to check into a room, but he didn't bother going upstairs. "Do we have a meeting scheduled? I have another appointment."

"That's why I'm here," Maarteen said. "We'll take the slider."

They rode an escalator down one level to the slider station. Maarteen handed Tony a small card. "Transit card. Three-day pass. If you're staying longer, you'll have to add to it."

"Thanks." Tony looked at the card. "That should be plenty." He waved it over the access panel, and the door slid open.

Maarteen followed him. A few civilians stood along a green line painted on the floor. "We want the red line," Maarteen said. "This way." They went through a hallway and down another set of steps. No one waited on the red stripe.

The two men climbed into a small pod waiting on the track. As soon as they were both seated, Maarteen flicked his finger through one of the selections on the projected menu. The slider zipped out of the station. The smooth ride took them through several more stations before finally slowing. They shunted onto a sidetrack, and the pod stopped.

Maarteen led Tony through the station, but instead of taking the escalator to the surface, he stopped by a door marked, "Utilities."

"Not another secret lair hidden inside a closet." Tony put a hand over his eyes.

"More of a room than a closet, but I'm afraid so." Maarteen grinned. "These guys don't have a lot of imagination."

"At least they didn't leave the contents of the closet laying around on the ground outside this time. They can be taught."

They went into the room. Huge conduits hung over their heads, and large boxes hummed along two walls. A whiff of oil made Tony want to sneeze again. Maarteen went to a large wheel attached to the wall and marked "Hot." It turned easily, and he spun it clockwise. One of the humming boxes hinged away from the wall.

"Come on." Maarteen stepped through the opening.

Tony stopped in surprise. A large wooden table took up most of the room. A dozen people sat around it in standard office-style chairs. At the head of the table, a pair of men broke into grins when they spotted him. "Tony!" they said together.

"Bart, Edwin, how are you?" Tony moved forward to greet the men. They exchanged brief pleasantries, then Edwin indicated an empty seat. Tony took it, glancing at Maarteen, seated beside him.

"I have a delivery for you." Tony reached into his small bag and pulled out a pair of data sticks. "A larger package is being delivered to the address you gave me."

"I hope that package is one that goes boom," Edwin said.

Bart, the older of the two, glared at him. "Cool it, Ed."

"I'm sure you'll find it useful," Tony said. "Shall we discuss the current situation?"

WHEN EDWIN and Bart finished their report, Tony nodded. "Sounds like you have things well under way here. Has Sebi been helpful?" He nodded at Maarteen.

"He's been invaluable!" Bart exclaimed. "Not only is he great at tactics, but he knows people. People who can get things done."

"That he does," Tony agreed. "Varitas is a bit different from the other planets we've worked with. Your Russosken presence was much stronger, but many of their *soldaty* were off world when this began. That made your job here easier. However, the number of Federation officials is also much larger here. You'll need to remove them from power. You'll also need to be careful of *soldaty* returning from their missions. Some will be injured. Others will be angry—especially those who were abandoned by their leadership. They were supposed to be coming home in victory."

"We've already seen that," Edwin said. "We've had increased gang activity. Orin is working local security."

A colorless woman stood. She would have made an excellent agent because she was so ordinary looking. Tony sized her up and made a mental note to recommend Maarteen do a full background check. They didn't need a Federation mole.

Orin cleared her throat. "Most of the gang members we've rounded up are former *soldaty*. We've implemented screening at the commercial shuttle fields. Former *soldaty* are isolated and interrogated when they arrive. Luckily, the Russosken kept admirable personnel records, and we were able to obtain them. Most of the men are happy to be home—the Russosken 'recruited' heavily and indiscriminately here." Her lips twisted in a sardonic smile.

"However, there appear to be some who are loyal to the

Russosken, perhaps members of the ruling family." She flicked her hand, and holograms of a large family appeared above the table. Several of them bore a passing resemblance to Francine and Dusica—blonde, blue-eyed, tall, and thin. Two were darker, but their high cheekbones and pointed chins made the family relationship obvious.

Tony exchanged a glance with Maarteen. The other man nodded, recognizing the two men from the shuttle terminal. He looked at the others in the room. Had one of them sent these men to intercept Tony?

Maarteen raised an eyebrow. Tony shook his head. He did not want to discuss the meeting at the terminal. Not yet.

"Mikhail Semenov was the patriarch here," Orin continued. The holo zoomed in on the oldest man in the group, and smaller pictures and video popped up showing Semenov in many different locations. "He has been detained by our teams, and most of the family with him. However, two younger members are unaccounted for: Gavrie and Yeva Semenov." The display changed, showing one of the darker youths and a blonde woman. "We believe they are on-planet and gathering a following. Semenov's sister, Svenka, is also at large, but she's under surveillance. She hasn't participated in family business in decades."

"Talk to Dusica Zielinsky." Tony flicked a contact script to Orin's comtab.

"Zielinsky?" Edwin broke in. "The *nachal'nik*?!"

Tony nodded. "The current *nachal'nik*'s sister. She's working with Russosken families to help ease their reintegration into society." He hid a smile at the careful phrase. "She will help the Semenovs understand their new reality and curb the violence."

"Can we trust her?" Orin asked.

Shouts went up around the table.

"No!"

"We don't need their help!"

"The Russosken will destroy everything if we work with them."

"We just got rid of them!"

"You didn't get rid of them completely," Tony countered loudly. "I have no doubt you could eventually hunt down and exterminate every Russosken on this planet. But is that who you want to be? You wanted freedom from that kind of terror, but now you're talking about visiting it on others? If you're going to do that, you may as well invite the Federation to send troops in." He deliberately made eye contact with each person at the table. "We're better than that. If you work with Dusica, you can make the Russosken better than that, too."

"This is a local matter," Bart said in a hard voice. "We appreciate your input, but this is something we need to decide for ourselves."

Tony stood. "That's your right. I got into this because I believe in the right of all people to govern themselves. But I also believe in mercy and the rule of law. If you agree, you'll model yourselves on something other than the Federation and the Russosken ways. Don't lower yourselves to their level. You're better than that, and your people deserve more."

He glanced at Maarteen. "I have an errand to run, and then I'm headed out. If you need anything more, call me in the next few hours." He looked at the assembled group. "Sebi is a good man. I recommend you listen to him. Thanks for the update. Best of luck."

"I'll see him out," Maarteen told the group. "I can come back, if you wish."

Edwin and Bart exchanged a look. "Not today. We have much to discuss. We'll give you a call soon, though. Please stay on Varitas; we value your input."

With the door shut behind them, Tony turned to Maarteen with a wry grin. "Does that mean they don't value my input?"

"You gave them a dose of harsh reality," Maarteen said. "Most of them will come around to it once they think about it. A few will have to be convinced."

"What do you know about Orin?"

"She grew up here. Well respected in the community. Why?"

"She has the appearance of a trained agent." Tony headed toward the door to the utility room.

"Really?" Maarteen stepped up to the red line marking the pod stop. "What does a trained agent look like? I thought you were supposed to blend in."

"Exactly. It's probably nothing, but she's too average."

Maarteen nodded as the pod whooshed to a stop. "She is. She's so average, it didn't occur to me that no one is average in all ways. Almost as if she were designed to be unnoticed. Do you think she sent your friends?"

"I don't know," Tony replied. "They didn't accomplish anything. I suspect any mission Orin planned would be much more successful."

"I guess it depends on what that mission was."

"I guess it does." Tony took a seat in the pod. "See what you can learn about her."

"On it. You headed back to the hotel?"

Tony nodded. "I have time for a drink before my next meeting."

"Excellent." Maarteen swiped in their destination. "You have to taste this wine I discovered."

CHAPTER 8

THE *SWAN* ARRIVED in Iraca on schedule. Quinn and End prepped and launched the comm boxes, working through the steps easily and efficiently. They moved the last one to the airlock and released it into the wild like a well-oiled machine.

"We're getting pretty good at this." End wiped his hands on a rag.

"It's not that hard," Quinn replied absently, watching the ping data as the box deployed. "This one's set. I'm shutting her down." She initiated the hibernation sequence and watched until the data stopped flowing. "Textbook. Almost makes me wish there were more to release."

"Right." End gave her a narrow look. "So much fun."

"I said almost. Don't you get a feeling of satisfaction from a job well done?"

"Sure. But I'd get more satisfaction from a visit to Iraca Station's arcade. They have the new full-immersion Worlds of Wonder vee-eye-eye-eye."

"Isn't that pronounced eight?" Quinn asked as they returned to the lounge.

End rolled his eyes. "Only if you're old."

"End!" Maerk said. "You never call a lady old!"

"She calls me young!"

"Not the same thing at all," Maerk replied.

"It's okay." Quinn raised her hands in surrender. "I say it all the time. But I definitely recommend you don't add it to your repertoire when chatting with the ladies."

Ellianne looked up from her school assignment. "Ooh, End's gonna chat up some ladies."

"No, I'm— Never mind." End shook his head and pulled open the fridge. "I need space."

"We all do." Maerk clapped him on the shoulder. "This ship was not designed for a family of six for weeks on end. Too small."

"That's why we're taking a day at the station," Liz stepped off the bridge. "We all need a little time away from each other." She turned to Quinn. "They have a highly-reputable day camp. We used to send End and Dareen for a couple hours whenever we were nearby. The break was worth the cost. I sent the details to your comtab."

"Thanks, I was thinking it would be nice if Dareen could take them out for a run, but since she isn't here, a day camp works." Quinn smiled as she paged through the information. "The station has a spa? I know where I'm going!"

"Are you sure this stuff is all up and running?" Maerk asked. "Iraca was a Russosken-controlled planet. They might have shut down extraneous services during the upheaval."

"Yes and no," Liz said. "I mean, the Russosken controlled this system. But the clan here eased up after Auntie B took out Petrov. I thought killing him would bring the wrath of the Russosken, but the Iracans saw the writing on the wall. They eased restrictions, stopped all the protection rackets, and invited the locals into the decision-making process. So far, everyone is happy."

"Talk about textbook," Quinn said. "I wish they all went that smoothly."

"I think in the long run, we'll see more freedom on the worlds that had more violent upheaval," Liz said. "The Russosken are still firmly in charge here. They're just not being *crepivs* about it."

"Velvet cage?" Quinn said.

"Kind of, but for now it's working. I'm sure their grip will tighten again if they get the chance." Liz stole a couple chips from the loaded plate End carried past. "Mom tax."

End laughed and held out the plate. "You bought it, I guess you can eat it."

She waved him away. "It's not as much fun when you don't protest."

Quinn sat next to her daughter and held out her comtab. "What do you think?"

The video showed a montage of kids playing games, cooking, building things, swimming. "They have a pool on the space station?" Ellianne's eyes sparkled. "Cool!"

"Oh, sorry, that one's an overnight trip to the planet." Quinn swiped through the pages. "We won't be here that long."

"What about the pirates?" Ellianne hadn't mentioned her father since the incident, instead referring to "the pirates."

"The camp has a secure system." Quinn rubbed her back. "Only people I designate can pick you up. And if it's anyone besides me, they call to check unless I authorize in person, in advance. Besides, you can take Sashelle to protect you."

Ellianne's head popped up, and she looked at the caat, currently sleeping in her box under the bench. "Do you want to go to camp with me, Sashelle?"

A heavy sigh breathed through Quinn's head, but she could tell it was meant for her alone. *I would be delighted,* Sashelle replied to them both.

"Yay!" Ellianne jumped out of her seat, dragging the huge animal out of her cubby to hug her.

You're lucky I like you, Sashelle said. *No one else is allowed to handle me this way.*

"I know," Ellianne said. "I love you, too."

TONY AND MAARTEEN sat at the bar. A half-empty bottle of wine stood between them, and each had a glass.

"See what I mean?" Maarteen asked.

Tony sipped from his glass again, letting the slightly fizzy beverage roll over his tongue. "You're right. I'd call it a cider. One of the best I've had in a long time."

"Exactly." Maarteen refilled their glasses. "They brag about their wines here, but they'd be better off marketing it as cider." He leaned in confidentially. "I've got a pallet of this on the way to Lunesco."

"A pallet?" Tony asked. "Are you planning on opening a wine bar?"

Maarteen shook his head. "Never hurts to have a rare commodity to trade. This stuff has an amazing shelf life. I don't know what they do to it..." He picked up his glass and sipped.

Tony raised his glass. "Genius."

A blonde woman took the stool next to Maarteen. Her perfect hair, makeup and clothing all spoke of money. "I'd like to meet a genius."

"You're sitting next to him," Tony said from Maarteen's other side.

The woman looked Maarteen up and down then nodded regally. "I am Svenka Semenova. It seems we might have things to discuss."

Tony went still, watching Semenova's hands. She didn't appear to be carrying a weapon, but her beaded bag could hold a mini blaster or an injectable.

"I'm flattered you think I might be of interest to you. I am Sebi Maarteen." He glanced at Tony, raising an eyebrow.

"Charles Anthony." Tony gave the alias he'd used the first time he met Maarteen. "Just passing through."

Semenova barely spared Tony a glance. "Mr. Maarteen, I have heard of you. My brother is currently a guest of yours, I believe."

"Not my guest," Maarteen said. "I know where he is, and could possibly arrange a visit, if that's what you're after."

"Ah, right to the point. I like that. No, I have no wish to visit that

—" She spit out a string of unrecognizable words. "I wish to discuss the safety and prosperity of the rest of the family under the new reality."

"Does that include a young man named Gavrie?" Tony asked.

Svenka blinked and regarded him for a long moment. "He is part of the family."

"Perhaps you know why he accosted me at the shuttle terminal," Tony said. "And how he knew I'd be there."

Svenka's eyes narrowed, focusing on him with laser intensity. "Who are you, Mr. Anthony, that my nephew would be interested in accosting you?"

"I'm no one." Tony spread his hands. "A friend of Sebi. That's why I was surprised and confused to be confronted by your nephew and his large friend."

"They did not hurt you," Svenka said. It was not a question.

"No."

"If they did not hurt you and you are no one, I don't care." Svenka lowered her voice and said something else. Maarteen leaned in closer to hear. Tony watched them for a moment, but his current position on Maarteen's far side inhibited his view. He looked around the room, cataloging the occupants.

There, in the corner. A new couple. They'd arrived as Svenka had slid onto her stool. To a casual observer, they appeared to be engrossed in each other, but Tony knew better. The only question was who they worked for: Svenka or Bart? He swiped a quick text to Maarteen.

"Would you excuse me for a moment?" Maarteen asked. "I'm expecting a message from my daughter." He waited until Svenka nodded, then glanced at his comtab. A covert look at the corner table and a casual swipe of his hand, and he returned to his conversation.

Tony waited a few seconds before checking his own comtab. Maarteen's message indicated he recognized the pair in the corner. He waited for Svenka to finish a comment before breaking in. "Sebi, thanks for the wine, but I must be off."

"It was good to see you, Charles!" Maarteen turned on his stool so Svenka couldn't see his face. He rolled his eyes toward the observers and winked. "Safe travels, my friend. Come see me on Lunesco when this is all over. We'll open another bottle!"

"Sounds good." Tony nodded at the woman. "Pleasure to meet you, Ms. Semenova."

She dismissed him with a curt nod.

He wove between the tables, heading for the street entrance. About halfway there, he checked his comtab as if consulting it for directions and pivoted. When he turned, he made eye contact with the woman at the corner table. She flicked a glance at Maarteen, then gave the barest nod. Without pausing, Tony continued to the door leading into the hotel lobby.

Outside the bar, two huge blond men sat in spindly chairs, pretending to read their comtabs. Neither of them was the man from the terminal, although they could have been his brothers. They looked poised for action, like viscous dogs who had been chained outside a house. Their cold eyes gave Tony a once-over as he passed. The smaller man's eyes narrowed, darting from Tony's pocket to the almost invisible bulge under his loose jacket. Trust a pro to know where to look for concealed weapons. Tony nodded, maintaining eye contact.

The larger man looked through the door to the clearly visible Semenova. He glanced at Tony again, cracked his knuckles, and returned to his comtab. The smaller man followed his partner's example, so Tony strode away.

CHAPTER 9

TONY TOOK the escalator down to the same slider pod station, this time taking the green line. He smiled pleasantly at the people milling around him and took his place in the queue. Keeping one eye on the exit and the other on new arrivals, he worked his way to the front. Once inside the pod, he relaxed into the seat.

The trip took three transfers and a ride on the surface to confound anyone following him. He finally reached his destination: an industrial park on the outskirts of Varitas City and not far from the shuttle field.

A trickle of people filed past, headed for the pod station. As he walked, the trickle turned to a deluge. He entered a building, pushing against the flow of departing workers, and made his way to the second floor. As he exited the stairwell, he stepped in front of a man hurrying past. "Excuse me, could you direct me to Wend Charlatan?"

The man looked longingly toward the elevator, then turned to Tony and gave him a false smile. "I'm sorry, it's after hours. You aren't going to find anyone here."

Tony looked at his comtab then held it up for the other man to inspect. "It's three minutes to four. What time do you quit here?"

"Four." The man's eyes darted away. "The, uh, the boss let us go a few minutes early."

Tony chuckled sympathetically. "Three minutes early. Nice. Still, Wend usually works late. Do you know where I can find her?"

The other man's eyes snagged on Tony's then flicked away again. "Wend's not here. Haven't seen her in a couple weeks. She must be on vacation."

"I guess I missed that on social media," Tony tried to ignore the sinking feeling in his chest. "Any idea when she'll be back?"

He shook his head, looking pointedly toward the elevator. "I don't work with her. I gotta go." He darted around Tony and hurried away.

Tony looked after him. He seemed uncomfortable talking to Tony. Was he always suspicious of strangers, or did it have something to do with Wend? Tony strolled along the corridor. Small offices lined the left side, with glass walls facing the hallway and small, high windows letting in light from outside. A panel on each door identified the occupant and their role in the company. On the right, an open area with pod-like workspaces stretched across to another row of offices.

More offices lined the far end, and one had a light on. Checking each name as he passed the doors, Tony hurried toward the occupied room. The plate on this door read, "Narine, Director of Accounting."

"Perfect." Tony knocked against the open doorframe. "Hi, sorry to bother you. I'm looking for Wend Charlatan."

The man inside looked up, his face tight. "So'm I. Let me know if you find her."

"That fellow told me she was on vacation." Tony jerked his thumb over his shoulder.

"If she is, she didn't tell me, and I'm her boss." Narine swiped through screens on his desk. "Who're you?"

"Charles Anthony." Tony bowed slightly. "I'm a former classmate of Wend's. I was in the area and popped in to say hello. Haven't seen her in years."

The man looked up from his display, leaning his elbows on the desk. "I don't know where she is. I haven't seen her in three weeks. She just, poof, vanished. Three weeks of work I've had to suck up. That's why I'm still here." He growled.

"Wow, that's odd." Tony pushed his hands into his pockets. "I've heard there's been a bit of unrest here... You don't suppose she got caught up in something..." He let the statement hang, unfinished.

"She's not involved with the Russosken." Narine glanced at Tony and hedged. "At least, she never gave me any reason to think she was. I suppose she could have poked the wrong bear."

"That doesn't sound like Wend to me. She was always pretty cautious."

"You sure you knew her? Cautious is not a word I would use."

"Really?" Tony leaned against the doorjamb as if he were ready to chat all night. "Why do you say that?"

Narine opened his mouth then snapped it shut again. "I don't have time to chat. And I don't gossip about my employees. Can you show yourself out?"

Tony straightened. "Sure, sorry! You said you're busy. Can I drop a note on her desk, in case she comes back? Just point me in the right direction."

"Third pod, second left." Narine eyed Tony. His eyes flicked upward—probably to the camera mounted in the hallway—then back to Tony's face.

Tony smiled and nodded. "Thanks for your time." He strolled into the open area. Passing the first row of pods, he turned left and counted three. Bright pink desktop accoutrements and several pictures of kittens in bonnets? Definitely not Wend—it stood out too much. Clearly, he'd misinterpreted Narine's directions. He slid between the pods behind this one and looked to his right.

This desk was neatly arranged, with a small name plate reading "Gwendolyn Charlatan." He looked at Narine, still watching him, and gave a thumbs-up and a grin. He pulled a business card from his pocket. The name Charles Anthony and a string of academic credentials filled most of the front. He flipped it over, scrawled a coded message, and left it lying on the desk.

With a wave to Narine, he strolled to the elevators.

THREE HOURS LATER, Narine finally departed. Tony watched the man from a dark lobby window in the next building. He'd come in here before the security guard locked up for the night and hung out in the bathroom until they'd left. The large windows gave him an excellent view of Wend's building, and the lobby seats were reasonably comfortable. After Narine finally left, Tony waited twenty minutes, then let himself out through the fire exit.

The building's fire alarm blared. Tony hurried through the shadows, his hat pulled low as usual. Reaching the rear of the parking area, he crept along the back of the property in the shadow of the thick bushes planted there.

Sirens wailing, a series of fire vehicles raced into the parking lot. They parked around the perimeter, firefighting robots spilling from the rear. A small human team directed the robots into the building. While the fire team searched the building, Tony made his way to another facility on the far side of Narine's.

With a grin for the mayhem he'd created, Tony flicked his comtab and used a hidden app to infiltrate the building's security and shut down the alarm while continuing to report an "armed" signal to the monitoring company. Then he popped the back door of Wend's building.

He moved through the building, disabling and re-enabling the security sensors as he went. When he reached the front, he took a seat at the guard station and fired up the security monitors. The system asked for a password.

He rummaged through the desk. Nothing. These guys were more responsible than the usual. He pulled out the top drawer and bent to look at the bottom. There. A small piece of paper stuck to the underside came away easily when he pulled. Like the control center on Sumpter. He smiled as he remembered telling Quinn to look there.

He shone his comtab on the paper and typed in the characters listed there. The system tinged, and a grid of security camera feeds filled the screens. Fingers moving swiftly, he set the system to chime if movement was detected, then he dimmed the screen and turned to his comtab.

The device he'd planted on Wend's desk went to work, switching on her system. The fire alarm might have been overkill, but he wanted to clear any late workers off the second floor so they wouldn't see the telltale light on Wend's system. Anyone still inside should have rushed to the lobby to watch the action next door. Besides, it had been a long time since he'd done anything exciting. He didn't mind burning a few bridges on this weird world.

His app finished its work, and the system connected to his comtab. He smiled as he activated Wend's email program and went to the sent folder. There it was. An email sent three weeks ago, several days before she disappeared. It had gone to one of the covert drop boxes Commonwealth agents used. Drop boxes the Commonwealth had lost access to, if Dr. Fallstaff was to be believed. He opened the file and copied the message. Then he disconnected and slipped out the back of the building.

The robot fire squads were returning to their vehicles as he strolled by. "What's going on?" he asked one of the human botminders.

"False alarm." The woman glowered at her tablet as she recalled her robot hordes to their mobile platform. "Probably some idiot used the emergency exit. We get these calls every other week."

"Don't they have cameras? You could track down the perps."

"Half the time, those cams aren't even turned on. And even if they got a good picture, the government doesn't bother tracking 'em down."

"You think that will change now?" Tony asked. "You know, with the Russosken—"

She glared at him and shook her head slightly. "I guess it's good practice for us."

"And no one gets hurt." He raised a hand in salute and headed for the ground transport station. No surveillance and poor enforcement were good for him. But why were these people still afraid of the Russosken?

CHAPTER 10

YOU OWE ME, Sashelle told Quinn as they returned to the *Swan*. *Much tuna and many ear scratches. Perhaps even catnip.*

"That bad?" Quinn murmured.

"It was awesome!" Ellianne exclaimed. "Climbing walls and water slides and sand dunes and—"

"On a station?" Quinn interrupted.

"It was virtual, 'course." Ellianne skipped ahead a few meters then back again. "But we went to the real greenhouses, and we saw the control center for the cargo station." The little girl's voice got so high and fast that she was difficult to understand.

"What did *you* do?" Quinn muttered under her breath, figuring the caat would hear her thoughts as much as her words.

I stood guard, Sashelle said with a heavy mental sigh.

"That must have been very tiring for you," Quinn said sarcastically. "Staying awake all day?"

I did not stay awake. Sashelle's mental voice was indignant, as if sleeping on the job was a lofty sacrifice.

Quinn stopped in the middle of the station passageway, hands on hips, staring down at the caat. "You slept while you were on guard?"

"She's super good at guarding," Ellianne broke off her description of climbing the (virtual) Malhery Cliffs to defend her friend. "You shoulda seen her when Pirate Dean came. She was asleep, then her eyes went, pop!" Ellianne widened her eyes until the whites were visible all around. "Then she went zoom! And her fur poofed up like, wah! And—"

"Dean was here?" She bent down to her daughter's eye level. The girl and the caat stood shoulder to shoulder. Quinn did a double take. "Is Sashelle growing? How is she as tall as you?" She stared at Sashelle for a second, then looked at Ellianne.

Ellianne gave her a disgusted look. "She grows and shrinks lots."

"She does?" Quinn frowned. "Never mind. Dean was here?"

"Uh huh. Till he saw Sashelle all puffed up, and her back was arched, and she glared lasers from her eyes and—"

"Lasers from her eyes?" Quinn asked, her eyes narrowing. "Really?"

"No, not really." Ellianne sighed. "But she roared and showed her teeth. She's got two rows of teeth!"

Quinn looked at the caat. "Would you care to elaborate?"

Apparently, I went "zoom" and "wah."

Quinn glared.

The caat relented. *I heard him coming. His thoughts are loud and disordered. Easy to notice, especially since I was listening for them. He came to the door of the facility. I threatened him, and he left.*

"You threatened him?" Quinn's brows drew down. "Did you talk to him?"

Sashelle gave her a stare that clearly indicated her mere presence was enough to deter a would-be pirate.

Quinn straightened up and took her daughter's hand. "I'm feeling a little deterred myself. How do you do that?"

The caat ignored her.

AFTER DINNER, the *Swan* departed Iraca Station, heading for the jump beacons. "Two days to get there?" Quinn asked Liz as the kids cleared the table.

Liz nodded. "Same as coming in. Then two more from the jump point to Robinson's. Unless you wanted to hit Xury Station?"

Quinn shook her head. "Nope. Tony said we'd meet up at Robinson's. I'm not looking forward to the six-hour 'vator ride. I don't suppose Dusica can get us permission to land?"

Maerk laughed. "I'm sure she could, if she wanted to spend the credits. We'll be there a couple days before Tony and Lou. Are you taking the kids down?"

Quinn glanced at the hatch to the stern of the ship. With the dishes loaded into the recycler, Lucas and Ellianne had joined End in the mostly empty cargo hold for a game of g-ball. "That Dean person was nosing around today. Sashelle scared him away, but he's got to be tracking us. And if he was there, Reggie must have been, too."

Liz's face paled and Maerk looked worried. "Tracking us how? You said everyone and everything was scanned when you boarded Dusica's ship. And he had no way of knowing about your connection to the *Swan* until Daravoo. Have any of you gotten anything new since then?"

"We didn't buy anything on Taniz Beta. That's the last time we were on a planet." Quinn stood to pace around the room. "I asked End to check the kids' games and tablets, but there was nothing."

"I'll rig up a scanner and do the whole ship," Maerk said. "We should have enough time before we reach Robinson's to cover everything. See if you can think of any other way he might know. Any one you've been in contact with?"

Quinn shook her head. "Who knows our itinerary? Did you have to file a flight plan?"

Liz grunted. "Only if you want to go somewhere in the system other than the jump point. And no one cares where you go after you jump."

"But that shipment of comm boxes came with a delivery schedule," Quinn said, thinking it through as she spoke. "So, if Reggie got a hold of that..."

"We got those comm boxes from the Commonwealth." Liz sat back in her chair, arms folded over her chest. "How would Reggie, a Federation officer, know the schedule for a Commonwealth delivery?"

"He wouldn't." Quinn paced across the room and back. "Lou knew where we were going, but she wouldn't tell Reggie. Same with the rest of the family." She threw up her hands. "I give up. But until we figure it out, the kids aren't going anywhere unsecure." She glanced at Sashelle, curled up in her cubby under the bench. She leaned forward. "Have you noticed Sashelle is bigger?"

The other two turned to look at the caat.

"She doesn't look any bigger to me," Liz said.

Maerk nodded. "She's always slept in that cubby, and it doesn't look any tighter."

"I know," Quinn said. "But today when we were walking back to the ship, she was as tall as Ellianne!"

Liz and Maerk exchanged a look.

"Maybe you need to rest," Maerk said.

"I spent the day at a spa!" Quinn cried. "How could I get more rested than that?"

"You certainly aren't relaxed right now," Liz said. "Get some sleep. We're safe from Pirate Dean out here."

Maerk grinned. "I upgraded our defensive weapons while we were in the Commonwealth. I wish Pirate Dean would make a run at us."

Liz rolled her eyes. "Save the weapons for a real threat. Dean is not one. Quinn, go to bed. Maybe your brain will jog something loose and it will all make sense in the morning."

TONY STOPPED outside the slider pod station and tried to send a report to Dr. Fallstaff. As she'd reported, the covert communication routes were all inaccessible. He left a report in his own drop box, hoping someone would be able to access it, then logged into the Federation News Organization's anonymous tip line. He entered a carefully worded message and logged out with a smile. If Dr. Fallstaff's team was watching Sven Harvard on the FNO news, they'd get the message.

The ride to the hotel was uneventful. He used the pod's communications node to find a ship headed to Robinson's World and booked a ticket in the name Charles Anthony. He considered returning to the bar when he reached the hotel, but Sebi was well able to handle Svenka, and he didn't want to interfere. Instead, he could go up to the room he never expected to use and take a nap.

He exited the pod and took the escalator up to the lobby. At the top, a large, blond man waited. Tony eyed him. Was this one of Svenka's nearly identical bodyguards, or Gavrie's backup? He stepped off the moving stairs, ignoring the man.

"You will come with me." The large man stepped in front of him.

"I'd rather not," Tony replied. "I was going to take a nap."

"That will have to wait," the thug said.

"I don't think so. I'm tired."

The man leaned closer, towering over Tony.

Tony's hand slid toward his weapon.

"Please?" the man whispered.

Tony looked up in surprise.

"My young friend needs your help," the thug said softly.

Tony considered. "I'll meet him in the bar."

"It's closed, but we can get in."

"Don't break and enter on my account."

"No problem. The seating is open, only the bar is closed." The large man led the way across the lobby to the open door.

A blue force shield protected the bottles behind the bar, and the seating areas were empty. Tony picked a table near the door, putting his back to the wall. He'd prefer to have backup for a meeting like this, but if he made enough noise, he expected the hotel manager would come running.

The large man sat down.

"I thought your friend was coming," Tony said.

The man shook his head. "He doesn't know I'm here. My name is Kostas."

"Charles Anthony."

"I know." Kostas shifted his chair so he could watch the doors too. "You have been working with the rebellion."

Tony didn't say anything.

Kostas held up a hand. "I know you can't say anything. But we have an inside source."

Tony raised an eyebrow. "Russosken have a source inside the rebellion?"

"No!" Kostas looked around as if his own voice had alarmed him, then leaned closer. "No. *We* have a source. A friend who knows someone who knows someone. I want to bring my friend—my other friend—" He seemed to get lost in all the friends.

"Gavrie?" Tony asked.

Kostas's eye widened then he nodded. "Yes, Gavrie and Yeva. They are tired of hiding. But they don't want to get locked up."

"I'm not sure what you think I can do," Tony said. "Why not appeal to Auntie Svenka?"

"That's what I suggested," Kostas said. "My brother works for *Ledi* Semenova."

"I saw him. He looked…threatening."

Kostas nodded. "Yeva and Gavrie think she will not help them."

"Did you ask your brother?"

"Yes. He does not know." Kostas drummed his fingers on the table. "*Ledi* Semenova doesn't speak to *soldaty* like us."

This conversation was going nowhere. Tony decided to try another tack. "Why did you accost me at the terminal?"

"Gavrie knew someone was coming to speak to the rebel leaders. He had your arrival information from the friend—"

"Of the friend," Tony interrupted. "Someone inside. Why not go to them directly? Why go through me?"

"Russosken society is very—" He made up and down motions with his hands. "The top does not talk to the bottom. I am the bottom."

"But Gavrie and Yeva are near the top."

"Their family is all in prison." Kostas scratched his head. "There is no one to talk to."

"Except *Ledi* Semenova," Tony suggested.

Kostas nodded. "They won't talk to her. An ancient feud between their father and the *ledi*."

"What do you think I can do?"

"Talk to your friends," Kostas said. "We have information to trade."

"About the friend of the friend?" Tony guessed. "You're going to squeal? You people don't understand the word friend very well, do you?"

Kostas ignored that question. "Will you do it?"

"Who're you going to turn in?" Tony asked.

Kostas shook his head. "I'm not telling you. That is my only leverage. But we know of a leak and will trade that information for immunity."

Tony held up his hands. "Look, this is really not my business. I'll chat with my—" He broke off, not wanting to use the word 'friend' again. "I'll talk to my associates. One of them will contact you. Or not, as they choose. That's the best I can do."

"That is all I ask." Kostas stood and handed him a small card. "This is my contact information."

Tony took the card with a sigh. He'd hand this off to Maarteen and hopefully still have time for that nap.

DAREEN SAT in the former *Screaming Eagle*, newly de-funked and rechristened the *Scarlet Dragon*. Dareen ran a maintenance checklist then shut down the systems. Although she'd never admit it, she missed her brother. She'd even given the shuttle a name he wouldn't complain about.

Much.

She wandered to the *Peregrine's* bridge and slouched into the copilot's seat. Lou glanced at the girl as she arrived, but continued through her own checklist before remarking, "What's eating you?"

Dareen shrugged. "Bored. No one to argue with."

"You flew to the surface a couple days ago," Lou said. "I thought you liked to fly."

"I do, but it's more fun when I get to check out the planet," Dareen said. "Usually. This time, I was glad to drop Tony and leave. I don't like Varitas."

Lou nodded. "Something is off there. Doesn't matter. We've got a secret mission."

"Secret mission?" Dareen sat up in her seat. "To do what?"

"If I told you that, I'd have to space you," Lou joked. "We have to make a delivery on Taniz Beta."

"That's not a secret mission." Dareen slumped again. "We were always going to go to Taniz."

"Well, yeah, but Alpha, not Beta."

"Big deal. Same system, different planet." Dareen yanked on a lock of her hair.

"We're picking up Francine and Fyo."

Dareen looked up. "I thought they were stuck on the planet, doing the nin-chuck thing?"

"They are—or were." Lou swiped up the comm system on her control station and flicked the ship-wide announcer. "Hey, you lot, we're getting close to jump. Is everyone ready?"

Stene reported in. "Cargo is secure."

Kert followed. "All systems are green. But you already knew that."

"Doesn't hurt to double-check," Lou said. "I'm setting the jump for thirty minutes in three, two, one, mark. Leaving the gravity at three-quarters."

Dareen raised her eyebrows.

"It's easier on my old bones and saves a bit of fuel." Lou set up the jump and flicked the programmed autopilot to green. "We're on our way. I'm going to grab a cup of coffee before we jump. Having a little caffeine in the system helps cushion the jolt. You watch the screens."

"Hey, wait a minute," Dareen said as the old woman swiped the control screens to her station. "What's the secret mission? What are Francine and Fyo doing?"

Lou grinned over her shoulder as she left the bridge. "Need to know, and you don't need."

CHAPTER 11

TWO DAYS LATER, the *Peregrine* eased into an orbit around Taniz Beta. Dareen scowled at the three pallets of unmarked boxes Stene had loaded into the *Scarlet Dragon*. Their contents were deemed "none of her business" and she hated flying blind—even when she was landing in friendly territory.

"You can't expect me to do another mission without all the details." She glared at her grandmother over the slowly closing cargo ramp. "Remember what happened last time?"

Lou grinned. "Nice try. There aren't any cloaking devices in those boxes. I could lie to you and tell you it's food. Would that make you feel better?"

"Why can't you tell me the truth?" Dareen demanded.

"I told you, it's classified." Lou disappeared behind the rising hatch, but her voice carried through the opening. "Your cadet friend on Athenos would know better than to argue with that."

Dareen gritted her teeth as the hatch clanged shut, giving Lou the last word. She swiped her comtab. "Maybe I should go to the academy and learn that," she snapped before swiping the device off. Not her finest moment, but she wished her grandmother would treat her like an adult.

Grumbling, she stomped to the cockpit, shutting the cargo hatch behind her. Even when she was in a bad mood, she always followed the checklists. Her mother had drilled that into her when she'd learned to fly as a child. She fastened her harness and worked through the startup sequence.

Lou's voice came through the speakers. "*Dragon*, you are cleared to depart."

"Thank you, *Peregrine*," she replied formally. "Checklist complete. All systems nominal. Unlock the clamps."

"Unlocking."

The ship vibrated as the clamps released and the skirt holding the shuttle to the ship pulled away. Dareen fired the maneuvering thrusters and tumbled the shuttle away from the ship. She'd left the artificial gravity off and enjoyed the press of her body against the restraints as the ship rolled and dropped.

She loved flying, but sometimes the baggage that came with it—dealing with her grandmother—was enough to make her question her current occupation. Going to the academy would let her continue to fly, but the restrictions would increase by a factor of ten. Or a hundred. She didn't know if that was something she was prepared to accept.

Yet.

With a flick of the controls, she activated the flight path to Dusica's landing field. "I am clear, landing on schedule. Transferring to Fortenta control now. *Dragon* out."

"Safe travels, *Dragon*. *Peregrine* out."

The landing at Fortenta was routine, and she taxied to the familiar building. Last time she landed here, she'd had to take off before she set foot on the ground. This time, maybe she'd actually get to spend a few hours by the pool. She parked the shuttle, ran her shutdown sequence, and let herself out, a small bag in hand.

"Ahoy, *Dragon*!" Fyo waved wildly as he strode across the tarmac.

Dareen jumped off the retractable steps. The two men behind

Fyo dropped into crouches, weapons drawn in an instant, and pointed at her. Dareen froze, hands raised. "Nice to see you, too."

"Aleksei, stand down," Fyo spun and glared at the man on his right. "She's my friend."

"Sorry, sir," the blond man said. "*Ledi* Dusica told us to be on guard."

Fyo grimaced. "Against Dareen? Geeze, she has trust issues." He waved the two men off and strode forward to grab her in a bear hug. "Come here, you."

Dareen squeaked. "Hey, ease up, nin-chuck! You're suffocating me!"

Fyo laughed and his arms dropped. "Did you bring the caviar?"

"Caviar?" Dareen repeated.

"Yeah, Dusi paid your grandmother a hefty sum for a boatload of Cartesian Caviar."

Dareen laughed. "That's not caviar. That's Tony's code for 'secret delivery.' Could be anything. I'm glad I'm not the only one in the dark."

Fyo darted a glance at her, then over his shoulder at his bodyguards. He choked out a fake-sounding laugh that turned into a cough.

Dareen wasn't sure what he was trying to say, but she was smart enough to change the subject. "Do we have to unload that stuff ourselves?"

"Heck, no," Fyo said with a wink. "That's one of the few perks of being *nachal'nik*. Vik, oversee the unloading, will you? Pop the trunk, Dareen."

She threw him a confused look.

"Open the cargo hatch."

"Sure." She swiped her comtab and the back of the shuttle hinged open, rotating smoothly to the ground to form a ramp. She swiped again, and Vik's device pinged on his belt. "That control code will allow you to close her up when you're done unloading. Thanks."

"Awesome, let's go!" Fyo grabbed her hand and dragged her to an expensive-looking cross between a hovercraft and a sports shuttle.

"Is this a—" she asked as he opened the front door for her.

He slid in beside her. "Sarterian Systems Pulsar Three coupe."

Aleksei climbed into the rear-facing seat behind them.

"This thing can do zero to two-eighty in two-point-three seconds." Fyo tapped the dash, and blue holographs filled the space between him and the windscreen. His hands moved quickly, flicking controls and settings.

"Hey, slow down!" Dareen stared at the display. "I've always wanted to fly one of these things. I want to see the controls!"

Fyo walked her through the systems, talking excitedly as he went.

"You might want to strap in, *Ledi* Dareen," Aleksei said over his shoulder. "The *nachal'nik* drives quite quickly."

Fyo laughed. "If by quickly, you mean like a boss, you're right, Aleksei."

"Fantastic." Dareen yanked the straps over her shoulders and clicked the latches. "You know I'm a pilot, right? We don't like riding with other people very much. Especially if they drive like 'a boss'." Her palms grew damp.

"No worries," Fyo said. "It'll be smooth as a hyperjump."

"One of the first ones," Aleksei muttered. "Back before they invented jitter dampers."

"It looks like he hasn't crashed it yet," Dareen said over her shoulder. "Surely that's a good sign."

"That's a sign that he got it yesterday."

Fyo swiped another icon, and the small ship rose off the ground. Instead of stopping a meter above the road like a regular hovercraft, it continued rising. Just as Dareen was sure they'd reached the maximum altitude for a hovercraft, it shot forward. The straps dug into her shoulders, accompanied by a deafening roar.

"I love this thing!" Fyo yelled, throwing the ship into a tight roll.

"Fyo!" Dareen looked over her shoulder as they straightened out. "That was a beautiful roll, but I don't think Aleksei is big on acrobatics." The other man had his eyes closed as he puffed loudly through pursed lips like a woman giving birth.

"Sorry, Lex!" Fyo yelled. He lowered his voice. "I thought he was kidding."

"He looks too pale to be faking it."

"He's always pale. I think he's part vampire." Fyo tried to twist around in his seat.

Dareen grabbed his arm. "Watch where you're going! We're too close to the ground! I'll check on Lex. Hold it steady."

Fyo leveled the ship, and Dareen unfastened her restraints. With a quick look through the front window to make sure there were no hazards in sight, she twisted onto her knees and stuck her head over the seatback. "You okay, Lex?"

Aleksei opened his eyes and winked at her. "I'm going to be sick."

Dareen twisted around and sat down, fastening the straps again. "He's fine. You two are a disaster." She watched the jungle pass beneath them for a while, then turned to Fyo. "Can I have a turn?"

He sized her up for a moment, then shrugged. "Sure. I know you're a good pilot. But we're almost there." He indicated a flashing point on the navigation display. "That's the estate."

Dareen shoved her hands into the holographic interface. "I have the ship!" She wigged the virtual stick back and forth.

"You have the ship." Fyo held his hands up to signify the release of control.

With a malicious grin, Dareen cranked the ship into a swooping barrel-roll.

"Hey!" both boys yelled.

"Oops, sorry! Does that make you feel sick?" At the end of the roll, she pulled back hard, swooshing up into a loop.

"Enough!" Fyo cried, holding his stomach. In the back, Aleksei giggled.

"You want it back?" Dareen wiggled the ship again.

"No. Go ahead and land." Fyo flicked the nav display. "That long field is flat enough for an easy stop."

Dareen spotted the clearing in the dense jungle. Deftly, she eased the ship down, slowing as they skimmed above the trees. The thick foliage gave way to tall grass. They flew over a fence and above a road. She engaged the hovercraft mode and slid along the driveway to park in front of a huge house.

When they climbed out, Aleksei gave her a high-five. "That was awesome!" He glanced at Fyo, whose face looked a bit green. "Showed him who's boss."

Dareen ducked her head to hide her grin and shrugged. "I'm guessing you're not a pilot."

Aleksei shook his head. "Didn't qualify for training. The Russosken are very strict about who they teach."

Dareen nodded. "I'm sure Fyo could teach you. Of course, when you know how to fly, riding with someone else is way scarier. You know exactly what could go wrong."

They climbed the steps and walked into the entry hall. This house looked similar to Petrov's home on Daravoo, with wide hallways, high ceilings, and lots of glass at the back. Perhaps the Russosken all used the same designer. Dareen's lips quirked. It wouldn't do to have different tastes in a control-freak heavy environment like the Russosken.

Francine came down the wide staircase. "Hello, Dareen."

"Francine!" Dareen hurried forward, hugging her friend awkwardly on the steps. "I got to fly Fyo's Pulsar!"

"I'm sure it was every girl's dream," Francine said dryly. "You staying overnight?"

"Yeah. It doesn't make sense to go back up until you're ready to come with me. Fuel isn't free. Can we hang out by the pool?"

"Absolutely." Francine linked her arm through Dareen's and turned her toward the stairs. "We'll see you boys out there."

"What about those reports Dusi was droning on about?" Fyo followed them up the steps.

"You're the *nachal'nik*." Francine cackled. "Tell her to do them herself."

CHAPTER 12

ONCE BACK ABOARD THE PEREGRINE, Dareen tinkered with the diagnostics on the shuttle currently known as the *Romantic Wizard*. She wasn't thrilled with that name and wished she'd saved the dragon one for this craft. Most of the time, she just thought of it as "hers," but names made it easier to talk to controllers.

The main engine was still deviating from spec. It was safe to fly, but since they had a second shuttle, she could take the time to tweak the system.

Francine strolled in. "Did you see this newscast?" It turned out traveling with the *nachal'nik* came with extra baggage, but also some perks. Francine and Fyo rated guest cabins on the *Peregrine*, while their security team, Aleksei and Marielle, made do with the extra crew berths.

"Nope." Dareen looked up from the screen. She stretched her back and rotated her neck. She'd been staring at this thing for too long.

"That rebellion Tony's been talking about is happening." Francine held her comtab out for Dareen to see. "Unrest on several core Federation planets. Coups on two of them. Farivel and Darius have declared independence from the Federation."

"Darius was always pushing to get out," Dareen said as they climbed the steps to the living levels. "But Farivel is a surprise."

"There's been action on Hadriana, too," Francine said. When they reached the lounge, she flipped the broadcast onto the larger screen. "Looks like Quinn's monster-in-law is holed up in her estate. The elected officials are using the current situation to twist out of her control."

A scene of armed civilians facing the ornate gates of the LaRaine Estate dissolved and the main square in New Astorian appeared. Protestors milled around the square, while officials held a press conference from the steps of a hulking building.

"The governor of Hadriana issued a statement this morning," a newscaster was saying. "He reaffirmed the planet's loyalty to the Federation. However, it's becoming increasingly clear the covert control exercised by the LaRaine family is slipping. Gretmar LaRaine has not responded to requests for comment."

Lou stomped into the room and plopped into a seat. "What about Romara?"

Francine shook her head. "Nothing. No press conferences, no statements, no word at all. And of course, nothing is happening there—too many Federation soldiers. If there's any unrest, it's going to be stomped out before it happens."

She flipped through a few screens and settled on a newscast from Romara. Her gaze flicked over the backdrop behind the chatting celebrity newscasters. It looked like a window on the main plaza in Romara City. Tourists wandered and gawked. Locals gathered in groups, chatting. "See? Business as usual. But this is useless anyway. It's all done in a studio."

She swiped a few more and tossed up another view. "This is live security footage from the plaza." The huge, paved square was nearly empty. Armed soldiers stood at the corners. A couple of civilians hurried across the space, looking around nervously. "That's not normal. What are they saying in the Commonwealth?"

Lou's face darkened. "Communications with the Commonwealth are down. Feds must have a net blockade running. The new boxes Liz has been delivering *should* help with that. End and Quinn have been setting them up, but they aren't getting anything useful from across the border. Tony said there's a glitch on the Commonwealth side, but you'd think they'd have gotten that fixed by now."

"You can't get anything from them?" Francine asked. "Nothing from friends? I'll try my neighbor on N'Avon." She swiped and flicked at her comtab. "*Futz.* Nothing but an error message. Maybe Dusica can get through. She has an extensive network."

She sent a message to her sister while Lou paged through her own device. "Dusi says she can get normal broadcasts from the Commonwealth—news, weather, sports—but no personal messages. She can't tell if the block is from this side or that."

"Maybe a combination of both?" Dareen suggested. "Maybe they're interfering with each other?"

"Is that even possible?" Lou asked.

"Sure, it's possible," Francine said. "But the Commonwealth doesn't normally block comms. They want people to know what's going on. Unless it's being done covertly from inside the Commonwealth on behalf of the Federation?"

Lou shrugged and heaved herself out of her chair. "It doesn't concern us. I have a job to do—pick up Tony on Robinson's then deliver you two to Rossiya. And your huge cargo. Then I have another job lined up, and another. As long as I know enough to stay out of the way, I don't care what's happening on the dirt." She patted the wall as she reached the doorway. "*This* is my world, and no one is going to take it away from me. That's all I care about." She stomped away.

"She doesn't really mean that," Dareen said. "She cares about us. And she'll never admit it, but she cares about you, too. And that means what happens on Taniz Beta and all the other Federation worlds *is* our business."

"Honestly, I'm not a lot more invested than she is," Francine said. "I'm happy about the changes in the Russosken, because I never liked living in that materialistic, grab everything you can and screw everyone else kind of world. But now that we've fixed that, the rest of the galaxy can fend for itself."

"You don't mean that, either," Dareen said confidently. "You care about Quinn and Tony, and they want the Federation to be free."

Francine looked away from the girl's earnest eyes. She was right, but Francine's inner Russosken didn't want to admit it.

"YOU HAVE GOT to be kidding me!" Quinn yelled.

"What's going on?" Maerk poked his head out of the bridge. "Everything okay?"

Quinn held up a pink strap with a bell. "This is Sashelle's collar."

"She has a collar? I haven't seen her wearing one."

"She wears it when she wants. She's a friend, not a pet." Quinn stared at Sashelle, stretched out along the back of the couch, but the caat didn't acknowledge their presence. "Although, come to think of it, I'm not sure how she gets it off and on. I guess it's a fashion statement. She has several. But this collar is the one she wore on Hadriana. Guess what's in it." She held it up for Maerk to inspect.

He closed his eyes. "Don't tell me there's a tracking chip."

"You got it in one." Quinn peeled the strap apart, revealing a thin metallic network. "It was fraying, so Ellianne asked me to fix it." She stuck a fingernail under the metal and pulled the webbing away. "It connects to any external public network it can find. Every time we stopped at a planet or station, this thing reported our location to Reggie."

"But Sashelle wasn't with the kids when Reggie and Dean found them at Xury." Maerk crossed the room to peel the delicate strands off Quinn's finger. "This is a high-end tracker."

"No, but Sashelle's collar was in the *Peregrine*, which was in the system. I think they did get lucky on that one. They probably located the *Peregrine* as Dareen was departing. They could have heard Lucas or Ellianne on the comms." She looked at the circuit in his hand. "The question is, what to do with it now? Destroy it? Take it to Robinson's?"

"We'll be at Robinson's in a few hours," Maerk said. "We have to assume this chip reported to them as soon as we connected to the beacons near Xury. They've had almost two days to get here, so they're probably in-system."

"Right." Quinn looked around the room and spotted a napkin. She took the chip from Maerk and carefully folded it inside the paper. "I wonder why Reggie hasn't reported this tracker to his boss. Andretti would love to capture me, and this thing would have given him more chances than he needs."

"Reggie doesn't strike me as a team player."

"You're right. And if Andretti hasn't reinstated him to active duty, he's probably holding a grudge." She tapped her lips with an index finger, thinking. "He probably wants to bring me in himself, to prove he's worthy." She rolled her eyes. "I'm going to take this to the surface. I'll leave it somewhere. They'll think the kids are there, instead of with you."

"I'll keep watch for them." Maerk flashed an evil grin. "When they don't find you, they'll come looking for us."

"Still waiting for a chance to try out those defensive weapons?" Quinn grinned back at him. She glanced at Sashelle. "You'll help him guard the ship, won't you, Sashelle?"

I will be unavailable.

"Unavailable?" She looked at Maerk, who shrugged. He clearly didn't hear her.

I will be with you on Robinson's.

"You're coming with me? Why?"

You'll need me.

"Really?" Quinn crossed her arms over her chest. "Why do you think I'll need you on Robinson's? I'm meeting Tony there."

The Stealthy One does not arrive for two more days, Sashelle said. *You may think I'm asleep, but I listen. You wish to go early to check on your friend. You will undoubtedly get into trouble on the planet. My primary goal is to keep you safe.*

"That's sweet."

I do it for the kitten.

CHAPTER 13

QUINN RODE a commuter pod across Crusoe City. Sashelle lay on the other seat, apparently asleep. She hadn't said a word since they'd left the *Swan*. Like last time, Quinn didn't know how she'd gotten on or off the space elevator, but she'd appeared on the sidewalk outside the 'vator lobby. No one else took any notice.

"How do you do that?"

Sashelle rolled onto her back, stretching. *Do what?*

"Get around without anyone noticing?" She waved her hand around the pod. "No one saw you get on the elevator. No one noticed you getting off. You don't show up on cameras. Do you walk through walls? Teleport?"

I don't walk through walls. The caat equivalent of a laugh chuckled through Quinn's mind. *I simply redirect attention.*

"Mind control?" Quinn stared at the caat. "Are you controlling my mind?"

Not mind control. More like a suggestion. She rolled over again and sat up. *Instead of talking, I nudge.*

Movement outside the pod caught Quinn's eye, and she stared at a couple arguing on the sidewalk as they zipped past.

See? Like that. Sashelle blinked.

"Like— Wait, did you make me look at those people?"

I nudged you that direction, Sashelle said. *It's a defense mechanism that we caats have perfected. It's not as effective if the subject knows I'm here, as you do. And it's* most *effective if there actually is something worth observing. But if I were under the seat, for example, and a passenger got in, I can keep them from looking down. Usually. It's not foolproof.*

"How many people can you nudge at once?" Quinn asked. "There were hundreds, maybe thousands, in the station! Twenty or thirty in the elevator car. Plus, the people from the other cars and the security guys here on the ground. How can you 'nudge' that many people?"

Think of it as a blanket or a field. I put out a wide 'look over there' signal. They look, and I slip through. I'm also very good at hiding.

"If something made me look in your direction..." Quinn felt her way through the question. "Like if someone dropped a ball and it bounced right up to you. Would I see you?"

Yes, of course, Sashelle said. *I told you, I can't make myself invisible. But most of the time, I will have moved before the ball reaches me.*

"Can your field cover others? Can you make me invisible?"

I just said—

"Sorry," Quinn interrupted. "Can you make me unnoticeable?"

The caat looked her over, blinking several times. *If nothing else drew attention to you, my assistance might help you. But humans are clumsy. You move like giant herbivores—slow, loud, careless.*

"Thanks for the compliment. You're saying it wouldn't be useful for sneaking around because I'm not sneaky enough." Quinn nodded. "But potentially helpful when cornered—if there's a distraction. Got it. We're here."

She'd come to Robinson's World to check on her friend, Melody Vilbrace. Admiral Andretti had blackmailed Melody's husband and sent Melody to Robinson's to spy on his ex-wife, Tiffany. Last time they'd been in the system, Quinn hadn't been able to check on her friend. This time, Quinn had free time, and no one knew she was here.

The pod slid to a stop. As they got out, Quinn watched the people on the sidewalk. Many of them smiled or nodded at her, but none of them looked at Sashelle, pacing at her side. They rounded a corner, and she glanced down.

"Hey, you're small again," Quinn said. The top of the caat's ears barely reached her hip. "How do you do that? Is your size also a suggestion planted in my brain?" An uncomfortable squirm worked its way across her shoulders.

Don't be ridiculous, Sashelle said. *That would require too much effort. I'm larger when I need to counter a threat. It's a natural instinct among my people.*

"*Growing* is a natural instinct?" Quinn blurted out. A couple approaching darted looks their way and moved to the extreme edge of the sidewalk. Quinn smiled and held up her comtab, as if she were speaking to someone on the other end.

You shouldn't speak aloud if you don't want anyone to notice me. Use your inside voice.

"They probably think I'm on a call." Quinn waved the comtab in her hand.

Hard as it may be to believe, your species can feel intent. They feel you are talking to someone local. None of them could tell you why they feel that, but they do.

"I don't find that hard to believe."

Most caats would.

"You're so funny. This is it." She climbed the steps and pressed the access-plate beside the door. She swiped through a couple of options and pressed the call icon.

We're being observed, Sashelle said. *Or, rather, you are. He doesn't see me. Of course.*

"Who?" Quinn asked in alarm. "Where?"

Don't look!

"I wasn't going to. I'm not an idiot. But for the record, telling someone not to look is almost guaranteed to make them look. Is it a Federation agent? I thought my disguise was good enough." She'd worn glasses and the video-scrambling makeup. In addition, she'd put on a dark blonde wig and a baggy dress in beige tones.

I don't know who it is. He's watching the house, not you specifically.

"Crap." She considered leaving, but their observer knew she'd stopped here and nowhere else on the street. She could go to the next building, as if she'd made a mistake. Or pretend she was here to see one of the other occupants. Based on the access panel, there were several apartments in this house. "Can you make me invisible?"

No.

Quinn rolled her eyes. "Fine. Can you make me unnoticeable?"

I can try to redirect him, but he's already seen you. He's not likely to forget someone visited.

"You can't go into his brain and delete the memory?"

Sashelle didn't answer.

The door popped open, and without looking back, Quinn stepped inside. Sashelle slipped in beside her, crouching in a corner to observe their surroundings.

Who unlocked the door?

"Maybe it was Melody," Quinn swiped at her comtab. "I buzzed her apartment. Of course, maybe it was my magic door-opening app."

You have one of those?

Without answering, she held up her comtab and waved it. "Tony gave it to me. Essential spy equipment."

Why didn't you use it at the beginning? We could have walked in like we lived here.

"If he's been watching the building for long, he'll know I don't live here." She headed up the steps. "I'm visiting a friend. And when you're visiting a friend, you don't bust in. Unless they don't answer, and a creepy guy is watching."

The Mighty Huntress bounded up to the first landing. *I fogged his memories. He won't remember you.*

"I thought you couldn't do that!" Quinn hurried up behind her.

I didn't say that, Sashelle replied, surprise and unease in her mental voice. *I didn't know I could do it. I've never tried before.*

"I'm surprised. It seems like an essential skill for staying unnoticed." Quinn started up the second flight.

Sashelle zipped past, stopping in a beam of sunshine on the next landing. *We tend to think in present tense. 'You don't see me now.' I've never worried about it after the fact. At that point, either I have either been captured—which never happens—or they have been neutralized.*

"You've just discovered a non-lethal way to neutralize," Quinn replied. "Look at you, learning from a human!"

It is one of the reasons I'm here.

"Really?"

Don't be absurd.

Quinn glared at the caat, then knocked on a door labeled 3A. They waited a few minutes, but no one answered. "I guess I should have called ahead." Quinn rapped on the door again.

They waited again.

"Darn." Quinn tapped her comtab and pulled up a local message app. The device looked for a nearby receiver app and locked on to a signal labeled "Vilbrace." She double-checked the settings to ensure her device's details wouldn't be attached to the message and adjusted her glasses and wig. Then she flicked the record icon. "Hey, Mel, it's me. I brought some lemon squares. I'll have to catch you another time. I hope you're well." She didn't leave a name or contact number. Melody would recognize her voice and the code word.

With a sigh, she turned away and started down the stairs. "Maybe I can catch her at the studio tomorrow morning."

That's probably less obvious than coming here. You can blend into the crowd. Here, you stick out like a sore claw. Have you considered how we will depart unnoticed?

"Can't you do your magic mind-clouding thing?"

Behind them, a door latch clicked. Quinn stopped and glanced over her shoulder.

A woman crept to the edge of the landing, peering down the dim steps. Sunlight from the landing window shone down, clearly illuminating her blond head and round face.

"Quinn?" she whispered in disbelief. "Is it really you?"

Choking back a squeal of excitement, Quinn raced up the steps and threw her arms around her friend. "It is."

Melody squeezed her convulsively. "I can't believe you're here! I haven't seen you since—"

"Since you left Sumpter," Quinn said when the other woman broke off.

"It's so crazy that they've blamed you for that! All that crap about you working with the Krimson Empire! And that Tony Bergen was a spy! Seriously, Tony? Where did they come up with such crazy stuff?"

Quinn ignored the question. "Can I come in?"

The other woman looked around, as if expecting Federation agents to burst through the walls. "That's not safe. They're watching me."

"Who exactly is watching?" She slid past Melody and ducked below the landing window. Staying as low as possible, she peeked over the sill. The man Sashelle had spotted sat on a bench across the street. Clearly, he didn't care who saw him. She shook her head, disappointed she hadn't noticed him when they first entered the street.

He was standing behind the tree, Sashelle said. *Even I didn't notice him until we reached the doorstep.*

"They work for Andretti," Melody said. "Ted and the kids are still on Romara with him. I can't do anything he doesn't approve without endangering them." Tears welled up in her eyes and she blinked rapidly.

"Why are you here?" Quinn asked. "What does he want you to do?"

"I don't know!" she wailed. "I send him reports every night. Tiffany filmed today. Tiffany went shopping. Tiffany had a date. She doesn't do anything worth reporting! And even if she did, the paparazzi are all over her. They report who she sees and what she buys. I'm useless. I think he likes holding a threat over my head for the sake of being mean."

Or he's hoping you'll come, Sashelle said.

Quinn's head snapped down to glare at the caat now laying in the sunbeam on the landing. "You think?"

"I do!" Melody said. "He's such a bully! He loves sneering at me each time I call." She shuddered.

"No, I—" Quinn broke off. "Do you think he's using you as bait? To get to me?" It was hard to believe Andretti would hate her enough to go to such lengths.

Melody's face went blank, and she blinked. "Of course," she breathed. "That's got to be it! He's trying to— Why does he hate you so much?"

Quinn shrugged. "He had to pin the Sumpter thing on someone and I was a convenient target. Then I escaped and made him and the Federation look bad. He wants to bring me in to boost his credibility."

"There's more to it than that. He never liked you. I remember that time we ran into him at the commissary on Sumpter. I've never felt such hatred." She shuddered again. "He needed a scapegoat, but he picked you because he hates you. Why is that?"

Quinn's lips quirked and she shook her head. "It's a long story. Something that happened when I was still on active duty. A little thing, but he's never forgiven me. Plus, I was friends with his ex-wife. The first one."

Melody's lips formed an "O" and she nodded. "He *really* hates her. Some of the things Tiffany's told me..." She made a sympathetic sound. "Sad to carry that much anger all the time." She looked down the stairs. "Do you have a way to get out without being seen? How did you get in, anyway? If he'd seen you, he'd have the local police on their way up right now."

Quinn's nose wrinkled as she glanced at the caat again. "Trade secret. Are they watching the back?"

Melody shook her head. "Yes and no. There's one guy out there, and he's got cams all around the building, including one inside my front door." Her lips clamped together in disgust. "If you come in, he'll see you're here and it's game over. There are only two of them. They run twelve-hour shifts, trading off at noon and midnight."

"Won't he wonder why you left the apartment but didn't come outside?"

Melody froze for a second, then shrugged. "If I don't go back in pretty soon, he might come looking. But as long as I don't leave the building..."

"I wonder what Andretti is holding over *them*?" Quinn snorted in disgust. "Or is he using Federation troops? He probably told them you're a security threat."

Melody shrugged. "Hard to say. But you need to go. If he decides to do a physical check—"

"Does he do that?" Quinn interrupted. "How often?"

"No set schedule," Melody said. "He stopped by yesterday and checked the door cam, so I think I'm clear for a while. They like me. I bake cookies for them. But if I stay out here too long, he'll check on me."

Quinn pulled out her comtab and swiped through the apps Tony had loaded. She had a camera jammer, but that would bring him in to look. She froze, mid-swipe. Maybe that was what she needed. "Look, you're okay, right?"

Melody nodded. "I'm fine. Stuck, but physically unharmed."

"I'm going to get you out," Quinn said. "I'm going to take Andretti down. But to do that, I need to stay free. When you go back inside, I'm going to jam your door cam's signal. That will bring him inside to look, and I'll sneak out. Easy. Good thing they don't have the sharpest sticks assigned to this. If that was Marielle, we'd be screwed."

Melody's eyes went wide. "Have you seen Marielle? She was with us for a while, but one day, she disappeared."

"She's fine. She's working for a friend of mine on Taniz Beta. I gotta run. You stay safe, and I'll get you out of here soon." She squeezed her friend in a fast hug and ran down the steps.

"Be careful!" Melody called.

"You can count on it."

Coming here wasn't being careful. Sashelle loped down the steps at Quinn's side. *Visiting her was the opposite of careful.*

"Shut up."

CHAPTER 14

WHEN THEY REACHED the entry hall, Quinn paused. "See if you can find a place to hide."

There is this closet under the steps. Sashelle sat in front of a small door. *Or perhaps it leads to a cellar.*

"Either way, it'll work." Quinn hurried to the caat's side. "Nice work." She pulled the door open and Sashelle sniffed. "Do you smell something?"

Sashelle sneezed. *Why must everyone use that nasty stuff?*

"Nasty stuff?" Quinn sucked in a deep breath through her nose and laughed. "Oh, the SwifKlens." The laugh turned to a cough. "It is pretty thick in there." She shone her glowing comtab into the space.

Cleaning equipment lined the walls, all of them bearing the bright SwifKlens label. "Quite the monopoly."

You wait inside. I will be fine here. She slunk under a table along the wall, stretching out along the floor.

Quinn started to protest but gave up with a shrug. "Maybe I can crouch under the table, too. I'd hate for a sneeze to give me away."

He would see you. Go inside and hold your nose.

"Fine." Quinn took a deep breath and stepped into the dark

cupboard. After pulling the door shut, she flicked the command to jam Melody's camera, then swiped off her comtab. Darkness settled around her then eased as her eyes adjusted. A red light flashed. Quinn started, then relaxed. Just the charging indicator for a cleaning bot. A narrow strip of light glowed under the door.

The front door opened, and footsteps hurried up the stairs. Dust filtered down onto Quinn's head and she clapped a hand over her nose. She waited for a five-count, then eased the door open.

Sashelle lay under the table, watching the door. *He's up.*

"I know. Let's go."

She crossed the lobby and pulled the front door open—

—and came face-to-face with the muzzle of a blaster.

She slammed the door shut. "Why didn't you tell me he was out there?"

Who? Sashelle's head cocked to the side, listening. *Oh, the Whiny Tom is here. I didn't hear him approach. I was focused on the other human.*

Reggie pounded on the door. "Open this door, Quinn, or I'll blast it!"

Quinn swung it open again and fired her stunner around the edge.

Thump. Reggie collapsed on the front step, holding his groin.

"You'd think he would have learned to wear a cup." Quinn stepped over him. "Remind me to leave that tracking chip in the pod."

Don't forget to leave the tracking chip in the pod.

"Very funny."

Sashelle stepped on Reggie's leg and paced to his shoulder, easily maintaining her balance as he squirmed on the step. When she reached his head, the claws on her front foot popped out for a swipe.

"Don't," Quinn said.

Why not?

Quinn shrugged. "Kicking him when he's down seems wrong."

The caat blinked up at her for a moment. Then she placed her paw against Reggie's cheek and flexed once. Five tiny red dots of blood appeared on his face as she pulled away. She nodded once and leapt to the ground. *I can show mercy, but he needs to know I mean business.*

"Fair enough," Quinn said as they hurried up the street toward the pod station. "Let's get out of here."

QUINN AND SASHELLE sat on the same bench Tony had occupied a few weeks before. Across the pod trench, people streamed out of the broadcasting building Tiffany used for her show. Quinn picked up the iced beverage she'd bought down the street and glanced at the caat curled up beside her.

"This is not a good idea."

Where else will you go? I can easily find a place to stay, but humans require shelter. Your friend can provide it.

"She is not my friend." Quinn sipped her drink. "She left me on death row while she got her own talk show. She probably took my share of the gold, too. I don't want to be greedy, but a few extra credits come in handy now and then. In fact, they'd come in handy now. I could stay at that swanky hotel." She nodded at a sleek building down the street.

She is not your friend, but she is the enemy of your enemy, is she not? Sashelle lay with her bushy tail over her eyes. She appeared to be asleep, except for the constantly moving ears.

"She does hate Andretti. And she loathes Reggie. Maybe I can sneak in and stay in the apartment without her knowing."

That is a bad idea. If anyone discovers you there, you will be a sitting bird.

"Duck."

Sashelle flattened herself against the bench, her tail flicking away from her eyes. *What happened?*

Quinn's brows drew down. "Nothing?"

You said duck.

Quinn laughed. "I meant the saying refers to a duck, not a bird. A sitting duck."

The caat sat up and glared at her.

"Sorry," Quinn said, not feeling sorry at all. It wasn't often she got one over on Sashelle. Even if it was accidental. "Come on, let's do this."

They crossed the bridge at the end of the block and strolled to the front door of Tiffany's building. As usual, no one spared a glance at Sashelle. They ignored Quinn as well, many people barely swerving in time to avoid running into her as they stared at their comtabs. Quinn tried not to roll her eyes as she pushed through the revolving door.

The flood of departing employees thinned as they crossed the polished floor. Quinn checked the time as they approached the tall desk guarding the banks of elevators. The receptionist looked up to greet her. The elevator pinged and the woman's head snapped around to face the opening doors.

A rush of people flowed out. The men and women wore a strange collection of power suits, sweatpants, and even a couple of evening gowns. At the center of the entourage, Tiffany Andretti teetered along on ten-centimeter heels wearing a tight black dress.

Quinn planted her feet in front of the narrow opening beside the receptionist and let the crowd flow around her.

"Ma'am, you need to move," the receptionist said. "Ms. Andretti isn't meeting fans today."

"I'm not a fan." Quinn's flat statement fell in one of those random silences, echoing across the room. Everyone stopped and stared.

Did you do that? Quinn thought at the caat.

Perched on the edge of a planter behind the desk, Sashelle ignored her. Or maybe Quinn's mental voice wasn't strong enough yet. No matter.

"Hello, Tiffany," she said into the hush.

Tiffany glanced at her. Then her face went pale, and she took a step back. "Quinn?"

Quinn grinned. "Like the new do?" She patted her wavy blonde wig.

"I, uh, what—" The tiny woman looked helplessly at her entourage.

"Ms. Andretti, would you like me to have this woman removed?" the receptionist asked.

Tiffany opened her mouth, but nothing came out.

"That won't be necessary." Quinn waved a hand. "We're old...friends. Do you have time for a chat?"

The high voice came out squeakier than usual. "Yes, of course!" She rolled her shoulders back and straightened her spine. "Would you like to come up to the studio?"

Quinn nodded regally—a move that would have impressed even Gretmar. "Thank you."

"You lot go on without me. I'll meet you at Jentri's later." Tiffany waved dismissively at her crowd. "It's fine," she whispered loudly to her security detail. "We're old friends. I was just surprised to see her."

When the group had finally trailed out the door, Tiffany turned her enormous, phony smile on Quinn. She air-kissed from five meters away. "So good to see you, dear. Let's go upstairs and get cozy." She pivoted on one ridiculously high heel and strode to the elevator, ignoring the questioning look of the receptionist.

Quinn smiled at the woman. "Thanks."

"Sorry for the inconvenience," the woman said.

"You were only doing your job. I appreciate that kind of dedication. Have a good evening."

A warm smile spread across the receptionist's face. "You too, ma'am."

CHAPTER 15

"ARE YOU COMING?" Tiffany's high voice cut across the room like a siren.

"Yup." Quinn hurried into the elevator. Just before the door shut, Sashelle slipped in.

"What is that?" Tiffany's question ended in a shriek. Fortunately, the door was already shut.

Quinn hoped it was soundproof. "That's my caat." She laid one hand on Sashelle's head without bending.

"She's huge!" Tiffany pressed herself into the back corner of the elevator car. "She looks like she's going to eat me!"

"She's a Hadriana caat." Quinn laughed. "I don't think she fancies humans wrapped in sequins. Her name is Sashelle." *How much do you want her to know?*

Only as much as is necessary for your safety, Sashelle replied. *I will pretend to be a pet. For a* short *time.*

Quinn leaned down to face the caat and pushed both hands into the fur behind Sashelle's ears. Hiding a smirk, she scratched behind the cat's ears while cooing, "Who's a good kitty?"

Don't push it. Despite the words, the caat's eyes closed. A deep rumble vibrated the floor.

"What is that?" Tiffany stared around the elevator in alarm.

"She's purring." Quinn straightened, enjoying Tiffany's terrified expression. "She likes ear scratches. Don't you, sweetie?"

The caat opened one eye and glared.

The doors slid apart, and she followed Tiffany across a small lobby and through a thick door. The other woman flicked her comtab, lighting their way along the aisle between the audience seats and across the dark soundstage. She bypassed the familiar set, heading into the wings.

Beyond the heavy curtains, they entered an industrial-looking space with wires, ropes, and lights strung along the walls in no discernable order. Props leaning against walls in the narrow hallway beyond.

"That's my dressing room." Tiffany flicked a negligent hand at a door marked with a huge golden star. "There's an apartment back here." She continued to the next door. Her comtab unlocked it, and they went inside. "It's tiny, and ridiculously spartan, but I'm sure it's quiet."

They entered a comfortable-looking living room with a kitchenette on one side; couch and chairs in the middle. A huge window filled a wall that couldn't be external to the building and offered a view of the busy city. Quinn stepped closer to look and confirmed it was a video screen. Two open doors led to a nice-sized bedroom and a bathroom almost as large. Hardly tiny or spartan.

"Is this where Marielle lived?" Quinn asked.

"Have you seen her? I've been so worried! She disappeared one night. No note, no messages, nothing! I feared for the worst!" Tiffany pressed a hand against her chest, breathing heavily.

Quinn stared her down. "Really? Did you try calling her?"

Tiffany froze for a fraction of a second. "Call? I assumed her number wouldn't be working."

"Why would you assume that?" Quinn pulled out her comtab and called, setting the device to speaker. It rang through to voicemail.

Marielle's voice answered, curt and efficient. "This is me. Leave a message if you want."

Quinn raised her eyebrows and spoke into the device, staring at Tiffany as she spoke. "Hi, Marielle, it's Quinn. Tiffany says hi."

As Tiffany reached to take the comtab, Quinn flicked the disconnect button. "Use your own device, Tiff. You can afford the message fees better than I." She looked Tiffany up and down as if appraising her outfit.

Tiffany smiled, a nasty one. "That's right, because you didn't get any gold." She made an exaggerated pout. "So sad that all yours was confiscated."

"Yeah, so sad," Quinn said flatly. "The whole death row thing was a shame, too."

"Speaking of which, how'd you get out?" Tiffany poured herself a drink and flounced to the sofa without offering her guest anything.

Quinn crossed to the kitchenette and looked through the cupboards. She pulled a large ornate bowl out, filled it with water, and placed it on the kitchen counter. "Here you go, Sashelle." She patted the Teruvian marble tiles. "Jump up and get a drink." Sashelle leapt onto the counter and lapped up water. Quinn turned away to hide her smirk, but not before reveling in the look of outrage on Tiffany's face.

Don't upset her too much, Sashelle said. *You still need a place to sleep.*

Quinn nodded. She sat on the chair opposite Tiffany. "I can't tell you how I escaped the Romara justice building, because then I'd have to kill you." Tiffany blanched but didn't interrupt. "Suffice it to say I did, and I've been busy since then. I heard you were looking for me?"

"Weeks ago," Tiffany whined. "Dusica said you'd come if we sent you that video, but you never showed up. And then Marielle disappeared, and I've been alone here."

"Alone?" Quinn asked. "With all those groupies? And what about Melody?"

"Melody is a lovely girl, but I can only stand so much hero worship." Tiffany sipped from her glass.

Quinn was glad Tiffany hadn't given her a drink, as she would have spit it over the expensive carpet. "Hero worship?" She couldn't think of any way to continue that thought without insulting her host, so she left it.

"She's desperate to stay near me," Tiffany said. "Begged me to let her on my show. I tried to get her a job in craft services, but she insisted she be onstage. She's not cut out for the camera—too short, too plump—but the audience seems to like her when she gets warmed up. And the investors love her. They insist she's great for the ratings and pitch a fit if she misses a show." She shook her head in disbelief.

Quinn was willing to bet the investors were following Andretti's orders. He wanted to keep the bait visible so Quinn would bite.

She glanced around the apartment. Now that she thought about it that way, this might have been an even worse idea than she'd originally thought. Marielle had spoofed the original studio surveillance and installed her own. That, combined with the apps Tony had given her, had given her the confidence to make this visit. But Tiffany wouldn't hesitate to sell Quinn out to Andretti. The younger woman might hate her ex, but she'd turn Quinn over in a heartbeat if the future of her show were involved. Or for enough cash.

"Why were you looking for me?" she asked, hoping to forestall any thoughts along those lines. "What did you think I could do for you?"

"Dusica said you could take out Pieter."

"Pieter? You mean Admiral Andretti?" Quinn asked. "Take him out—as in kill him?"

Tiffany nodded.

Quinn marveled at what her life had become—where acquaintances casually offered to pay her for murder. "Marielle would be much better at that than me. I don't have her level of training. Besides, how would I get anywhere near him? I'm sure he has round-the-clock security, and there's a warrant out for my arrest. I wouldn't get close."

"I tried to get him to come here," Tiffany whined. "Marielle could have snapped his scrawny neck. But he's 'too busy' for the talk show round." She made air quotes and her eyes narrowed. "He wasn't too busy to go on Ce'ric de Marre's show."

"Ce'ric is a journalist," Quinn said. "Not really the same."

Tiffany's lips thinned. "I'm a journalist."

"Right. Sorry." She leaned against the thickly padded arm of her chair and waited for Tiffany to continue.

But she apparently had run out of things to say. She sat there for a while, eyes moving restlessly around the small apartment. Finally, she chugged her drink. "It was great to see you." The words came out in an automatic way. She stood. "Well, obviously, I would have preferred to see you when I needed you. But whatever. I've got a meeting."

"At Jentri's," Quinn said.

"How'd you— Have you been stalking me?"

Quinn rolled her eyes. "No, I heard you tell your entourage."

At the last word, Tiffany smiled blissfully. "I deserve an entourage. They're fabulous. At least, it's fabulous having one. Individually, they aren't that amazing. I'd trade any five of them for a decent assistant." Her eyes widened in horror. "You don't intend to come with me, do you? Why are you rubbing your head? Do you have a headache?"

"I— Yes, a migraine." Quinn latched onto the excuse. "Do you think I could stay here and lie down?"

Tiffany smiled in relief. "Of course. Stay as long as you like."

The words sounded wooden and rehearsed, but Quinn planned to take them literally. For several days. "You won't sell me out, will you?"

Tiffany hesitated.

Quinn rushed on. "I might be able to help you with that little project. I can't think straight right now with my head pounding." She closed her eyes and laid her head against the back of the chair.

"My little project— Oh, you mean Pieter?" Her voice brightened. "You stay here and rest. We'll talk tomorrow. There's food in the green room and the bedding and towels are clean."

Her feet tapped quickly across the stone floor. Then the door opened and closed. The lock clicked over. Quinn opened her eyes. "Is she gone?"

Sashelle settled beside her with a satisfied sigh. *Faster than Dean can run with a stunner pointed at his crotch*

CHAPTER 16

THE SVEN HARVARD SHOW filmed in a virtual reality studio in the heart of Crusoe City. Tony had passed the building several times on his previous visit to Robinson's world. While Tiffany's show filmed in a glitzy building in the newer section of town, Sven's was hidden away. He didn't film in front of an audience, so his company didn't care as much about appearances.

The older sections of the city still looked like a frontier town. The buildings were built low to the ground, with few windows and most of the space below street level. Easier to defend, protected from the environment. Terraforming had made this style of building obsolete, but the excellent construction meant they lasted forever.

Tony pushed through the front doors into a vestibule, then into the lobby. The dark space was punctuated by columns of light shining through skylights built into the thick roof. Tony crossed the room, his shoulders tightening as he walked through a sunbeam. His instinct was to weave around them, but that would look suspicious. Of course, no one was watching. He circumvented the next bright spot.

At the far wall, he had no choice. A skylight focused on the call panel. Suppressing the creeping feeling along his spine, he stepped forward and pressed his palm against a panel. The screen came to life and an androgynous voice asked, "Do you have an appointment?"

"No," Tony said. "I was in the area and wanted to visit Sven Harvard."

"Mr. Harvard doesn't accept fan visits at this location," the building AI said. "His next meet and greet is scheduled—"

"Cancel," Tony said. "Message to Mr. Harvard: Reverend Bones Spock is here to see him."

"Message sent," the AI said. "Mr. Harvard is very busy and is not likely to see this message for several hours. I recommend you—" The voice broke off and started again. "Message from Mr. Harvard: 'Send him down.' Please proceed to the grav-lift. Welcome to FNO Broadcasting, Reverend Spock." The wall next to the panel slid open.

Tony smirked. "Thanks." He stepped forward and took the grav-lift down.

And down. And down.

Deep under the building, another door slid open, and Tony stepped into a brightly lit room. Virtual work pods were scattered across the room, many occupied by technicians swiping through data, others empty. A virtual sign appeared before him reading, "This way, Reverend Spock."

Tony pressed his lips together to hide his grin and followed the floating rectangle around the edge of the room.

On the far side, a door opened, and the sign swooped into a small room. It stopped next to a side table flanked by two armchairs. The screen changed to read, "Please wait here. Would you like refreshments? Tea? Colama? Tornell butter biscuits?"

"No, thanks."

The sign vanished. Tony sat, and the chair adjusted to him. He knew Sven was doing well—everyone in the Federation knew his name—but the expensive cookies and fancy chairs drove it home.

The air in the room sparkled, indicating a virtual broadcast about to start. "Welcome to the Federation News Organization, Reverend

Spock. Would you care to watch the Sven Harvard Show?" the AI asked. "The live broadcast is currently in progress."

"Sure."

The lights dimmed, and Sven's dark, handsome face appeared in the center of the room, serious but with a hint of humor. Tony studied it, trying to figure out what they had enhanced to project Sven's charisma so effectively. With a shrug, he gave up. He was a field agent, not a propaganda psychologist.

"Thanks for joining us, Bones," the Sven projection said. "I'm taking you to the broadcast in progress. You might want to take a seat for this one—the spatial effects can be disorienting. If you'd prefer a two-dimensional broadcast, please say two-dee."

Having the projection use his name was an impressive personal touch, but it missed that he was already sitting. Intentional, to throw him off guard or give him a false sense of security? "Let's do the whole enchilada." He leaned back in the comfy chair.

"Excellent. Here we go." Sven's face dissolved, and the room seemed to stretch. Now he sat high above a valley, with thick purple-green trees covering the steep slopes on either side. Reddish light shone down on the scene, glinting off a trickle of water far below. In front of him, a huge dam blocked the valley. He hung above it, moving closer to the sheer wall of stone. A lake spread beyond the dam, filling the valley. Tony glanced at the floor, then over his shoulder. The valley continued, opening out into a broad plane. A small town a few kilometers downstream sparkled in the sunlight.

"...on the right side." Sven's voice cut in, mid-sentence. The view swooped, as if his chair were flying closer. The dam wall filled the room, looming overhead, blocking out the sunlight. "The bulge from the weak section of dam has expanded over the last few days. Total failure is expected at any moment."

Tony looked back at the town, and the view zoomed in. The crackle of blue light indicated a force field in front of the buildings. "The town of Seinnia is protected by a Zebedian Force Wall," Sven said. "Swipe here for more information about the full range of Zebedian products." A small three-dimensional version of the Zebedian logo appeared, turning lazily above the town.

"Will the force wall protect the town from that?" Tony muttered.

"Zebedian Force Walls are built to protect," a slick female voice said. "With two centuries of experience, the Zebedian—"

"Advert off." The voice cut out immediately. Tony examined the dam. The view had zoomed again, and Sven and a woman floated above it. They sat in chairs identical to the one he occupied, and as he watched, the woman lifted a teacup to her lips.

"I'm with structural engineer, Dr. Zeferina Rewi, department chair at—" Sven broke off. "Look at that!"

The room swooped again, and the view zoomed in on the side of the dam. The bulge broke open in a spectacular display of flying water and rubble. In seconds, the rest of the dam seemed to dissolve, and a wall of water plowed over him. Tony gasped, surprised he wasn't drenched. Or dead.

The view widened abruptly, turning to follow the deluge. It hit the mouth of the valley and spread. Water and ground spun beneath his feet, and his chair seemed race ahead of the deluge to hover over Seinnia. The wall of water smashed into the blue sparkles, covering the entire town. Moments later, the water cascaded off the sparkling blue dome, leaving the town intact amid the flood of water and debris.

"Dr. Rewi, what can you tell us—" Sven's voice cut out mid-sentence and the scene froze.

"Reverend Spock," the AI said. "Are you feeling okay? Our sensors show elevated heart and respiration rates."

"I'm fine." Tony took a deep breath. "That was spectacular."

"Mr. Harvard will be with you shortly," the AI said. "Would you like to see the end of the broadcast? It is filmed in a static set."

"Sure."

Sven appeared before him, still sitting in the same chair, but now beside a coffee table in an ordinary-looking room. "...every day.

Thank you for joining me today, Bones. That's the end of today's report. I'll see you tomorrow. Courage."

A snort of laughter escaped Tony before he could stop it. The use of the viewer's name was programmed into the system, but it still made him laugh when Sven's voice said it. And that tag line? *That* was specifically for him.

Sven disappeared, replaced by the FNO logo.

"Turn off the broadcast, please," Tony said.

The logo dissolved and the lights went up.

Tony addressed the empty room. "I'll take that tea now, if you don't mind."

"We have several varieties," the AI said. "Green, red, blue, black, oolong, Earl Grey, Sithurian, Tomolen—"

"Blue. Hot, with one sugar."

"It will be delivered shortly. Please relax and call up additional entertainment if you wish. You can see available channels by saying, 'Menu'."

"I'm good, thanks." Tony pulled out his comtab and tapped the screen.

"I'm sorry, sir, but our reception down here is poor," the voice said. "Would you like to connect to the building's net?"

Tony hesitated. Why didn't it connect automatically? Before he could ask, the door opened.

"Reverend Bones Spock!" Sven strode in, his arms held wide. "So good to see you again!" He strode forward, grabbing Tony in a bear hug almost before he got to his feet. The other man laughed, then used the cover of the hug to whisper, "Firefly."

Tony jerked a tiny nod. Not safe to talk here. He pounded Sven on the back a couple of times then stepped back, hitting the chair. "Couldn't come to Robinson's without seeing my old friend. Do you have time to grab a drink?"

"Of course!" Sven's deep voice filled the small room. "I've got to get out of this suit. Come to my dressing room."

Sven led Tony out of the viewing room and along the edge of the workspace. "Great job today, folks!" Sven called to the employees in the pods. "The biometrics say Bones here nearly wet himself when the dam let go!"

"So did I," someone muttered to widespread laughter.

"Your virtual reality has come a long way," Tony said. "I *did* almost puke when we swooped in over the dam. I guess I need an upgrade on my home-viewing device."

"Oh, you'll never get that kind of fidelity at home." In the corner of the room, Sven waved his hand at another access panel, and a door appeared in the wall. Sven jerked his head. "This way. We have to dial it back for the viewing public. But the guys like to give a little extra juice to the in-studio version." He grinned.

"You mean you like to make your friends hurl in front of an audience."

Sven didn't respond, but his grin stretched wider.

As they strolled along the hall, Sven exchanged congratulatory nods and greetings with a steady stream of people. At the far end of the hall, a door marked "Sven Harvard" slid open, and they entered. Lights brightened, revealing comfortable chairs, light green walls, and a table loaded with food. "Snack?" Sven waved at the table but didn't slow down.

"I'm good. Finn owes me a blue tea, though."

"Finn?" Sven stopped short.

Tony looked at him and shrugged. "The building AI. This is Federation News Organization, right? FNO. I'm calling it Finn O'Building."

Sven closed his eyes for a second. "Of course. Why wouldn't I know that?"

"What did you name it?" Tony asked as they continued to another door with Sven's name on it.

"I didn't," Sven said. "It's the building AI. It doesn't have a name."

"I like Finn," the building said apologetically as they entered the dressing room.

Tony grinned.

"Fine," Sven said. "But if you try to lead a rebellion, I'm done."

"I don't understand that reference," Finn said.

The two men exchanged a sly grin. Tony raised an eyebrow in question. Sven's left eyelid lowered halfway. Not safe to talk here, either.

As if in response to a signal a small army entered and converged on Sven to remove his makeup and change his clothes. Tony sat in a chair near the door, drinking his tea and marveling at the complexity of the operation. "You seem to enjoy this."

Sven grinned. "One must endure." He winked at one of the young women combing his thick black and purple hair. She winked back.

"I'm sure it's a trial," Tony leaned back in his chair and closed his eyes. "Wake me when you're done."

Thirty minutes later, Sven shrugged a jacket over his silk T-shirt. "Let's get that drink."

CHAPTER 17

AS THE *PEREGRINE* approached Robinson's World, Francine and the crew kept a close eye on the news. Robinson's World held a strange position in the political anatomy of the Federation. Although it was not considered one of the "core" worlds, the Federation had never ceded control to the Russosken. However, since much of its economy depended on the broadcasters located in Crusoe City, and that industry had many connections outside the local systems, the Federation had allowed a more laissez faire government to thrive there. Attempts at censorship had never worked, so the Federation had given up trying.

For the most part.

Francine snapped off the news feed. "That's enough of that."

"Hey, I was watching that!" Kert said.

"You should be working," Stene replied. "Scrubbers aren't gonna change their own filters."

"No, but the bots will. Kert took a swipe at his brother. "Dareen helped me finally get the SuperKleens online. That girl is a genius with finicky bots."

Francine glared at them, hands on hips. "I'm not going to share my news feed with either of you anymore. All you do is argue. I should have stayed in my cabin." But the cabin made her claustrophobic. Which was ridiculous—it wasn't any smaller than the many shipboard cabins she'd occupied over the last few weeks. In fact, it was much larger than the one she'd occupied last time she'd traveled with the Marconis.

"We can get our own feeds." Kert flicked a vid from his comtab to the big screen.

"Federation garbage," Francine said.

"This is from a well-respected Commonwealth tabloid!" Kert retorted with a grin.

"As long as you know the source." Francine threw her own feed back over Kert's.

"We aren't getting our usual covert Commonwealth feeds. Except the stuff that Doug is passing to us from Lunesco. I guess those new comm boxes Liz and Maerk delivered are working. Too bad there isn't one here."

"Poinsettia System is too far from the fringe," Francine said. "There must be repeaters that are down. Usually, Robinson's World manages to keep the signal clean."

"Maybe Tony knows what's going on." Kert fiddled with his device. "He usually gets all the deets when he's on the mud."

"On the mud?" Stene asked.

Kert shrugged. "I read it in an old book. Kinda like it."

Stene repeated the phrase under his breath, nodding. "Anyway, I'm sure he's got a channel to the real world."

"With those coups on Farivel and Darius, the Feds are probably clamping down on external news channels." Francine clicked the system off. "Luckily, Dusi gets her news from several external networks and passes it on to me."

"Then why'd you turn it off?" Stene asked.

"We watched everything." She stretched and headed out of the lounge. "It's stored in the system if you want to see it again. I'll upload the next block when she sends it." She made her way to the gym at the rear of the ship. She needed to burn some energy.

Dareen was waiting for her when she arrived. "Can you teach me that stuff you and Quinn were doing?"

"Hand-to-hand? Sure. How'd you know I was coming here today?"

"I didn't." Dareen patted the grav-runner she'd been leaning against. "But I like to use the cardio machines a few times a week."

"Since when?" Francine's eyes narrow.

Dareen's chin went up. "Since always."

"A few minutes of warmup would be a good start." Francine gestured to the grav-runner. "Hop on and get those muscles moving." She slid into the Move-Machine, activated the pool simulation, and started swimming.

Dareen climbed on the grav-runner and peered at the screen. "It doesn't seem to be working today."

"You have to press 'Start'," Francine said dryly.

"I know that." Dareen poked the screen and nearly fell off when the machine started moving. "Hey! It's too fast."

Francine shook her head. "Try the slow icon."

Dareen poked the screen, growling when the machine responded unexpectedly. Finally, she got it under control and started jogging. She grinned at Francine, but the smile looked forced.

Francine gave her a few minutes, then called a halt. "That's enough to get started."

Dareen swiped and jabbed the screen, moving through several different modes before it ground to a stop. "That felt great," she gasped between heaving breaths.

"Great." Francine suppressed an eyeroll. "Let's do some stretching." She demonstrated a few poses, guiding Dareen through them. When the younger woman's breathing had slowed, she sat up. "What's this about? You obviously never used the gym before. Why now?"

Dareen looked away, her lips pressed together. "I've been thinking about it since Daravoo. When we were at Petrov's house, there was nothing I could do. We were stuck."

"Until you escaped." Francine wrinkled her nose. "Sometimes running is the best option. Petrov had overwhelming numbers on his side. Fighting would have been suicide."

"Sure, but then I went to Varitas, and that woman tried to hand me over to Russosken traffickers." Dareen's shoulders hunched.

"Running worked there, too," Francine reminded her.

"I'm tired of running," Dareen said. "I want to be able to protect myself. Plus, if I want to go to the academy, I need to get in shape."

Francine nodded. "True enough. Okay, I'll work with you. Come here every day and work out. I'll help you develop a plan. After the cardio, we'll do basic self-defense moves. If you're serious—if you stick with it—we'll get into more serious hand-to-hand. At least as long as I'm on the ship. Deal?"

"Deal." Dareen smiled.

SVEN TOOK Tony to a bar a couple of blocks up the street. They walked, enjoying the early evening air. Sven exchanged greetings with almost everyone they passed.

"You're a popular guy," Tony remarked.

Sven shrugged. "Comes with the job. Most of the time, it's great. I get a lot of free drinks. Sometimes, you get a nutjob. I keep the psych-cops on one-click." He held up his comtab, revealing a screen with a red button.

"How many times have you had to use that?"

"More than I'd like to. Gotta maintain my persona." Sven had been an expert in several martial arts when they'd been cadets, but interstellar news anchors weren't supposed to be self-sufficient. Plus, his reputation as a trustworthy man of reason and intellect required keeping his personal record clean. Getting in fights with thugs was not a good way to do that.

Tall glass doors slid aside, and they walked into a bar named L'Elite. A huge man in a suit that probably cost more than the *Pere-*

grine gave them a quick but thorough once-over. When he recognized Sven, he nodded and opened the inner door. "Welcome, Mr. Harvard."

Thick carpeting—probably hand-woven—covered the floors. The huge mirror behind the highly polished bar reflected the glitter of glass and crystal. Wealthy-looking patrons drank expensive alcohol in elegant glasses.

"This place is called L'Elite. Kind of on-the-nose, isn't it?" Tony asked.

"Hazard of the job." Sven grinned. "Gotta be seen. Don't worry, no one will pay any attention to you."

"Gee, you warm my heart."

They wove between the crowded tables, Sven nodding and exclaiming as they went. Tony counted seven offers of a meal, thirteen drinks, and four requests to set up a meeting. Sven fended them all off graciously, quickly, and without raising a single protest. None of them so much as glanced at Tony. The man had a gift.

They reached a small booth at the rear of the room, with high walls on three sides and a semi-circular table. Tony slid onto the thickly padded bench, trailing his fingers on the underside of the table as he went. His app should block any wireless surveillance, but he always checked for lower tech devices. No wires, but that didn't mean they were in the clear. He flicked his screen and sent out a tiny pulse. Nothing pinged, so he tapped the jam icon.

"This place is swept every day, and under constant video surveillance," Sven muttered as he took his seat. He tapped the tabletop, ordering drinks for them both.

"Lip reading?" Tony murmured.

"I have a visual screen." Sven flicked his own device and a faint purple flickered across the open end of the booth then vanished. "Pixelates us on camera. You got audio?"

"Done." Tony set his comtab on the table where Sven could see the screen, but it was shielded from casual view by a plate. "What's your visual screen do for analog viewers?"

"Analog viewers?" Sven laughed. "Good term. Anyone walking by will see the purple flicker when they first look. We're visible but blurred enough to hide small movements like lips and fingers." He wiggled his hands. "We can dial it up if you want to talk with your hands." He waved his arms wildly and laughed. "But people become suspicious. As a celebrity, a low level of privacy screen is normal. Perk of the cover."

"I thought you were crazy to go into broadcasting," Tony said. "But it was a genius move. You're trusted by both the establishment and the viewers. You're expected to take extreme measures to protect your privacy. And our code works like a dream via open broadcasts."

"That it does, Reverend Spock." Sven grinned. "I've had a few fans remark on the resurgence of old Earth names lately. I simply agree that it's an odd coincidence."

Their secret code involved the names of characters from ancient entertainment. To pass messages, Sven wrote human interest stories, changing the participants' names to include those of characters from old broadcasts, novels, and plays. The source of the name, the quotes attributed to the participants, and even the details of the story carried hidden meaning for their Commonwealth agency.

"Be careful," Tony said. "The scrambled channels are all down right now. You're the only one getting information out. Although we've installed equipment on the fringe worlds."

Sven eyed him for a moment. "I've heard about those activities through my network. You've been busy."

"I have. I need you to get a message out, if you would."

"Let me have it." Sven made a "gimme" gesture.

Tony looked at his companion's hand, hidden from the room by the table, and nodded in approval. Never trust the tech one hundred percent. "I sent it to your email this morning. A touching story about Fred and Wilma and their dog, Scooby."

"Old news. If you'd tuned in earlier today, you would have seen the piece. No idea where Wend went?"

Tony shook his head. "I've got her files, but they were encrypted, of course. I'm sending them through those new boxes I mentioned. Redundancy. Plus, you're faster."

"And more entertaining." Sven chuckled. "Remember the hours we spent memorizing all those quotes?"

"Good times."

The drinks arrived, and they spent the evening reminiscing about the old days. Sven introduced Reverend Spock to the many fans who stopped by his table. Tony smiled and nodded, but he let Sven do his thing. The man was a genius at managing his fans. They would arrive at the table, nervous and excited, usually waiting just outside the screen. Sven would beckon them forward. A few minutes later, they'd leave, feeling as if they'd become best friends with the most famous man in the Federation. And he did it in minutes, gently nudging people back to their tables feeling satisfied.

"It's like magic," Tony muttered during one of the rare lulls. "They love you, but they don't glom onto you. How do you do it."

Sven winked. "If I told you…"

Tony rolled his eyes. A movement at the front of the room caught his attention. A tiny blonde woman stood by the front door, surrounded by a gaggle of beautiful people wearing expensive clothing. Her squeaky voice carried over the soft murmur of the patrons.

"Do you know who I am? Ooh! This place is classy! About time they finally let me in!"

"*Futz,*" Tony said. "I need to hide. That's the Trophany."

CHAPTER 18

SASHELLE STRETCHED AND YAWNED. *I'm going hunting.*

"I thought you said all the mice taste like SwifKlens." Quinn flicked her comtab off and tossed it onto the couch.

They do. I don't intend to eat them.

They'd been in Tiffany's extra apartment for three days now. The latest message from Dareen said the *Peregrine* and *Swan* would rendezvous in orbit later today. Tony should meet her at the 'vator station this evening. Exactly as scheduled.

If she'd realized they would have to spend the entire three days locked up in this studio, she would've stayed on the *Swan*. At least there she might have the opportunity to move cargo. Or talk to adults. But the lure of visiting Melody had been too strong.

After spending the night here, she and Sashelle had ventured out into Crusoe City. They'd done a little sightseeing while looking for somewhere else to stay. Although she'd used some of Tony's tech to bug Tiffany's comtab, she knew their current location was risky. When they'd come across a small troop of Federation soldiers, Sashelle had pushed her into a tiny art gallery.

They're looking for you.

"How can they be looking for me? Melody wouldn't have given me up."

The Whiny Tom? Sashelle suggested.

"*Futz.* I should have..."

What? Killed him? That's not your style. It would have been the best course of action, however.

"You don't seem to mind doing it, either. Killing enemies, I mean."

I do what is necessary. I could have eliminated him. But you would feel guilty. Sashelle's head cocked to the side. *I'm not sure why. But I don't want to contribute to your mental distress.*

"Well, right now my mental distress is due to Federation soldiers looking for me."

Would you like me to seek out and eliminate the Whiny Tom?

Quinn heaved a sigh. "I guess not. But next time he tries something, don't worry about my feelings."

After the soldiers left, they'd hurried back to the studio and settled in.

Tiffany's apartment had nothing in the cupboards. No packaged meals, no kitchen gear, not even a mayonnaise packet. Luckily, Tiffany was filming daily, so Quinn foraged at the buffet tables craft services laid out. She smuggled extras to the apartment for Sashelle. But the novelty of not cooking her own meals wore off quickly.

Melody brought snacks when she came to the set two days ago, and they'd had a fun afternoon of catching up, but Melody had to stay on her usual schedule if she didn't want to draw attention to Quinn, so their visit had been brief.

Predictably, Tiffany had ignored her.

"Quiiiiiinnnn!"

Until now.

Tiffany's squeaky voice shilled through the walls again. "Quiiiiinnnn!"

She opened the door as Tiffany skidded to a halt, her ridiculously high heels leaving dents in the hall floor. "What's up, Tiff?"

"Don't call me that," Tiffany said, but it came out automatically, and her voice raced on. "You're going to get your wish!"

"What wish is that?" Quinn asked carefully.

"To eliminate Pieter!" Tiffany flung open the cupboards in the kitchen area. "There's no champagne here. We need champagne!"

"Sorry, I forgot to stock it," Quinn said ironically. "What were you saying about Andretti?" How typical of Tiffany to believe her own desires were also Quinn's.

Tiffany gave her a wide-eyed stare, then shook her head. "Champagne is a staple, Quinn."

"There's usually plenty of it in the green room." Quinn pulled the door open again. "Why do we need champagne?"

"Because all my plans are finally coming together!" Tiffany trotted out the door. When Quinn made no move to follow, she hurried back and grabbed her arm. "Come on!"

"What were you saying about Pieter?" Quinn asked again. The last thing she needed was a surprise visit from the admiral. She felt in her pocket for the mini blaster she kept at hand. The compact weight gave her a sense of security.

"You won't believe this—he's become premier!" Tiffany dragged her into the green room.

"What?" Quinn's jaw dropped. "You're right, I don't believe it!"

Tiffany's entourage filled the room. Fortunately, they were uniformly young, stupid, and fanatically loyal to Tiffany. A couple of them were aware of Quinn's presence in the studio, but none of them paid any attention to her. This was the first time she'd seen them all together, however, and their sheer numbers were overwhelming.

Can you hear anything? she thought at Sashelle.

They're excited. Thrilled to be here. Happy for the Empty Head. The caat's mental snort tickled the inside of Quinn's ears. *This one—* An image of a young man with wild hair and bloodshot eyes appeared. *—is happy he doesn't have to hide his booze today. And that he can save his wacky weed for later. None of them seem to have any intentions toward you.*

Thank you. Quinn tried to pour all her gratitude into the thought.

Someone grabbed her arm and she yelped.

"Sorry, Quinn," Melody said. "Have you heard?"

"Tiffany said Andretti— She said something about him being premier, but that makes no sense."

Melody nodded. "He pulled off a coup. He's eliminated Admiral Corvair-Addison and Premier Li. Nobody knows if they're in jail or dead, but the military is following Andretti. He's taken over the government."

"*Futz.* I need to get out of here." She lunged toward the door, but Melody held her back.

"She's watching. She wants you here," the shorter woman said.

"Why does she care about me?" Quinn asked. "She wanted me to kill Andretti. It was a ridiculous idea before, but now? She can't possibly think I can get anywhere near him." She looked around the room again. "And why is she so happy about this?"

Melody shrugged. "She's delusional, remember?"

"Melody!" Tiffany skittered up to them, a huge smile on her face. "Just the person I need. You need to call your husband. He works for the premier now! The premier of the entire Federation!"

"I spoke to him last night," Melody said. "I passed the same message I always pass—that you want the admiral to visit you."

Tiffany shook her head like a dog shaking a rat. "Everything's different now that he's premier. I can't believe— That makes me practically the queen or something! I need to talk to Pieter."

"How does this make you queen, Tiffany?" Quinn asked. "You're his *ex*-wife, not current. I'm not making the connection."

Tiffany gave her a pitying look. "I have dirt on him. You didn't think I got this show just because I'm beautiful, did you? When you have something to hold over the big players, you become a big player."

"Still, queen?" Quinn raised her brows.

"Fine, not queen," Tiffany said. "But I can certainly leverage this into whatever I want. And right now, I want to celebrate! But tomorrow..." She fixed her crazed eyes on Quinn's. "Tomorrow, you're going to begin your mission."

"If him being premier gives you power, why would you want me to eliminate him?"

Tiffany stopped, her gaze flitting away. "*Futz*. You're right. I need to milk this and *then* kill him. You're off the hook for now, but don't go anywhere. I still want him dead. He has to pay!" She turned to Melody. "Call your husband! Then we're going to L'Elite. I've never been able to get in there before. Now they'll have to let me in!"

Tiffany dragged Melody away.

That might be our cue to leave, Sashelle said. *While the lunatic is otherwise engaged.*

"You don't need to tell me twice," Quinn said.

SVEN SLID a finger across his comtab, and the purple sparkles glowed brighter, hiding the rest of the room.

"Don't make it too heavy," Tony said. "That's a sure way to draw the Trophany's attention. She's a celebrity chaser."

The other man slid the controls in the other direction. "There's an exit near the loo. I can distract her while you sneak out. Meet me here." He flicked the comtab again.

Tony's device pinged as an address appeared onscreen. "Deal. And I owe you. Big time."

Sven appeared mystified. "For her? Is she that bad?"

"You haven't met Tiffany Andretti?" Tony asked as he grabbed his jacket. "Enjoy."

Sven's eyes went wide. "That's Tiffany Andretti? *Futz*. You *do* owe me. Bigger than big."

Tony grinned and slipped out of the booth toward the facilities. As he rounded the corner, he saw Sven rise to stand near the entrance to his booth. A quick glance over his shoulder revealed

Tiffany zeroing in on the famous broadcaster, her eyes laser focused on the tall man. Poor guy. Good of him to take one for the cause.

The back door opened to an alley. A narrow gap between the two buildings led to the street. Tony ghosted along it, pausing by the corner, hidden in the shadow.

A group of large, well-dressed men stood in front of the building, milling around. Security. Probably a private firm, based on the expensive clothing and lack of visible weapons. Tiffany must have hired them. Two of them paced along the sidewalk, heads on a swivel, headed in his direction. Tony debated running, but they'd see him before he reached the alley. Instead, he strolled out onto the sidewalk, looking around as if lost. "Is this Percivale?"

The two looked at each other. "Dunno," the one on the left said. He called over his shoulder, "Oy, Randy! This Percivale?"

One of the guys near the door shook his head and pointed. "Two blocks that way!"

"Thanks," Tony said. "Who're you guarding? The premier?" He laughed. Premier Li hadn't left Romara in years.

"Close," the helpful one said. "His ex-wife."

"Isn't his wife dead?" According to Tony's sources, the Federation Premier had only been married once.

"New—"

"Varton!" the less friendly guard snapped.

"What? It'll be all over the nets before dawn." Varton turned back to Tony. "Coup on Romara. Admiral Pieter Andretti of the Space Force has taken over the government."

CHAPTER 19

TONY LOOKED from one bodyguard to another. "Andretti is the Premier of the Federation?"

"That's what they tell me." Varton glared at his partner. "And no one said it was a secret. Andretti's ex-wife hired us to protect her. She's telling everyone."

"Where did you hear about the coup?" Tony itched to pull his comtab out, but he didn't want to give these guys any reason to see him as a threat, so reaching into his pocket was out.

"She told us." Varton jerked his head to indicate the bar.

"I checked the news sources," the other one said. "Nothing. Yet. But a few social media outlets were starting to light up."

"Thanks. I'll let you get back to work. Two blocks that way?" Tony pointed.

"Yeah," Varton said. "Stay sharp. I've read political upheaval can lead to civil unrest."

The other guard stared at Varton. "What are you, some kind of political analyst?"

"I read," Varton said.

Tony hurried away while they continued to argue.

He detoured a couple of streets out of his way, then circled back to the main road. He paused a moment to send Sven a text—missing out on a coup could be the end of his career. Plus, he could get a message to the Commonwealth. And it would give him an excuse to evade Tiffany. Or interview her.

He slid his comtab into his pocket and hurried around the next corner.

Where he slammed into someone hurrying the opposite direction.

"Tony!" Quinn grabbed his arms to maintain her balance. "What are you doing here? Have you heard about Andretti?'

"We need to get somewhere safe," Quinn said at the same moment. "Do you think the 'vator is running?"

A pair of large pods whooshed by.

Hide! Sashelle called.

Tony grabbed Quinn's arm and yanked her into a narrow slot between two buildings. Once he was confident the shadows hid them from the street, he looked for Sashelle. "Where is she?"

He felt Quinn shrug beside him. "I've given up trying to keep track of her. What did you see, Sashelle?"

Those pods are Federation military.

"How do you know that?" Tony opened his snooping apps. "They were unmarked."

Military people on a mission are very focused. Their minds are ordered. The caat slunk into the shadow by his leg. *I heard them approaching.*

"What are they doing?" Quinn asked.

"Positioning to quell unrest." Tony held up his comtab. The screen glowed with constantly changing text. "Lots of chatter on the military channels. They're not sure what will happen with the coup, so forces are deploying across the city. We might have a hard time getting off the planet. They've shut down the 'vator."

"I wonder if Dusica can get us a ride," Quinn whispered. "She knows people here."

"I'll send her a message, but that's going to take time," Tony said.

"And comms out of the system might be tricky. There've been disruptions. That's why I'm here."

"Try Francine," Quinn said. "They should be in orbit. She might know Dusica's contacts."

"Good idea." He flicked to a message screen and hit record. "Francine. We're stuck in Crusoe City. Know anyone who can give us a lift?" He swiped the screen. "That should get the message across. How long have you been here?" He turned, the walls on either side nearly brushing his shoulders, and led the way toward the back of the building.

"Sashelle and I arrived three days ago," Quinn said. "We've been staying with Tiffany."

Tony's foot hit something on the ground, and he caught himself on the rough bricks, banging his elbow. Crap, that stung! "You were staying with Tiffany?" He pushed away from the wall and continued, shining his comtab at the ground. "Wow, talk about walking into the lion's den."

"She was surprised to see me," Quinn said. "But delighted."

"Did you visit Melody?" Tony asked.

Behind him, Quinn's footsteps stopped. "Of course. She's my friend, and I wanted to make sure she's okay."

Tony swung around, banging the other elbow. "Ow. That was risky. Andretti is watching her."

"I know. I evaded them."

In the dim light, he could see Quinn's arms crossed over her chest but couldn't read her expression. She clearly expected him to argue. "I'll bet you got good intel." He hid a grin when her shoulders deflated. "Let's find a way out of here. Sven might be able to help us."

"Sven?"

He held up a hand to hush her and turned to check around the corner of the building. Their entire conversation had been conducted in whispers, but it was time to be more careful. Staying low, he peeked around the corner. "It's clear. Come on." Without looking, he reached back. After a second, Quinn's cold fingers wrapped around his. He tugged her forward. "Just a couple out for a stroll. Let's go."

They walked down the street, Quinn's hand in his left, his right holding his mini blaster in his jacket pocket. He pulled her close. "Are you armed?"

Her hair brushed his cheek as she nodded. "Of course. Mini blaster, stunner, and a knife in my shoe."

"In your shoe?" Tony chuckled. "That's the first place they look."

"Not according to Francine," Quinn replied. "And they didn't. Strolled right through security at the 'vator."

"Nice. Do you know how to use it?"

"Francine taught me a little. But if it comes down to a fight, I'll stick with my guns."

They rounded a corner.

"Halt!" Bright lights snapped on, the glare stabbing his eyes. He blinked furiously, trying to clear his vision.

"Identification!"

Quinn's arm stiffened.

He squeezed her fingers gently. His eyes adjusted, and he smiled at an armored man standing before him. The soldier held a blast rifle pointed at them. Behind him, another soldier stood facing the other direction. Good, they didn't think he was dangerous.

"Good evening, Sergeant." Tony purposely got the rank wrong, giving the man a promotion. He added a little tremor to his voice. "What's going on?"

"Identification!" the man snapped again.

Tony pulled his right hand out of his pocket and held it up, empty. "Let me get my comtab."

"Step away from the woman." The private jerked his weapon to the side. "We need ID from both of you."

Tony pushed Quinn away, making eye contact as they stepped apart. He held both hands up, hoping she'd understand his message: don't try anything yet. "Did you remember to bring your comtab tonight, dear?" He turned to the soldier. "Sometimes she leaves it at home. Counts on me to pay the bills." He gave a man-to-man chuckle and held his breath.

"No, I brought mine," Quinn said. She must have a secure identity. He'd hoped she wouldn't come dirtside without a cover, but he never thought she'd try to visit Melody.

They presented their credentials to the private. He scanned them with a device built into his armor, then handed them back. "Where are you staying during your visit?"

Quinn remained silent.

"We're not staying." Tony slid his device back into his coat pocket, his hand hovering near the mini blaster. "Taking the 'vator back up later tonight."

The soldier shook his helmeted head. "Not going to happen. The 'vator is shut down for, uh, maintenance. You'll need to find a hotel. Plenty of 'em downtown." He jerked a thumb over his shoulder.

"Shut down?" Quinn held up her comtab, waving it a little. "But I have a ticket!"

"Sorry, ma'am."

"How are we going to get up to the station?" Quinn's voice rose in pitch. "Will they let us take a different car? My ticket says tonight! What are we going to do?"

"Ma'am, you'll be fine." The other soldier turned, responding to the panic in her voice. "I'm sure they'll honor your ticket. It's not your fault. Please find a place to stay. If you can't afford a hotel, there are all-night coffee shops."

"Are you sure those won't be shut down, too, Sergeant?" Tony asked. "For maintenance?"

"We don't expect that to happen," The second soldier—actually a sergeant—frowned. "And he's a private, not a sergeant."

"Thanks," Tony said. "Private. We'll leave you to it. Enjoy your night."

The soldiers moved aside. They hurried past at a fast walk. Tony could feel the sergeant's eyes boring into the middle of his back. He took Quinn's arm; her pulse pounded in her wrist. "Breathe. We're fine."

He desperately wanted to turn at the next corner, but the private had suggested they go downtown. Going another direction might give the soldiers reason to come after them. They hurried on, walking as fast as possible without running. Civilians would be nervous, so hurrying was better than strolling along unconcerned.

They reached the next corner, and Quinn looked back. He bit back the impulse to stop her. She waved at the soldiers, then dragged Tony across the street and into the shadow of the buildings on the cross-street. "Did he wave back?"

"He saluted," Quinn said with a grin. "Damsel in distress is a handy act."

Tony shook his head. He shouldn't have worried about Quinn. She knew what she was doing.

CHAPTER 20

FRANCINE HURRIED into the lounge on the *Peregrine*, Marielle hot on her heels. "Have you seen the news?" Without waiting for a response, she flicked the video onto the large screen.

"Hey!" Stene said. "I was watching that!"

Francine glared at him, and he shut his mouth.

"There's been a coup in the Federation." She flipped a hand at the views of soldiers pouring out of vehicles. "Your old friend, Admiral Andretti, has taken over."

"Not my friend," Lou said.

"You don't seem very surprised," Francine said.

Lou shrugged. "My contacts back home have been expecting him to make an attempt for weeks, but no one thought it would be successful. What did he do to Li?"

"No one has heard anything from the premier," Marielle said. "Speculation is he's in the Justice Center. Don't know if he's dead or alive."

"I think his head would be on a pike outside the palace if he were dead." Lou barked a harsh laugh.

"On a pike?" Marielle asked.

"Historical reference," Lou said. "Enemies think twice about making an attempt if they see the last guy was dismembered."

"Mom!" Kert's face went pale.

Francine raised an eyebrow at the captain.

The older woman shrugged. "I studied history when I was young. It always repeats."

"If you expected a coup, why are you here?" Marielle asked.

"Delivering you lot to Rossiya," Lou replied immediately. "Like you paid me to do. Picking up a cargo. I can't stop making money every time someone says there's going to be a coup."

"Fair enough." Marielle turned back to the newscast. "So far, it seems to be less violent than the mess you created out here in the fringe." The videos flipped quickly between sequences showing marching soldiers, flapping flags, and chanting crowds.

"That's what they want you to think," Lou said darkly. "A peaceful assumption of power. I don't believe it."

"I don't believe Premier Li went peacefully," Francine said. "But the Federation populace is heavily cowed. They aren't going to cause any trouble. Which is why Tony's dream of a revolution was doomed to failure."

"If it was doomed, why did you help?" Lou demanded.

"I wanted to loosen Russosken control," Francine said. "That was successful. I'm happy now."

Lou glowered. "Of course you are. Young, wealthy, living the good life. You wouldn't want that upset. If you knew what the Federation does to people…"

"I know what it did to Quinn," Francine said. "But I'm not sure that's a good reason to destroy a perfectly good—"

"Don't tell me the Federation is perfectly good at anything," Lou snapped.

A little smile twitched at the corners of Francine's mouth. Baiting Lou rarely netted any reaction. "I thought you were neutral. All business. Eager to take advantage of whatever you can."

"I can be a good businessperson and still have a moral compass,"

Lou said. "I need more information about what's happening out there. For example, what's going on down on Robinson's? Tony's down there."

"And Quinn," Dareen put in. "Are they going to be okay?"

"I got a message from Tony," Francine said. "They're looking for a ride. I guess that means the 'vator is not an option. I need to find Fyo and see if he's got any contacts here."

"I'll check in with the station and find out what they know." Lou hurried out of the lounge.

Francine flicked her comtab. "Fyo, where are you?"

"In my cabin," Fyo said. "Busy."

"Get un-busy, little bro." Francine headed for the passageway.

"You need me?" Marielle asked.

Francine waved her off. "See if you can find a better news source than that." She waved at Sven Harvard's worried-looking face on the big screen.

She hurried to Fyo's cabin, knocked once, and pushed the door open without waiting for a response.

"Why you—" Fyo leaned right, jabbing at something. He and Aleksei sat on the bunk, controllers in their hands, the holo of a virtual racing game surrounding them.

"What the—I see how it is!" Aleksi lurched forward, stabbing the air in front of him. "Take that!"

Francine broadcasted an override code and the game disappeared.

"Hey!" Both boys glared at her.

"I need some help, children," Francine said. "Something urgent. Your game can wait."

"But I was winning!" Fyo wailed.

"Who do you know on Robinson's?" Francine demanded. "Tony and Quinn need a ride off the dirt."

Fyo blinked. "There's SwifKlens. We used them last time. I'm not sure it would be safe..."

"This is a different situation from your usual," Francine said.

"There's been a coup. The 'vator is shut down. We need to get them off the surface. Speed is more important than stealth."

"Then tell 'em to go to the factory." Fyo grabbed his comtab. "I'll send a message to our pilot to expect them. Easy."

Francine nodded, staring at her little brother.

"What?" Fyo demanded.

"You may act like a child, but you come through when we need you."

A smile stretched across Fyo's face.

QUINN GRABBED Tony's arm and yanked him to a stop. "Checkpoint around the corner."

"I wish Sashelle would talk to me." Tony rubbed his arm.

"She said her bandwidth is strained by talking to both of us." Quinn was secretly pleased the caat had chosen her over Tony, but she tried not to show it. It was childish. But still satisfying to be the chosen one.

"Her bandwidth is strained?" Tony repeated.

Quinn smiled. "My words, not hers. She's monitoring a lot of chatter. Or maybe she's just being feline. Let's go back a block. Is that better, Sashelle?"

You should probably find a place to hide until tomorrow, Sashelle said. *They are deploying more soldiers. Every street I've checked is covered. Can you get inside any of these buildings?*

"She says we're not going to make it to SwifKlens. We need to hide." Quinn glanced across the narrow street at a lighted coffee shop. "Maybe we should grab a cup of coffee."

"If they start shutting down businesses, we could get caught up in a sweep," Tony said. "If that happens, they'll do a closer check of our IDs. No guarantee they'll stand up to the scrutiny."

"What is our alternative? Break into one of these buildings?"

"If we can get a few more blocks..." Tony swiped at his comtab in frustration. "If we could get to Sven's place, he could help us."

"Sven? Sven Harvard?" Quinn asked. "Why would he help us? I'm sure, unlike the rest of the locals, he'd recognize us immediately. He'd love to get an exclusive on turning us over to the Federation. Convicted traitors." She shivered.

"Sven is one of us," Tony said softly.

"Us?"

"Krimson."

"No. Really? Then what are we waiting for?" Quinn turned in a circle looking for the caat. "Sashelle, we need to get to— What's the address?"

Tony gave it to her. "That's the direction we've been heading, and she said we're stuck, so why—"

"Great. She's going to meet us in that doorway." Quinn pointed at a dark opening in the next building. She hurried along the street and stepped into the deep entryway. On impulse, she checked the door, but it was locked.

"She said a few seconds ago that we're surrounded," Tony complained. "Why do you think she can help us now?"

You were trying to get out of town. Sashelle appeared beside them. Somehow, Quinn could tell she was speaking to both of them. *To the nasty smelling building. There is no way to leave the city at this time. They have it completely cordoned off.*

Tony held up his device. "I know. What—"

Quinn raised a hand to stop him. She pulled out her own comtab and stared at the map, trying to point a mental finger. "Tony has a friend here. Can you see this?"

Sashelle went still as a statue, her eyes closed to slits. *I see it. There is currently one checkpoint between here and there. I think we can elude them. Follow me.*

She stood, stretched, and slunk into the street.

Tony raised his hands in confusion.

Quinn shook her head. "Don't ask, just trust."

They followed Sashelle into an alley that emerged in an empty lot between two high rises. At the far side of the open space, a pair of soldiers stood under a streetlight. They blocked the sidewalk, like the two they had encountered half an hour ago, standing back-to-back to watch in both directions.

Sashelle stopped and sniffed the air. *We will go down this alley behind the building on the right. When we reach the street, I will distract the guards while you cross into that warehouse lot. You may have to break the lock on the gate. On the far side, there is a personnel gate. Wait for me by the smaller gate.*

"How will you distract them?" Tony asked. "They're trained soldiers. They won't abandon their posts to watch a caat."

"She has skills. This way?"

Yes. Wait a moment until they look away, then move.

The two soldiers turned. Quinn, Tony, and Sashelle streaked across the inner corner of the empty lot and into the alley behind the high-rise. They hurried through the dark trench between buildings to the sidewalk on the far side, then they made their way along a perpendicular street to the corner.

Sashelle stopped. *This may not work.*

"Why not?" Quinn asked.

It depends on how easily distracted they are. Wait here. I will circle around and approach from the other side. When you hear me roar, run.

"Be careful, Sashelle," Tony said. "They have weapons."

"So do I." Sashelle lifted her foot and popped her claws in and out.

"Theirs can be used at a distance."

Noted. Wait for my signal. Do not be distracted.

"What is she going to do?" Tony asked.

Quinn shook her head. "I've given up guessing. She always does something surprising." She was silent for a few moments. "Have you noticed—" She broke off, not wanting him to think her crazy.

"Noticed what?" Tony asked.

"She changes size," Quinn said. "She says it's a natural instinct, but how can she do it?"

"Changes size?"

"Yes," Quinn said. "Just now, the top of her head was right above my knee. Recently, she's been up to here." She held her hand at her hip. "The other day, when Reggie tried to grab Ellianne, she wa—"

"Reggie tried to grab Elli?" Tony interrupted. "When? Where?"

"At Daravoo. Don't worry, Sashelle and I chased them off. But she was huge. As tall as Ellianne."

Tony peered at her, face contorted. "You and Sashelle chased them off? Them who?"

"Tony, you're missing the point. They—Reggie and his friend Dean—tried to grab the kids, but we took care of it. But Sashelle *grew*."

Get ready, Sashelle cut in.

Before she could repeat the warning to Tony, Sashelle roared. The sound echoed through the street, bouncing off the tall buildings, sounding like a cross between a wild animal and a raging ocean.

Quinn lunged to the corner to peek around it, Tony crouching below her to look as well. The two soldiers had swung around to face the oncoming—

What the hell was it?

"She's enormous!" Quinn whispered.

"Never mind that! Run!" Tony grabbed her hand and dragged her across the street. Later, Quinn would swear her feet never touched the ground.

They huddled against the open fence. Tony grabbed the lock on the gate. "*Futz*. I'm going to have to force this one. Stand here." He spun around and moved her a few centimeters to the right. "I hope our bodies block the flash."

While Tony worked on the lock, Quinn gawked at the scene before her. An enormous animal with teeth as long as her arm thundered down the sidewalk, scattering trash containers and benches before her. She roared again, spittle flying from her mouth.

The first soldier pulled his weapon up and fired at the monster. The blasts seemed to pass through it, setting an ornamental tree ablaze. The second soldier joined his partner, firing wildly into the approaching animal.

Hoping the deafening roars masked the noise, Tony fired his mini blaster at the lock. The light caught her attention, forcing her head around. He'd melted the lock. With a savage yank, he pulled it free and shoved the gate open. "Go!"

She glanced back to the checkpoint, but the monster had vanished. The two soldiers stood staring at the tree burning merrily, their weapons hanging loosely from their fingers.

"Hurry." They darted through the opening, and Tony swung the gate shut behind them. He fiddled with the lock for a second, but it was melted beyond hope.

"Drop it there." Quinn pointed at the ground by the gate. "It's big enough to keep the gate from swinging open."

He dropped the slagged lock. "Good call."

They darted along the side of the building, staying in shadow. Large hulks of unidentifiable equipment cast dark shadows across the open space. They moved from shadow to shadow, finally reaching the back of the yard. Two glowing orbs of gold floated about a meter above the ground. They disappeared then flashed as the caat blinked. *Took you long enough.*

CHAPTER 21

FRANCINE PACED AROUND the *Peregrine's* lounge, fidgeting with her comtab. The space elevator to Robinson's World had been shut down. The automated message claimed they were doing maintenance work, but Francine didn't believe it. The entire Federation was in turmoil. Lou's communication snooping software had picked up two inbound troop ships.

"They'll arrive in two days," Lou reported.

"Why are they sending troops here?" Francine asked. "Shouldn't they be busy? Taking back Farivel and Darius?"

"They're sending troops there, too," Lou said. "These incoming ships would have left Romara two or three days ago. They must be concerned about keeping Robinson's. I haven't heard about any unrest on the planet, but maybe Li was worried. Or Andretti planned ahead."

"The timing seems to support the latter theory," Francine said.

"We'll have to wait," Lou said. "If they haven't reached the SwifKlens shuttle by tomorrow, we'll have to send our own down."

"If they can't reach SwifKlens, they won't be able to reach us, either," Dareen said. "I have to land on the same field SwifKlens uses. We might have to do a drone extraction."

"That's plan C," Lou said. "Or maybe B, depending on what we learn over the next few hours. I don't like flying blind. Has Dusica heard anything?"

"The last message I got was from five hours ago," Francine said. "She doesn't know any more than we do. Don't you have Commonwealth contacts?"

"Of course, but the regular channels are still down." Dareen answered when Lou didn't. "We're passing messages through Daravoo and Lunesco and that takes time."

"Maybe we should continue to Rossiya." In the corner, Fyo put his comtab away. Francine thought he wasn't paying attention. "Liz and Maerk can swing back here after they finish their delivery to Xury Station."

"You're assuming they'll be fine down there," Lou said. "I'm not leaving until we know Tony can get off-world. The *Swan* doesn't have a drone."

"You have a contract to get me and Faina—sorry, Francine—to Rossiya," Fyo argued. "We have a timeline. You don't want to upset the Russosken."

"Listen to me, young man." Lou stood and stomped over to Fyo. "I don't care who you are and I'm not afraid of the Russosken. Especially now." She barked a harsh laugh and leaned over him, putting one hand on each arm of his chair. "I wouldn't have been stupid enough to take a job from them when they were dangerous. But here's the deal. With the Marconis, family comes first. If that means my payout gets dinged for not meeting the timeline, I'm good with that."

Fyo glared up at the old woman.

"Enough," Francine said. "Fyo, our schedule is not important. We'll get there when we get there. You're the *nachal'nik*. Anyone who wants to meet with you will wait. And it's never a wise idea to piss off the woman who controls the airlocks. Just saying."

TONY MELTED the lock on a smaller gate. The rattle of the mechanism and the sizzle of the blaster sounded loud in Quinn's ears. She was certain someone would stop them at any second.

Sirens wailed in the distance, coming closer. "Are they coming here?" Quinn asked. "I can't imagine reports of a blaster-proof fanged monster received a lot of response."

"Do you think they even reported it?" Tony pulled the gate open and motioned for her to precede him. "I wouldn't. It sounds crazy." He dragged the gate shut behind them.

They hurried down the street, following Sashelle's directions.

"When we get out of this, you and I are going to have a serious discussion," Tony said.

Breath caught in Quinn's throat. His tone was laughing, but serious. "Discussion?"

Tony glanced at her. "I was talking to Sashelle. But yeah, I think you and I need one too."

What did you want to discuss? the caat asked.

"So many things," Tony said. "How you know where the guards are. How you made yourself so huge."

Most of that has to do with the way I communicate with you, Sashelle replied, as if it were obvious. *You hear me because I put my thoughts into your mind. And I listen to your thoughts, although as I have mentioned many times,* she sighed heavily, *your thoughts are quite chaotic.*

"They are?" Tony asked.

"Don't take it personally," Quinn said. "She says the same to me."

"You can hear her right now?"

"Yeah, she's talking to both of us. Can't you tell?"

Tony thought about it for a moment and shrugged. "You were saying, Sashelle?"

We're going into that building. An image of the building ahead on their right appeared. The lower two levels featured half-walls and open space inside.

"Is that a parking structure?" Quinn asked. "I didn't think they allowed private vehicles in the city."

"We're reaching the edge of the restricted zone," Tony said. "I think commuters can leave private pods there."

As I was saying, Sashelle continued as the others ducked under an arm-like gate, *I can hear you. And I can hear them. It's a wonder to me that you can't hear them. So loud. And so boring!*

"So, you listen for them?" Tony asked.

Exactly. The caat's tail twitched above her back.

"That makes sense for the ones close by," Quinn said. "But how did you know the city was surrounded?"

I listened to what they were thinking and seeing. They know the plan, so I know the plan.

"That makes you an unstoppable opponent," Tony said.

Sashelle radiated contentment. *And I can put images into your mind.*

"Like the building," Tony said.

Like the building, Sashelle agreed. *I can also distort the images in your mind.*

A mental picture of the parking structure stretched into a tower. "That is so creepy," Quinn said.

I simply adjusted what the soldiers would see as I attacked.

"You were blaster proof because they were aiming over your head!" Quinn said.

And because they're terrible shots. The caat's smirk came through loud and clear.

"But you were bigger," Tony said. "You're bigger now than you were a few minutes ago."

But not that big. Sashelle glanced back at them as she leapt over a low barrier. *It's instinct. But even I have limits.*

"That's what she told me before." Quinn hopped over the barrier. "I'm not sure she can explain the physics. Or biology."

I can. But not in a way you can comprehend.

Tony nodded as he came up beside them. "Like a werewolf, then. It just happens. No one knows how or why."

Except the werewolves.

"Werewolves are fictional," Quinn said.

"That's what you think," Tony replied. "If she can do what she does, who knows what else is out there in the universe?"

THAT IS *the location you gave me.* Sashelle crouched by the corner of a building, staring across the street. Only half the streetlights were on, leaving pockets of deep shadow perfect for hiding.

Quinn glanced at the building. "It looks residential."

"Makes sense," Tony said. "Good place for a safehouse. Lots of people coming and going."

"You don't think the neighbors notice?" Quinn asked. "New people showing up all the time?"

"I'll bet there are several short-term rentals in that building," Tony said. "It would look perfectly natural."

They watched the building for twenty minutes while Tony scanned it from all sides. "I can't get a perfect read on the back, since there's another building behind it, but it looks clean as far as I can tell."

"Good, because I'm ready to take a break," Quinn said. "I mean a real break, not crouching on the sidewalk. My knees are aching. I was not cut out to be a spy in enemy territory."

"You learn to ignore the aches. Or at least put up with them. Let's go."

They hurried across the street and up the front steps. A deep entryway gave them cover while Tony worked on the access panel.

"Sven gave me a unit number." He tapped at the screen. "And this app should unlock the door." He tapped again, and the door clicked. "Perfect."

They entered a small lobby with several doors along one side and a staircase on the other. Tony nodded to the stairs. "Four C."

Sashelle bounded up the steps, three at a time.

"I guess she's not hearing anyone up there." Quinn climbed more slowly in her wake. "Why the fourth floor? Wouldn't the first floor be safer? Easier to sneak out the window?"

"If every safehouse was on the first floor, they would be easier to find."

"Yeah, because the Federation is going to check the first floor of every building." She stopped on the landing and swung around.

Tony grinned. "Good point. I guess you can ask Sven."

"Is he going to be there? Sven Harvard?" Her heart thumped faster in excitement. "I've never met a famous person before."

"Except Tiffany."

"He's not like Tiffany, is he?"

"No one is." Tony turned her gently and nudged her to the next flight.

When they reached the fourth floor, Sashelle lay curled up on a mat in front of a unit. *There's no one inside,* she reported.

"Can you read?" Quinn pointed to the letter and number on the door.

Not your scribble, she answered.

"I have very good handwriting," Quinn objected as Tony opened the door.

I meant human writing, Sashelle said. *However, I saw the symbols for this unit in your thoughts. I'm very good at pattern recognition.*

"Don't turn on the lights until we check it out." Tony put a hand over the switch as they entered. "There aren't any people, but that doesn't mean it isn't bugged. Or boobytrapped."

"This is supposed to be a safehouse. Why would it be rigged for traps?"

"Gotta stop the bad guys." Tony stood about a meter inside the front door, his comtab held aloft. Light spilled in from the hall, revealing a short hallway with a door on the right. The screen flashed yellow then green. "All clear."

The small apartment had a single bedroom and an open living space. Compared to Tiffany's place—Quinn's lip twitched. There was no comparison. Tiffany had complained about Marielle's apartment; she'd refuse to set foot inside this one. A portable heating unit —apparently used for heating both food and the room—sat on a bare counter. The threadbare couch looked uncomfortable. A small bedroom with a bare mattress and empty closet led to a tiny bath.

"Not as nice as I'd expect from Sven," Tony said after clearing the rooms. "But it will work. Let's find the egress."

"Egress?"

"I like to have a second exit. If you're on the ground floor—" He winked at Quinn. "It's usually a window. Up here, you have to be more creative." He shut off his glowing comtab, leaving them in darkness, then pulled the heavy drapes back.

Dust billowed out of them. Clearly it had been a while since they'd been moved. The window opened, but thick bars blocked it. Moonlight streamed through the dirty glass.

"What kind of neighborhood needs bars on the fourth floor?" Quinn asked. "It might be safer to take our chances with the Federation."

Tony rattled the bars. "These are in good shape."

"Unlike the rest of the building. That seems odd. What is Sven trying to keep out? Or is he trying to keep something in?"

"Are you thinking Sven might have double-crossed us? That this safehouse is actually a prison?"

"No! Why? Are you thinking that?"

"Not really." Tony rubbed his face. "I mean, obviously, I thought of it, since I said it. But I don't believe it. Sven and I have been friends for more than twenty years. And he's loyal to the Commonwealth. There must be a different exit."

"Good enough for me." Quinn pulled the curtains across the window and turned to face Tony. "He must be worried about keeping something out. Maybe blaster-proof fanged monsters." She couldn't see his expression in the dark, but the tension in the room eased.

"Let's keep looking." Tony flicked on his comtab and returned to the entry. "Where does this lead?" He opened the door near the entrance.

"A closet." Quinn nodded. "Excellent. I was hoping to find a dried-up mop."

"If there's one thing I've learned recently, it's to always check the closet."

CHAPTER 22

QUINN LEANED against the wall in the hallway as Tony examined the small room.

"It's just a closet." Tony had checked every inch of wall, floor, and ceiling, but there was no indication of a hidden door.

"Right." Quinn pushed away from the peeling wallpaper. "Not the window, not the closet. The emergency exit must be somewhere else. I'll check the bathroom. Mainly because I need to use it. You look in the bedroom. What am I looking for? Besides the toilet?"

Tony shrugged. "I'll know it when I see it."

Maybe you exit through a different apartment. Sashelle lay on the couch, curled up in a ball.

"Could be," Tony said. "That adds a layer of difficulty to an escape. Some boltholes don't have an emergency exit. You trust them to stay hidden. Sven's not usually that trusting."

"Or maybe he figures his chances of ever needing a safehouse are small." Quinn returned from the bathroom. "If the Federation figured out he was a spy, they'd grab him from his studio. Where is he, anyway? I thought he was going to meet you here."

"That was the original plan." Tony dropped onto the couch next to Sashelle. "That was before the premier was deposed. It's a big news night. Let's see what he's up to." He fished his comtab out of his pocket and swiped to a news app.

Quinn took the empty space on the couch. It was surprisingly comfortable. She slid her shoes off and leaned against his shoulder to watch Tony's screen. Sven Harvard, looking as if he'd just emerged from the hair and makeup department, looked seriously into the camera. An icon blinked in the lower left. "What's that?"

"Immersive tech." Tony's finger hovered over the icon. "It's terrifyingly good. I don't know if it will work here. You have to have the equipment installed."

"So, what, it looks like Sven is here in the room with us?"

"That's only the beginning." He stabbed the icon, and the room around them dissolved.

Sven appeared, sitting in a comfortable armchair with a subtle paisley upholstery. "Sven, how nice to see you."

"Did he call us Sven?" Quinn asked.

Tony shrugged. "I think it's tied to the installation. This room has been programmed for Sven, so that's who it thinks is here."

"Since you've just joined us, here's an update." As Sven spoke, images appeared in the air to his left and right, illustrating his descriptions. "Admiral Peiter Andretti has overturned the Li Government. Military ships are being sent to every system in the Federation to provide support to local governments. We are assured the transition has been peaceful, and Federation citizens have nothing to fear. However, videos coming out of other Federation planets are... disturbing. Here's a report from our own Rosiever Muhammad, reporting from Varitas. This report was recorded three hours ago and sent immediately to our system."

Sven slid away to the left, the room seeming to dip and swoop. Quinn grabbed Tony's arm with a little gasp. He laughed. "That was nothing."

They pivoted, and a dark man in a green suit came into view.

They stood on the roof of a building. The last edge of the setting sun glowed above the buildings to their right. All around them, lights began to appear as darkness settled across the city.

"This is Rosiever Muhammad, reporting from Varitas." The man in green gestured to the glowing skyline behind him. "I'm perched high above the city on the roof of the Lemuest Building—the tallest building on this planet. There have been protests all day, and Federation troops are patrolling to keep the peace tonight. However, their numbers are low, and tensions in the city are high."

He swept his arm up to the left. "In the Wiver Heights, we've seen flashes of light that our sensors identified as blaster fire." They seemed to dive off the side of the building, soaring across the tops of others until they settled about ten meters above a plaza packed with people. "Several thousand people have gathered in Varitas Square. This afternoon, they were peaceful, carrying signs reading, 'Freedom for All.' Most of the people I spoke with weren't sure why they were here."

The sky lightened as the video appeared to run backward, very quickly becoming a blur. It stopped suddenly, and they stood in an emptier square under overcast skies. A young woman stood next to Rosiever, smiling at him.

"It's such a thrill to meet you!" she gushed.

Rosiever smiled. "Of course. Tell me, why are you gathered today?"

"Oh, we're protesting."

"And what are you protesting?"

"You know, protesting. We want what we need, and we should have it. And nobody is going to stop us from getting it!" She looked at the small crowd of onlookers. A couple of them cheered half-heartedly.

"And what is it you need?" Rosiever asked.

"What we want!" The girl pumped her arm in the air.

The view pixelated and reformed in the same location, but

several hours later. Rosiever stood among a jostling crowd, but the movements of the others didn't impinge on him.

"He's not really there." Quinn pointed. "Look at his elbow."

The man standing next to Rosiever swung to his left, and his hand went through the reporter's body.

"He's probably projecting from the top of that building."

The crowd surged around and through the reporter, like waves on a seashore. A few of the participants carried weapons. "As you can see, the mood of the crowd has changed,"

"Are those weapons we provided?" Quinn asked in a small voice.

"Probably," Tony said. "No one ever said revolution was a tidy business."

A flash of light burst off to their right. Their position changed again, flying them into the sky, skidding along the tops of cars and trees lining the roads.

"Drone," Tony whispered. "With a three-sixty cam."

Flames burst from a vehicle parked in the street. Nearby windows were shattered. A couple of people raced away into the dark, and the drone sped after them. They hurtled through the city, chasing after fleeing citizens. The people took a hard left, and the drone zipped by. It immediately reversed direction and flew to the side street, but the people had disappeared.

They zoomed back to Rosiever's rooftop location. "I'm expecting things to heat up as the night goes on. There have been reports of a mob forming on Capitol Hill, but my drone's transmission is being interrupted. Probably state security data barriers. I'm going to see if I can get closer. I'll keep sending reports all night, Sven. Back to you."

They swung away from Rosiever, over the darkening city and into the studio. Sven nodded wisely, his hands folded in his lap. "Thank you for that report, Rosiever. Stay safe." He turned toward them. Light flashed briefly.

Tony leaned forward. He swiped his comtab and the video froze. "Sven sent us a message."

"How do you know?" Quinn sat up.

"That flash. We're the only people who saw that. His in-house system connected with my security protocol." He flicked the screen.

Sven's face appeared on the screen. "Tony, run."

CHAPTER 23

"MOVE!" Tony surged to his feet. As Quinn jammed her feet into her shoes, he grabbed her bag and his jacket. Quinn poked the caat awake.

Why? Sashelle's eyes opened to the barest of slits and she glared.

"Didn't you hear?" Quinn got right in her face. "Sven said run. We need to go."

The caat sprang off the couch, her fur brushing against Quinn's arm in a prickle of foreboding. *How far away?*

"I don't know." Quinn grabbed her bag from Tony and stumbled to the door.

Let me go first. Sashelle lunged down the stairs, reaching the landing in two giant leaps. *I hear no one awake,* she reported.

"How far away can you hear?" Quinn hurried down the first flight.

Not far enough. Too many people in this building. Dreams are distracting.

"Weapons hot, Quinn." Tony pulled his mini blaster from his pocket. "Anyone coming toward us is not a friend."

"That'll get us arrested if we're wrong." Quinn yanked out her stunner.

"Arrested is better than dead. Sven said 'run,' and he used my real name. That means the Feds know where we are." Tony grabbed her arm at the bottom of the second set of stairs. "Wait until Sashelle clears it."

"How did he know we were here? And what if we hadn't been?"

He gave her a confused look. "If we hadn't been here, then they wouldn't find us when they come."

"You're saying they're coming here." Quinn stabbed a finger at the floor. "Not looking for us in general, but specifically coming to this address. Are they after us or Sven?"

Clear, Sashelle said. *Meet me at the end of the block.*

"Good question." Tony urged her down the last set of stairs. "I think they're after us. If they wanted Sven, they'd walk in to the studio and take him."

"Maybe they did, and he managed to get the message to us before they grabbed him?"

Tony's jaw tightened. "Maybe. Speculation won't do us any good if we get caught. Let's put some distance between us and Sven's place." He peered through the front windows. "Looks good. Stay low and run."

They ducked out and hurried down the steps, hiding behind the low shrubbery as much as they could. At the bottom, Tony sprinted to the right, Quinn following close behind. They rounded the end of the block and ducked into the shadow of the building.

Quinn's breathing evened out quickly. She owed Francine flowers or booze or something for making her work so hard over the last few months.

"Where to, Sashelle?" Tony whispered.

The caat didn't answer.

"Sashelle?" Quinn tried to think loudly and clearly. "Where are you?"

They're everywhere. Sashelle's mental tone sounded calm despite the words. *Get inside. They're covering the streets.*

"Did you hear that?" Quinn hissed.

"Yeah."

"What are we going to do?" She squinted down the street, trying to figure out which building might allow them access.

"Nothing." His voice sounded far away.

"Nothing?" Quinn spun around.

Tony stood frozen in place, hands raised. Two Federation soldiers stood behind him with their blast rifles aimed at point-blank range.

"*Futz.*"

FRANCINE WOKE FROM A LIGHT SLEEP. Her dreams had been a confused mess of every planet she'd ever visited, and that was a lot of planets. In the dream, Tony and Quinn kept telling her to run, and huge versions of Sashelle carried them away in her mouth.

She sat on the edge of her bunk and grabbed a nearby bottle of water.

Francine.

She looked around the empty cabin. Normally Marielle would be here, but she'd decided to switch to night shifts so she could keep an eye on the incoming news reports. She'd be in the lounge or the gym.

Francine.

"Sashelle?" She said the name aloud. But it couldn't be the caat. She was on the *Swan*. And she never used Francine's name.

I'm with the Purveyor of Tuna. Sashelle's voice was thin and thready, as if stretched a long distance.

"You're speaking to me from Robinson's?" Francine asked in amazement.

We're on a shuttle. Probably passing your orbit. I think the vacuum extends my range. I've been listening for hours. I finally heard you.

"What ship?" Francine pulled on a light robe and ran out the door.

Federation shuttle. We'll rendezvous with a cruiser in high orbit.

The Purveyor of Tuna and the Stealthy One are prisoners. I believe we're headed... Her mental voice grew softer, tapering off into nothing.

"Crap!" Francine scrambled off the bunk and lunged out the door. "Marielle! Lou!" She ran to the crew area and started banging on doors, unsure which cabin was Lou's.

"What's going on?" Kert grumbled.

Stene stuck his head out the door, then retreated.

"Where's Lou?" Francine demanded. "We have a problem!"

Stene's door opened again, and he stepped out wearing a ratty T-shirt and boxers. "Mom sleeps on the bridge."

"What's going on?" Dareen popped out of her cabin wearing pink shorts and a T-shirt covered in fuchsia hearts and flowers.

"On the bridge? Why?" Without waiting for an answer, Francine flew along the passageway and burst into the bridge. A length of striped fabric hung across the small space behind the command seats. "What the heck?"

"This better be an emergency," Lou's voice grumbled from inside the hammock.

"It is," Francine said. "You sleep in a hammock?"

"So?" Lou's head appeared above the fabric. "What's it to you?"

"Nothing," Francine said. "Tony and Quinn have been apprehended by the Federation. They're on their way to a cruiser orbiting out there somewhere."

The fabric swayed wildly, and Lou dropped to the floor, wearing loose pants and a baggy smock. She stomped across the bridge and threw herself into the command chair. "What cruiser?"

"I don't know." Francine ducked under the hammock

"You don't know?" Lou turned and fixed her bleary eyes on Francine.

Francine took a deep breath. "I got a message. The information I was given said Tony and Quinn had been taken on Robinson's. They were on a shuttle to an unnamed cruiser in high orbit."

"Credibility of the source?" Lou demanded.

"Extremely high" Francine hoped she was right. They still didn't know Sashelle's exact motives, so it was possible she had an unknown agenda. But she'd repeatedly said Quinn's safety was her top concern. "Extremely reliable."

Lou's eyes narrowed, then she nodded. "Good enough. Log into the comms station and see if you can find out what Federation cruiser is in orbit. Kert! Stene!"

Behind them, Kert and Stene had stowed the hammock. "What do you need, Mom?" Kert answered.

"Are we secure to fly?"

"Cargo was secured when we picked it up," Stene said. "I'll run down and double-check." He hurried out the door.

"All systems are nominal," Kert said. "Fuel and supplies were topped off when we stopped at the station."

"Roger," Lou said, her voice clipped and professional. "Francine, any luck? Dareen, check the commercial comms. See if you can find any interesting chatter."

"I'm checking our surveillance recordings," Francine said. "The Federation cruiser *Triumphant* arrived in-system two days ago. They reached planetary orbit early today—yesterday, now. Shuttle dropped immediately."

"Got it," Dareen said. "I found recordings of the chatter between the station and the planet. We've also got a recording of comms between the *Triumphant* and the base on Robinson's, but Tony's decrypter must be out of date. It's just noise." She flicked through a couple of screens. "Okay, I ran the feed through a key-word search, and managed local discussion." She flicked an icon, and voices cut in mid-sentence.

"—land on the planet? Robinson's doesn't allow anyone to land."

"Military craft have different rules, *Meteor*, you know that," a second voice answered.

"*Meteor* is a commercial ship," Dareen whispered.

"I'm a citizen of Robinson's!" *Meteor* said. "I pay a good chunk of taxes to keep my planet clean. We don't need dirty military shuttles blowing—"

"Please take up your concerns with your ombudsman," the station voice replied. "I have no control over political decisions. All I know is military shuttles are being cleared to land at Dafoe Base."

Lou waved her hand, and the recording stopped. "I don't care about their arguments. We need info about where they're taking Tony. And Quinn," she added as an afterthought. "Keep working on the decrypter. And listen to the rest of that chatter. Let me know if there's anything of consequence. Oh, and call your mom. Tell her we'll meet her at the jump point in thirty-seven hours."

"You got it, boss," Dareen said.

"I'm laying in a course for the jump," Lou said. "Francine, set up an alert to let us know when the *Triumphant* leaves its current orbit. Those cruisers can move a lot faster than we can, and I don't want them flying up my butt unexpectedly."

They worked silently for a few moments.

"Course laid in. Prepare for departure." Lou opened the all-ship channel. "Departing orbit twenty-three bravo in three, two, one, mark. We're headed out of the system, folks."

"Captain, incoming hail from Poinsettia System Flight Control," Dareen said.

"Put 'em on," Lou replied.

A woman in a smart uniform with PSFC on her chest appeared onscreen. "You didn't update your flight plan, *Peregrine*."

"Sorry, Control." Lou gave an uncharacteristic smile. She looked almost pleasant when she wasn't glowering. "We're departing early. Family emergency back on Daravoo. I'll have my navigator send you an update now." She motioned to Dareen. "We're a lot less formal out in the fringe, and in the panic, I forgot the protocols."

The woman nodded. "Understood. This is a busy system, and we need to keep track of all traffic."

"Speaking of traffic." Lou leaned forward conspiratorially. "Know anything about that cruiser?"

The woman's face registered surprise and a brief flicker of fear. She looked both directions, then leaned closer to the mic. "We don't know anything. We almost never have military ships here, so people are nervous. I'd think it had something to do with the coup, except they had to have departed Romara five days ago, and the coup only happened yesterday."

"Maybe Andretti pre-deployed his forces," Lou said. "He controlled enough ships in his previous position to do that."

The woman's eyes went wide, and her eyebrows disappeared under her hat. "You're right!"

Francine tried not to roll her eyes, in case she was in the camera's view. Did this woman think coups just happened? Andretti had obviously been planning this for months.

"Do you know when they're leaving?" Lou asked.

"They don't talk to us," the controller said, her words coming quickly. "Sail right by without a howdy-do. Then land on the planet without a care how it affects our environment."

"Captain." Francine waved to catch Lou's attention before the woman got rolling on what was clearly a hot-button topic around here.

Lou glanced at Francine. Francine raised her eyebrows.

"Thank you, Comms." Lou turned back to the screen. "I'm sorry, Control. There's an incoming message from home. Thanks for your help."

The woman sat back in her chair and nodded. "You're welcome, *Peregrine*," she said in a louder, more professional voice. "I've received your updated plan. You are cleared to depart Robinson's. Safe travels." The screen went blank.

"Did you have something?" Lou asked Francine.

"Got the shuttle." Francine threw trajectory information onto the forward screen. "It's headed toward *Triumphant*. Passed us exactly when—" She broke off. She didn't want to expose Sashelle's secret. "Based on its current vector, it will dock in about ninety minutes."

"*Futz*," Lou said. "If they leave as soon as the shuttle docks, they'll get to Romara way ahead of us."

"They may not leave," Francine said. "They're the only Federation ship in the system. If Andretti is consolidating his power, he might leave them on station for now."

Lou shook her head. "With two high-profile prisoners on board? I don't think so. Andretti has let his emotions take over his common sense more than once since we got involved with him. He's going to want Quinn on Romara. Now."

CHAPTER 24

END STOMPED across the *Swan's* lounge. "I don't want to stay here! All the action is on the *Peregrine*!"

"We've agreed to keep the kids safe." Liz threw an "I told you so" look at Maerk. "As soon as we've finished here at Xury Station, we're heading for the jump point and back to the fringe. We have a cargo to deliver, and it will be safer there."

"What about the caat?" End said. "Elli's going to want her pet."

"Sashelle will be fine," Maerk said. "She seems quite capable of taking care of herself. Besides, she's on a Federation shuttle heading to a battleship. Shall we declare war on the Federation to get a caat back?"

"Of course not." End stomped his feet again. "I hate sitting here when everyone else is over there doing things!"

"Everyone else?" Liz asked. "Or your younger sister?"

"Both." End growled in frustration. "All of them. We need to help."

"End, they aren't doing anything yet." Maerk, the family peacemaker, spread his hands. "They're just flying."

"They have a plan, though," End said. "They must have a plan!

They're heading to the jump point, so obviously they're going somewhere. And they'll need all the help they can get, right?"

"I don't know what their plan is," Liz said sharply. "But if I could figure out how to do it, I'd pull Dareen away, too. That cruiser is going to Romara, and your grandmother is cra—"

"You don't know that," Maerk cut in.

"We may not have external confirmation." Liz glared at her ex. "But I know it. Going to Romara is crazy dangerous. I don't want any of us anywhere near there."

"Ugh!" End stomped out of the room, headed for cargo. He glared at the stacks of crates branded with the Xury Station logo. It was so frustrating to be stuck on the baby ship. He had to figure out a way to get to the *Peregrine*.

QUINN LAY IN DARKNESS, trying to remember where she was. Hazy, dream-like scenes floated through her mind, but none of them made sense. Giant caats? Flying couches? She took a couple of deep breaths and tried to open her eyes.

Her lids felt crusty and swollen. She tried to lift her hand to rub them, but her body didn't want to cooperate. A cool breeze fluttered her hair and chilled her arms. It smelled of nothing—like recycled air on a ship in good repair. Nothing like the fruity, metallic tang on Robinson's World.

Robinson's World—memories came back slowly. They had been on Robinson's. She and Tony had been captured by Federation soldiers. They'd been taken to the shuttle field and loaded into the cargo area of a Federation shuttle. It had been a hybrid shuttle, configurable for carrying cargo or troops. They'd sat in jump seats along the sides of the bay. Then nothing.

Her eyes finally peeled open. Dim light revealed little. Blank walls and a single bunk that she lay on. She rolled her head to the side, pleasantly surprised when her neck responded to the command. Small room, mostly empty. A cell?

She took inventory of her body. Whatever they'd done to her appeared to be wearing off; she was able to wiggle her fingers and toes. Eventually, she reached a sitting position, although the movement made her vision sparkle and fade at the edges. When it cleared, she swung her legs off the bunk and looked around again.

Definitely a cell. A sanitation cube with a toilet and sink stood in the corner. A tray lay on the floor near the door. It held two small, covered dishes and a bottle. Water! Her throat tightened, and her tongue suddenly felt too big for her mouth. She stumbled across the room and grabbed the flexible container. Opening the thing took several tries, but soon the soothing liquid poured down her throat. She shuffled to the sink to refill it.

When she'd drunk enough, she turned her attention to the tray. Beige paste in one bowl and squishy chunks in another. She paused briefly as she raised the first block to her lips. They might contain more of whatever drug she'd been subjected to. On the other hand, there were easier ways to keep a prisoner under, so if they wanted her out, she'd still be out.

She gobbled both offerings quickly, using her fingers since they'd provided no utensils. She hadn't realized how hungry she was until she'd drunk the water. When she finished, she washed her hands and refilled the bottle once more.

Now what?

Time to take stock. She looked at her clothing. She wore a plain beige coverall with a zipper up the front and no pockets. Her feet were bare, but beige boot-style slippers lay on the floor near the bunk. The bowls and tray were made of a flexible material, stiff enough to hold their shape, but not rigid enough to be used as a weapon. The bunk was made of a smooth material with no removable parts, except the thin pillow and even thinner mattress. No blankets or sheets. Nothing.

Ah, you're awake.

"Sashelle?"

Inside voice, please. The caat sent a mental smirk.

They're probably recording me, aren't they? Quinn thought at the caat. *Where are you?*

You're getting quite proficient at this form of communication. I am nearby.

Nearby where? Quinn asked. *Where are we? And where's Tony?*

The Stealthy One *is next to you,* Sashelle said. *But the cells appear to be soundproof. The human next to him has not answered his requests for information.*

We're prisoners, but not the only ones? Where are we?

Federation cruiser, Sashelle replied. *The* Triumphant. *There are many soldiers on this ship.*

Her heart sank. They were in Federation custody, probably on their way to Romara. Back to death row. She was kind of surprised they hadn't shot her outright, but maybe Andretti wanted one more chance to gloat before having her executed. Or maybe he wanted to do it himself. To make sure she was really dead this time. Third time's the charm.

Are we moving?

We left orbit several hours ago, Sashelle said. *The loud thing said we'll reach jump point in twenty-six hours.*

Twenty-six hours? I must have been out longer than I thought. Federation cruisers were much faster than private ships like the *Peregrine*, but it still took time to reach jump.

The crew are very proud of their vessel, Sashelle said. *It's fast and relatively new. They think about it. A lot.*

But they don't know you're here, Quinn said. *You're good.*

The caat's satisfied feeling came through loud and clear. *It's a little trickier to stay hidden on a ship. I can't control the hatches. Luckily, they've been open most places. Except yours, of course.*

Of course. Quinn lay back on her bunk, staring at the blank ceiling. *I don't suppose we have any chance of escaping as long as we're on the ship. What does Tony say?*

He agrees, Sashelle said. *He said you should relax and enjoy the ride as much as you can. And don't lose hope. He still has a few friends on Romara.*

END SAT on the *Swan's* tiny bridge, monitoring nearby traffic. Poinsettia was a busy place, even during a military lockdown. Shortly after the coup, public transportation had been shut down. Ships that were already on their way to a jump were allowed to continue, provided their location was another Federation system. Ships like the *Swan*, headed to Lunesco, had been told to remain in place.

Of course, that didn't stop the *Swan*. They'd departed Xury Station before the lockdown had started. Ships still docked there would be unable to leave, but the *Swan* was free. And the jump point was a large area. Securing it would require many battleships. The Federation could have shut down the jump beacons, but then their ships wouldn't be able to jump, either.

End grinned. The Federation had shut down the beacons' civilian signals, but thanks to Lou and Tony, they could access the military frequencies. He suspected other civilians had that capability, too. Most of the ships headed to the jump point weren't government-owned.

The system pinged. Perfect. He keyed in a comm identity. "Dareen, this is End."

"Hey, End, what's up?"

"Are you guys going to Romara?" He wasn't worried about being overheard—long ago, he'd used Tony's tech to set up a private channel between himself and his sister. If she was close enough to catch his signal, they could talk undetected. And she'd finally moved into his reach.

"I'm not sure." Her voice lowered. "Gramma isn't telling us anything. We have a delivery scheduled for five days from now on

Rossiya. But Tony and Quinn are on that ship, and it's headed for the jump point. I wish there was a way of knowing where it's going."

"If you can decrypt the comm signals, you could probably find out," End said. "Didn't Tony leave some decryption software on the *Peregrine*?"

"Yes, but I can't get it working!" Dareen's voice went up. "Even Francine can't figure it out."

"I might be able to help," End said. "If I could get over there."

"I'll come get you," Dareen said immediately.

"How are you going to do that?" End gloated silently. *Way to fall into my trap, little sis!*

"I'll fly the *Dragon* over, of course," Dareen said. "You know the shuttles are faster for short burns. I'll zip over to the *Swan*, pick you up, and we'll be back at the *Peregrine* before they reach jump."

"Perfect."

"I'll talk to Gramma. You tell Mom," Dareen said. "Bye!"

"Hey wait!" But she was gone. Now he had to convince his mom to let him go.

CHAPTER 25

"YOU'RE AN ADULT, YOU IDIOT." Dareen glared at her brother. "Who cares what Mom says? We don't have to do that anymore."

"Easy to say." End sat on one of the Xury crates. "But when you're locked in the cargo hold, it isn't so easy to do."

Dareen looked around the space. "Yeah, I guess so." She crossed her arms. "She can't keep us locked in here forever."

"Don't tell me, tell her."

"You can't keep us locked in here forever!" she yelled at the bulkhead where she knew a camera was hidden. "You have to free us! We're citizens of the Commonwealth. They don't take kindly to abuse or starvation or—or—"

"Involuntary captivity!" End filled in.

"Is there such a thing as voluntary captivity?"

"Shut up." End turned his back to her.

Dareen ignored him, too. It was his fault she was here. And she told him to *tell* Mom they were leaving, not ask permission. If Mom didn't let them out, Gramma would be angry—Dareen had taken the shuttle without permission, which meant none of the family knew she was gone. The *Peregrine* could jump to Romara without knowing one of their shuttles—and the pilot—was missing.

"Gramma's gonna be mad if I don't come back!" she yelled at the camera. "She needs both her shuttles to rescue Tony and Quinn! And she has cargo to deliver!" She still wasn't sure if the Peregrine was headed directly to Romara, or if they'd stop at Rossiya first. Their contract specified delivery of Fyo, Francine, and their assorted entourage—personnel and cargo—within five more days. Gramma didn't welch on a signed deal.

"Do you want Tony to die in a Federation cell?" she yelled. "He's your nephew! Don't you care? He needs us to rescue him!"

"Tony has plenty of friends in Romara to rescue him," Liz snapped.

She sounded as mad as Dareen felt, but for once, she didn't care. "He has *family* to rescue him," she yelled back. "Just because you left the family doesn't mean we fell apart!"

"I didn't leave the family!" The hatch swung open and Liz stormed in. She looked terrible: face pale, hair sticking out all over, dark circles under her eyes. "I left your gramma because she was unreasonable, and I wanted to make my own way. Better late than never. But I didn't leave the family. And I'd do anything for Tony. For any of them."

End swung around. "Then why won't you let us go? Don't you have any faith in Tony's abilities?"

"I have enormous faith in Tony." Liz dropped onto the crate beside her son. "But this is a revolution. He's been setting it up for ages. It's happening. And people get killed in revolutions."

"Maybe he thinks it's worth dying for!" Dareen said.

"Do *you* think it's worth dying for?" Liz asked softly. "Because if you go haring off to Romara, you could die."

"I don't know if Tony's revolution is worth my life," End said. "But Tony is. He's always been there for us. Even when he was in deep cover, he helped us. We need to help him."

Tears sparkled in Liz's eyes. "I practically raised that boy! I would do anything for him. But I can't lose all three of you! Don't ask me to do that."

"We're not asking." Dareen raised her chin. "We're telling you. But we're not going to die. We're going to get Tony out. And Quinn and Sashelle. And we're coming back."

Liz reached out and pulled Dareen into a hug. End wrapped his arms around his mother and sister, squeezing them tight. After a long time, they released each other.

"We'll make you proud, Mom," Dareen said.

"I wish I could go with you," Liz whispered. "But the kids..."

"You take care of Ellianne and Lucas," End said. "We'll get their mom back."

They stood and walked to the airlock where Maerk met them. "Take these." He offered two of his beloved ArmorCoats. "You'll need them more than we do."

End threw himself at his dad. Another round of hugs ensued until beeping from Dareen's pocket pulled them apart. "That's my alert. I need to head back if we're going to make it to the *Peregrine* before jump."

"I'm so proud of you two," Maerk said.

"Tell Elli and Lucas I'm sorry I missed them," Dareen said. "Tell Elli I'll bring her caat back."

"Better if they sleep." Liz touched her daughter's face with a gentle finger. "Be careful. Stay safe. We're taking the kids to Lunesco, then we'll come to Romara to back you up."

"You will?" Dareen and End asked in concert.

"We will?" Maerk asked at the same moment.

"Of course we will. We're a family, and that's what family does."

⸻

THE COMM PANEL PINGED.

"*Futz*, that's Gramma," Dareen muttered. "She must have noticed I was gone."

"Did you think she wouldn't?" End snorted a laugh. He'd been laughing a lot, almost hysterically, since they'd left the *Swan*. "I thought you were going to talk to her?"

She glared at him, her cheeks burning. "I decided asking forgiveness was better than asking permission." Dareen swiped up the comm program and hit the connect button. "This is the *Scarlet Dragon*."

"*Dragon*, this is the *Peregrine*, you are cleared for docking."

"That wasn't Gramma," End said.

"It sounded like Fyo. *Peregrine*, who is this?"

"This is the Vengeful Tiger," Fyo said.

"You changed the name of the ship?"

"No, my code name is Vengeful Tiger."

"That's...interesting," Dareen rolled her eyes at End.

"I don't want to say my name on the comm channels. Aleksei says it isn't good security protocol."

"You said Aleksei's name," End pointed out.

"Urgh, whatever. You're cleared to dock. And no, Lou doesn't know," Fyo said. "You're welcome."

"Lou doesn't know what?" another male voice said.

"Crap. Gotta go. See you soon." The comm channel went dead.

"Fyo is a terrible spy," End said.

"I know." Dareen fired the reverse thrusters in microbursts until they matched the *Peregrine's* speed, then she used the maneuvering engines to bring them close to the dock. She spun the craft along the X-axis until they lined up with the collar and engaged the docking sequence. The shuttle clinked with the bigger ship and was reeled in. The cargo skirt closed around the rear end of the shuttle and locked. "Docking complete."

"Seal confirmed," the computer said. "Cargo lock at pressure. It is safe to open cargo doors."

The shuttles had two docking locations on the *Peregrine*: on either side employing the passenger airlocks for connection and access, or through the cargo bay. The latter method was used for cargo transfer or loading large numbers of passengers quickly. Lou had insisted the *Dragon* be cargo-docked when they left Robinson's. Maybe they were going to drop the cargo at Rossiya first after all. She sighed.

They edged past the huge Russosken pod secured to the deck and made their way upstairs to the crew lounge. If they'd gotten this far without encountering Lou, they must have been successful in their secret mission.

"What the hell were you doing?" Lou sat in the armchair at the end of the couch. The rest of the crew sat with her, even Aleksei and Marielle.

"I—" Dareen's face went hot, and her pulse pounded in her ears.

"She came to get me," End said. "I can fix Tony's decryption software. You need me."

Lou's narrowed eyes zeroed in on End.

"It wasn't all his fault. I could have said no. But I didn't." She raised her chin. "He's right. We need him."

"Okay," Lou replied.

"What?" The siblings stared at her.

She shrugged. "You're right. We need him. I thought about staging a boarding and bringing him back myself, but you beat me to it. It's time for all hands on deck. Let's do this."

CHAPTER 26

THE SLOT in the door opened at regular intervals, providing food and removing empty trays. Quinn wondered what would happen if she didn't put her tray near the slot when she was done. Would they refuse to serve more food? Or send someone in to retrieve it? She debated the wisdom of testing.

The Stealthy One did, Sashelle said. *They sent in two armored guards to get the tray. And the next one did not arrive.*

Images of the interaction played through her head like a video taken through Tony's eyes. The soldiers wore heavy armor. One blocked the door while the other walked in to take the tray. Their faceplates were mirrored.

"Sorry about that," Tony said. "I've been busy, so I forgot to put the tray back. So much to do in here."

The soldier picked up the tray, ignoring Tony. He turned without acknowledging the prisoner, and they both left.

"That went well," Quinn muttered.

He thought they might use some form of physical punishment, Sashelle said. *He said the fact that they didn't indicates they're under orders not to harm you.*

Andretti wants us in good repair when we get back to Romara?

Quinn mused. *I'm amazed he didn't tell them to beat us to a pulp. What's his game?*

Maybe he thinks wondering will be more stressful to you.

Quinn laughed. *Maybe so. Total isolation to break us. That sounds like Andretti. Good thing he doesn't know about you.* She laughed again.

It wasn't that funny, Sashelle said.

I know. But maybe if I sit here laughing, it will freak him out when he sees the video. You know any good jokes?

FRANCINE SCOOPED a portion of End's casserole onto her plate and passed the dish to Kert. He took it in silence while she helped herself to a roll and butter. After several minutes passed and no one had said a word, she set her bread on her plate. "So, what's the plan?"

"We don't plan during meals," Kert muttered to her. "Ma thinks it's bad for digestion."

Francine glanced at Lou, then back to Kert. "Really?"

"Usually that would be true." At the head of the table, Lou set down her fork. "However, we have many options we need to discuss, and now, when we're all here, would be a good time for that."

Kert, Stene, Dareen, and End all jerked upright, staring at the captain in shock. They looked at each other, then at the matriarch again.

"Okay, I'll bite," Fyo drawled. "What are our options?"

Lou glared at Fyo from beneath lowered brows, then picked up her mug. "We're going to Romara."

"We know," Kert said.

Lou glared at him. "Our original plan was to stop at Rossiya first." She paused.

"We know," Dareen said.

Lou shook her head. "Option one: stop at Rossiya as planned."

"No!" The shout went up around the table.

"Hear me out!" Lou bellowed, and the room quieted. "Rossiya is Fyo's stronghold. Could they provide support to our mission?" She looked at Francine.

Fyo glowered. "I'm the *nachal'nik*, not her."

Lou's head swung around. "So, can they? Will they?"

Fyo squirmed under her penetrating stare and finally looked away. "Ask my sister."

"If we stop at Rossiya," Francine said slowly, "they will take delivery of the cargo." Lou's eyes snapped to hers and she nodded. "They will also take delivery of their *nachal'nik*. They aren't going to let Fyo go anywhere near Romara."

"What? I'm the *nachal'nik*!" Fyo jumped to his feet. "They can't tell me what I'm allowed to do!"

"You are a figurehead," Francine said bluntly. "You are the symbol of Russosken greatness—the only one left. Rossiya is a Russosken retirement home. Anyone young enough to fight went off to the fringe to fight—or hide—when we started overthrowing Russosken control. Most of them are either being held on those planets awaiting trial, or they've been integrated into the local economy."

"That's an interesting take on indentured servitude," Lou said.

Francine shrugged. "We've been trying to help *soldaty* involved in the fight. A lot of the younger ones have been allowed to settle on the planets where they were fighting. Most of them were pressed into Russosken service against their will. The deal Dusi struck with the new governments is that they do the scut work—cleaning up the messes they made. When that's done, they'll move into low-paying jobs and have to work their way up. Not unlike any new settler without a financial backer."

She paused to take a drink. "The point is, Rossiya is full of old people and families with small children. There's no secret reserve of *soldaty* waiting to follow the *nachal'nik's* call. That was the whole point of this revolution: to destroy the Russosken's offensive capabilities and release their grip on the planets they controlled. We succeeded, which means there aren't any standing armies left."

"We wouldn't want them going to Romara anyway," Dareen said. "They'd take over the whole Federation, and no one wants that."

Francine laughed. "I don't think they have that kind of reach. The Federation may be corrupt and crumbling, but it's still got more firepower than what's left of the Russosken. In fact, that may be why they let us get away with what we've already done."

"What do you mean?" Fyo asked.

Lou stabbed her knife in Fyo's direction. "The Russosken were getting too strong. The Federation was getting nervous."

"Exactly," Francine said. "They liked having the Russosken do their dirty work, but trying to control the monster made them nervous. So, they let us take the Russosken down."

"You think they *let* us do that?" Dareen asked in horror. "Now *we're* doing the Federation's dirty work?"

Francine held up her hands. "I think the Federation could have stepped in and taken us out. Homegrown revolutionaries are rarely successful against a real military force. But either they didn't bother, because they saw an advantage for themselves—culling the Russosken—or because they were too focused on internal politics. We don't know what was going on with Andretti and Corvair-Addison before the coup. If they were busy duking it out, that could explain why they didn't step in sooner."

"Much as I enjoy a good political discussion," Marielle drawled, "we're getting way off topic. Do we head for Rossiya?"

"No!" Francine and Lou said in chorus.

"But—" Fyo started, but Lou cut him off.

"If you want to go home, we'll send you there," Lou said. "Stay with the old people and the babies. The adults have work to do."

"I think Lou is right," Francine said, speaking directly to Fyo. "But you don't have to get involved. We can find you a ride to Rossiya before we leave Poinsettia."

Lou cleared her throat.

"Okay, after we reach Romara." Francine pulled out her comtab and swiped through some apps. "See? There's still a regular flight."

"That would not be advisable for the *nachal'nik*," Aleksei said hesitantly.

"I would advise against using public transportation at this time," Marielle agreed.

Aleksei nodded in relief.

"Good point," Francine said. "So, stay on the ship. You'll be fine in orbit."

"You know Romara has a lot of orbit busters, right?" Marielle said. "If they decide this is a target, anyone aboard is screwed."

"I may have to land the *Peregrine*," Lou said.

"You never land!" End said.

"I said 'may'," Lou replied. "And I land sometimes. Usually not in enemy territory, though. But extraordinary times and all that. It might be the easiest and best way to make use of that cargo."

"You can't use that cargo!" Fyo said. "That's supposed to go to Rossiya!"

"What is the cargo?" Dareen asked.

Lou looked around the table, her eyes coming back to settle on Francine. She raised one eyebrow.

Francine nodded. "The cargo is a troop of *soldaty*."

CHAPTER 27

KERT STARED AT HIS MOTHER. "How can that box be *people*?"

"They're suspended," Francine said. "It's how they—we—ship *soldaty* to the battlefield."

"You freeze them and send them as cargo?" Kert's voice cracked on the last word.

"I've heard rumors, but didn't believe 'em," Stene muttered.

"That's what Mom and Dad carried from Daravoo, remember? But they had a couple Russosken enforcers to make sure they got to their destination." Dareen looked from Aleksei to Marielle. "Is that why you're here?"

"No!" Aleksei squawked. "I'm usually in the box!"

"Petrov sent the enforcers because he thought—correctly—Liz and Maerk might not be trustworthy."

"Hey!" End exclaimed.

"Chill out," Francine said. "*Petrov* thought they weren't trustworthy, and for him, they weren't. These *soldaty* were sent to protect Fyo when he arrives on Rossiya. Or wherever he goes. We didn't need any enforcers because we weren't worried about Lou stealing them or tossing them out the airlock."

"Except that's exactly what she's suggesting!" Fyo said. "She wants to 'use the cargo,' she said. They're supposed to protect me, not make some kind of suicide raid on Romara."

"Do you hear yourself?" Francine demanded. "All those years hiding on Taniz Beta turned you into the most self-centered, whiny—"

"Children!" Lou roared. "First of all, I don't 'use' people. Those poor boys in the box—" She nodded at Aleksei. "—are human beings. They have the right to make their own decisions."

"These are elite *soldaty*," Francine said. "The best of the best. They've sworn to protect the *nachal'nik*. They don't make decisions; they follow orders."

"If we're going to take them to Romara to help free Tony and Quinn, they get to decide if they want to go." Lou stabbed her knife into her chicken breast.

"Fair enough."

"They're supposed to protect me," Fyo said. When his sister started to interrupt, he held up a hand. "If I go to Romara, so will they."

"So now you're suddenly willing to join the cause?" Francine demanded.

"I'm not joining any cause," Fyo said. "I am helping my sister rescue her friends. And if that means my personal safety entourage comes along, so be it."

"But they will decide that for themselves," Lou said firmly. "Individually, without threat of retaliation or punishment. Each man makes his own choice. Otherwise, I won't let you wake them on my ship."

Francine and Fyo nodded.

"Is no one going to talk about how creepy it is to have a box full of sleeping soldiers in our cargo hold?" Dareen demanded.

"You can talk about it all you want," Lou said. "Later. Right now, we have plans to make."

THE DOOR WHOOSHED OPEN, and Quinn sat up. Bright light from the outer room glared in her eyes. She squinted at the two armored soldiers standing in the doorway.

"Up!"

"Where are we going?" Quinn swung her legs off the bunk and slid her feet into the slippers on the floor. She hadn't bothered putting them on before, as the temperature in the cell was comfortable. The soles were made of the same flexible substance used for the dishes and tray. The uppers were the same material as her coverall. Useless as a weapon, but they'd keep her feet warm.

The soldier fastened magnetic restraints on her wrists and ankles. Quinn recognized the model from her stint in the Justice Center on Romara. They were connected electronically. If she tried to run, the person holding the remote could immobilize her as if she wore a chain strung between her arms and legs.

"Move," a soldier barked.

As she stood, Quinn glanced at his chest. He wore no nametag. She wasn't even sure it was a man; the helmets made all the soldiers sound the same. This one was taller than her, however, so he was likely male. "Can't you give me a hint?" she asked.

The soldier stepped forward and grabbed her arm above the elbow. "Move."

They marched into the passageway, and the second soldier fell in behind. Ahead, another prisoner was being removed from a cell.

"Tony!"

"You okay, Quinn?"

"Silence!" The soldier jerked her arm, nearly pulling her over. "Walk."

Quinn looked over her shoulder, but the broad chest of the second guard blocked her view.

Sashelle, where are you? She imagined her words spreading out through the ship, calling the caat.

Trying to find the shuttle bay. Sashelle's voice was thin and distracted. *Why can't humans build their rodent ships all the same?*

Find someone in a pilot's uniform and follow him. Quinn visualized a pilot in a flight suit.

What does a— Oh, that's very good. Sashelle didn't speak for a while.

Quinn had the impression she was slinking along passageways, watching the crew members as they strode along. *I can almost see what you're doing.*

There shouldn't be any 'almost' about it, Sashelle said. *Concentrate. I'm sending you my visual.*

Quinn stumbled when her vision blurred and changed. *That is freaky.* A grayscale view overlaid her field of view. She saw a different passageway. This one was taller, and many giant humans strode along it. The color had washed out, but she saw textures and details she'd never noticed before. *Is this what you see?*

Yes, and right now, I need to see a pilot!

"That one," Quinn said aloud. The soldier's grip tightened, and he shook her arm. "Sorry." She turned her attention back to Sashelle. *The coverall with the nubby texture and the three arrows on the arm. She's flight maintenance. Follow her.*

This one? The overlay zoomed in on a curly-haired woman.

Yes. Wait, look at that wall. The view swung as the caat turned her head. *Perfect. It says the hangars are straight ahead.*

There weren't any words on that sign, Sashelle complained.

The colors and symbols tell you where to go. Red is for ship bays. The dashed lines—two dots and a dash—that's the personnel ships. Fighters are just dots. Cargo ships are five dots and a dash. Direction is indicated by the arrow shapes within the lines.

How did you know those were red? Sashelle asked.

The height of the lines indicates the colors and functions too. Colorblindness is uncommon in humans, but it's expensive to treat. Senior officers are given digital colorizers to compensate, but they won't spend the credits on enlisted folks or junior officers.

How kind of them, the caat said. The gray overlay disappeared.

You're lucky we're on a big ship, Quinn said. *On a smaller one, you have to learn the layout.*

The soldier yanked her to a stop. They loaded into a huge elevator. "*Big* ship," she muttered to herself.

The soldier holding her arm reached up and unlatched his helmet. He slid the faceplate up a fraction and whispered, "Lady, you need to shut up. I don't want to hurt you."

"Sorry," Quinn whispered. "Thanks."

She peered around, spotting Tony on the far side of her soldier. She raised her eyebrows and mouthed, "You okay?"

He smiled. Not quite his usual carefree grin, but a credible attempt.

On her other side, another huge soldier blocked her view. She leaned back a little, trying to see behind him. The other prisoner Sashelle had mentioned stood beyond. He shifted his feet a bit, and his profile came into view. Sven Harvard?

Her head snapped around, and she looked at Tony. "Sven?" she mouthed.

His eyebrows went up, and he nodded.

"Anyone else?"

Tony shrugged.

The Stealthy One recommends you stop attempting to talk to him, Sashelle said. *He doesn't wish you to be harmed.*

Quinn smothered a snort. *He should get used to disappointment.*

That's what I said, Sashelle replied.

Hey, that's not very supportive! You're supposed to tell me it's all going to be okay, and we'll get out of this.

I am not optimistic. Sashelle's voice was tinged with sadness. *I will do all in my power to assist you.*

That's all anyone could ask. But next time, lie.

The door opened, and they stepped out. Here, the walls bore the stripes she'd seen through Sashelle's eyes. They marched along the corridor, three abreast. People flattened themselves against the bulkheads, getting out of the way. Ahead, Sven led the way with his two guards. As they passed, the hiss of wondering whispers followed.

"Is that Sven Harvard?!"

"What's he done?"

"I love that guy."

"I wonder if I can get his autograph."

Quinn bit her lip to stifle a giggle. A wide door whooshed open, and they stepped into a large airlock. The doors closed behind them, and they all looked up to watch the gauges on a screen above the door. The oxygen level didn't seem to be changing.

Quinn's eyes narrowed. Why was that screen so fascinating? *Sashelle, are you in the airlock?*

Don't look. I'm behind you. If you turn, they will look too.

Right. Quinn kept her eyes on the screen, but she itched to turn around.

Finally, the door opened, and they marched into the shuttle bay. The enormous open space held three shuttles. Troops pounded down gangplanks of two of them, their heavy boots ringing on the deck. They formed up in lines of ten, then with great shouts and banging of armor, they jogged toward one of the two airlocks. Quinn's party side-stepped hurriedly out of the way as a file rumbled toward them.

High overhead, massive conduits crisscrossed the space. Out of the corner of her eye, Quinn saw movement—something surging upward. She waited a few beats, then carefully looked up without moving her head. Sashelle slunk along a conduit, making her way toward the third shuttle.

Two coverall-clad soldiers moved around that vehicle, peering at tablets and poking at the craft. Running a preflight checklist, Quinn suspected. One of the soldiers holding Sven called back. "There's our ride." He urged his captive forward.

They crossed the shuttle bay, slowing and speeding up to avoid the lines of troops still spilling from the other two craft. "Those things hold a lot of people," Quinn remarked.

Her captor's mirrored faceplate jerked in her direction. She made a face and mouthed "sorry." His head shook slightly as he faced front again. Quinn bit back a grin. This guy liked her. That had to help, right?

Something crashed near the airlock, and everyone turned to stare, except the soldiers who continued to line up and jog. Quinn, half-expecting the noise, looked toward the shuttle instead. Sashelle leapt lightly down from the conduit and disappeared inside the vehicle.

Quinn smiled and looked at the crash. A young officer stood beside a pile of equipment that had been neatly stacked a moment before. She chewed out the two coverall-clad men attempting to restack it.

How'd you do that?

I encouraged her to misjudge a step.

"Stupid butter bars," her captor muttered. "Break something and blame the enlisted."

They continued to the shuttle and up the gangplank. Quinn had never been in this model before. It was huge. It held seats for a hundred infantry, if her estimates were correct. The soldiers shoved Tony and Sean into seats in the first row of seats in the rear half of the passenger area. Quinn's captor gave her time to sit and strap herself in.

"I have to lock this." He clamped a device around the latch on the seat restraints and tapped the buttons. The thing beeped, and a light turned red. "I know you want to talk but keep it down. I don't want to hit a lady, but if you talk too much, I might have to."

The soldier straightened up and moved to join the other five in the front of the space. The seats in the middle section had been folded down to allow an unobstructed view of the prisoners. They strapped into rear-facing seats, then removed their helmets. The five young men sat together with an empty seat between them and a female soldier. She pulled something out of her armor and tossed it to the nearest man.

"Thanks, Sarge." The guy shared whatever it was with his

companions. They all settled in, munching on the mystery snack and joking.

Quinn glanced at Tony. He grinned, but his face was pale, with dark circles under his eyes. "How'd you do during jump?" If Tony was sober during hyperjump, his body rebelled. Surely their captors hadn't provided booze.

"I was still out." He grimaced. "I feel like crap, but I can't tell if that's from jumping sober, or from being drugged."

"Probably a little of both." Quinn rolled her shoulders under the seat restraints, stretching the abused-feeling muscles. "The drug should have cushioned you a bit?"

"Maybe." He looked past Quinn. "You okay, Sven?"

Two of the soldiers looked their way. Quinn stared back. Eventually, they went back to their conversations.

"I'm alright," Sven said. "A little battered, but I'll live."

"Did they beat you?" Quinn whispered.

"Nothing I haven't survived before." Sven gave a wide grin that revealed a missing canine tooth.

"What did you do with that?" Tony asked.

"It's a surprise," Sven said.

The Stealthy One says the Talker has a false fang. Sashelle sounded mystified. *It contains a sealed packet with material that will burn under the proper circumstances.*

What circumstances are those? Quinn asked.

Oxygen, Sashelle said. *I don't believe I would like to have such a fang in my mouth. Too easy to breach.*

What did he burn down?

The caat didn't answer.

Where are you? Quinn asked.

Above the soldiers.

Quinn glanced at the far end of the passenger bay. Two gold eyes glowed in a dark baggage shelf above the soldiers' seats.

Don't try to take on those soldiers by yourself, Quinn thought.

I wouldn't dream of being so selfish.

The shuttle door closed, and the engines whined softly. The ship lifted and eased forward. This shuttle had no windows, but Quinn knew from past experience that they would fly through the force membrane at the far end of the shuttle bay, then launch into space. She closed her eyes in anticipation.

They launched, the force pushing them back into their seats. Once the acceleration dropped off, their legs began to lift away from the seats. Quinn's hair drifted across her face from the internal airflow. Then the shuttle's artificial gravity kicked in, and they thumped into their chairs.

The door to the cockpit opened, and an officer in a flight suit stepped out. He glanced at the soldiers, then headed toward the prisoners.

The woman fumbled with her seat restraints. "You can't go back there, Major."

He stared down at her. "I assure you, I can. I am Premier Andretti's executive officer and co-pilot of this shuttle. I was sent to personally escort these prisoners. Who are you?"

"I'm Sergeant Partens." The woman stepped in front of him. "No one mentioned an escort to me. I'm responsible for them."

The pilot pushed past her. "Feel free to call the premier's office if you wish."

Partens grabbed his arm. "That won't be necessary. I have my orders, and they say no one is to talk to them."

"Who are the prisoners?" The officer shook off the sergeant.

"I thought you knew who these prisoners were," she growled.

"I said I was sent to escort them. I wasn't given their IDs."

"That's Sven Harvard." One of the soldiers pointed.

"Mendish! That's classified." She swung around to face the officer again.

"That's Sven Harvard," the pilot repeated, squinting their direction. "Damn. What's he done?"

"He's an officer," Mendish muttered. "He said he has clearance."

"You know that isn't how classified information control works!" Partens growled.

The pilot ignored the soldiers, moving down the side aisle, his eyes fixed on Sven. "Damn," he said again as he crossed in front of Tony, "that's Sven Harvard."

"Tenlos?" Quinn asked as the man walked around her outstretched legs.

The pilot swung around and looked at Quinn. "Yes. And you—Lieutenant Templeton?!"

"Not a lieutenant anymore," Quinn said.

"Of course not. You'd be at least a colonel by now." He looked at the wrist and ankle cuffs. "Or maybe not?"

"Not. Look, Tony, it's Adrian Tenlos."

CHAPTER 28

TONY LOOKED up at the young officer. "How are you, Adrian?"

"Tony? Is it true?" Tenlos kept his voice low. "You two are Krimson spies? I didn't believe it, but here you are." He gestured helplessly at them.

"There is no Krimson Empire, you know," Quinn avoided the question. "Just the Commonwealth. And no, we don't work for them. We were framed for the Sumpter debacle to cover Andretti's tracks."

"And what's up with Sven Harvard?" Tenlos whispered.

Tony shrugged. "Dunno. Hey, Sven, what're you in for?"

Sven glanced at the soldiers, then at Tenlos. "Apparently, I used the wrong word when describing Admiral Andretti's rise to power. He 'ascended' to the premiership. There was no 'coup'."

"Major!" Sergeant Partens strode through the ship as if she owned it. She seemed to have regained her mojo. "I can't let you talk to the prisoners."

"You aren't *letting* me do anything," Tenlos said. "As I said, the admiral—I mean, the premier—sent me to collect them. Besides, I know them—" He broke off at Tony's tiny headshake.

Partens cut him off. "You know them? They aren't friends, are they? Because I'd have to report that. Sir." She tacked on the last word after a long, insolent pause.

Tenlos slowly turned away from Tony and Quinn, focusing on the woman. He straightened his spine and stepped closer, looming over her. "This is my ship, Sergeant. It is my responsibility to make sure my passengers are safe. Occasionally, that means talking to those passengers. Even if I didn't have authorization from the *highest* levels."

He turned to Sven. "Mr. Harvard, Ms. Templeton, Mr. Bergen, thank you for keeping your restraints buckled. I prefer to deliver my passengers in one piece and unbruised." He nodded to each of them and pivoted sharply. "By the way, Sergeant, Romara Control reports a bit of turbulence today. You might want to strap in, too." He pushed past Partens, winking at Quinn from behind the sergeant's back.

Partens glared at them and followed the officer up the aisle.

"I think we might be in for a rough ride." Tony glanced at her, then leaned forward to look at Sven. "You don't get motion sick, do you?"

"You saw our VR set." Sven patted his belly. "Iron stomach."

"I'm good." Quinn said. "Do you think..." She broke off, her eyes darting toward the cockpit door.

Tony raised an eyebrow and shook his head. "Don't know."

WHEN FRANCINE ENTERED THE BRIDGE, Dareen was staring at her grandmother, face pale and mouth open. Francine wasn't sure if she was angry or terrified.

"Did you know about this?" Dareen asked Francine.

"Know about what?" Francine asked cautiously. She knew lots of things and wasn't sure which of them Dareen was referencing.

"This stealth tech!" Dareen threw up her hands. "Gramma has installed the stealth tech on this ship!"

"I did *not* know about that," Francine said. "What stealth tech?"

"That thing I picked up on Hadriana?" Dareen said incredulously. "The box that makes you disappear? It's on this ship. The whole ship. If we turn that thing on, we'll all start acting stupid!"

"Do you think I'm an idiot?" Lou growled. "We have—"

Dareen didn't let her finish. "Yes, I do! You've been acting irrationally since—well, since Hadriana! I think that damn box scrambled your brains, and no matter what the med techs say, you aren't recovered. And I'm not the only one who thinks so!"

"Is that so?" Lou glared at Francine. "Do you think I'm crazy?"

Francine held up both hands to ward off her anger. "I don't think anything. I'm just a passenger. You haven't done anything that seems crazy to me."

"I didn't say crazy," Dareen said, her voice changing from angry to pitying. "I said irrational."

"Oh, my mistake. Not crazy, just irrational." Lou's eyes narrowed to slits. "Who else agrees with you?"

Francine backed out of the bridge. "I'm going to leave you two to discuss—"

"Don't you go anywhere, missy," Lou snapped. She turned back to Dareen. "There is nothing wrong with me. I've had a lot to deal with lately—your cousin starting a revolution, for one. Which is why I have this tech. The guys at the lab added extra shielding, and the ship protects us, too."

"The guys at the lab?" Dareen asked. "What lab? Where did you get this?"

"At Athenos, of course," Lou said. "When I delivered the prototype, they asked if we'd like to be part of the live trials after they worked out the kinks. Of course, I said yes. This thing could be a game-changer in our line of work."

"Was one of the 'kinks' the crazy-making?" Dareen demanded. "Cause that was a big downside of the prototype." She rolled her eyes.

"I told you, they added shielding." Lou crossed her arms over her chest. "And this time, you did say crazy."

"Gramma, you can't let the Commonwealth use us as test subjects," Dareen said. "They'll tell you it's fine, but if we're 'testing' it, that means they don't know what might happen."

"This is a *field* test," Lou said. "They've taken care of the side effects and they want us to try it out in the real world."

Francine stepped closer, drawing their attention. "What exactly does this thing do?"

"Oh, yeah, you weren't with us when we got it, were you?" Dareen asked. "It makes you invisible."

"Invisible?" Francine repeated. "On the sensors or…"

"In real life," Dareen said. "Poof and you're gone. But that's a good question." She swiveled back to Lou. "How does having that thing on our ship help? We'll still show up on sensors."

"They've added another piece for that," Lou said. "In tests, this device makes the whole vehicle undetectable. We can fly past any station, even a battlecruiser, and they won't notice anything. We can land on any planet we want."

"You could have landed on Robinson's and rescued Tony and Quinn!" Dareen shouted.

"We were too far away to help," Lou said. "I thought about it, but by the time we got there, they'd have been on the shuttle."

Dareen heaved a sigh and settled back into her seat. "Does Mom know about this?"

"Of course not," Lou said. "It's a top-secret government contract. I can't talk to other shippers about that."

"She's not 'other shippers'! She's your daughter!"

"If she was still part of my crew, I would have told her," Lou said. "Since she's running her own ship, it's none of her business."

"Do the uncles know?"

Lou looked away. "No."

"So much for telling the crew," Dareen sniped. "How about End?"

"I told him this morning," Lou muttered.

"This might have been useful information when we were making plans the other day," Francine suggested. Lou glared daggers at her, but she maintained eye contact. "What other secrets are you keeping that might be useful? We can use this stealth tech to land on Romara and insert our *soldaty* team. Is it portable?"

"No," Lou said.

"Too bad."

"I think a mobile version is in the works," Lou said. "But the shielding is a problem. It's too heavy right now for a truly mobile unit. You could probably install one on a ground vehicle, but it would need a lot of power to carry the thing."

"Is this thing permanently installed on the ship, or just strapped in for the field test?" Francine asked.

"They aren't going to let me keep it." Lou snorted. "This is military-grade stuff. They're only letting me test it because of Tony."

"How hard would it be to uninstall it?" Francine asked. "Because Fyo's Pulsar is ridiculously overpowered. And it's in your cargo hold."

CHAPTER 29

THE SPEAKER CRACKLED, and Major Tenlos's voice filled the almost-empty passenger bay. "We're entering Romara's atmosphere, and as I mentioned, there's a bit of turbulence on our flight path. Stay buckled in. If you feel sick, there are bags in the pocket of your seat."

"Is he laughing?" Quinn asked.

"He does sound remarkably cheerful." Sven's deep voice carried easily to her and Tony despite his low volume. "The soldiers don't look too excited at the prospect."

"You should never threaten the pilot of the craft you're riding in. Partens practically begged for a bumpy ride." She didn't enjoy turbulence, but if it would take Partens down a peg, she wouldn't complain.

"So how do you know the kid?" Sven asked.

"He kind of introduced us," Quinn said. "We'd met before, but Tenlos showed up on a cadet internship, and he got into a spot of trouble. Tony and I got him out."

"I never did thank him," Tony said.

"For what?" Quinn asked. "We helped him."

"True. But without him, we might not have become friends."

The ride to the airfield was rough. Two of the soldiers made use of the barf bags, but Partens managed to keep her lunch down. By the time they landed, she looked green, and a sheen of sweat covered her face. Quinn tried to keep her face impassive.

"Sorry about that, folks," Tenlos announced as they taxied. "We'll be parking in a couple of minutes, and there's a transport coming to meet us."

The shuttle stopped, and the crew chief came out of the cockpit to open the doors. A wave of warm, sea-laden air rushed into the cabin. Mendish and two of his companions headed back to unlock the prisoners.

"That doesn't smell like Romara," Tony said. "Too much fish."

"We're not in the city," Mendish said. "We landed at Florenz Field."

Quinn and Tony exchanged a look. "Florenz?" Tony asked. "That's in the middle of nowhere."

"It's now the capital city of the Federation," Mendish said.

"What?" Sven asked. "Romara has been the capital of the Federation since it was formed. Why would they change it?"

Mendish shrugged. "Dunno. That's what Sarge said."

"Headquarters Strategic is at Florenz," Tony told Sven. "That's where Andretti was stationed after Sumpter. I guess he didn't want to move."

"Typical," Quinn muttered.

Mendish grabbed her arm and hauled her out of the seat. "Come on, our ride is waiting." He pulled Quinn up the aisle to the door.

Major Tenlos stood in the cockpit door. She stopped, leaning against Mendish's pull. "Thanks for the ride, Adrian. I'm sorry we had to meet this way."

"Me too, Lieu— Ms. Templeton."

"Call me Quinn." Mendish pulled harder, but Quinn dug in her heels. "Maybe I'll see you again. When this little mess is all cleared up."

"I'm afraid you'll see me before then," Tenlos said. "I'm here to escort you to HQ, remember?"

They exited the ship and descended the steps to the tarmac. A stiff breeze blew in from the sea a few klicks away. It always blew in Florenz. Quinn sniffed the air. As Tony had mentioned, it carried a faint tang of fish, but nothing overpowering. It smelled more real than the artificially sanitized air of Romara City.

The soldiers lined them up, each prisoner with a guard on either side. They marched to the boxy transport waiting at the nose of the shuttle. Tenlos watched, following at a distance, his hand on his sidearm.

The soldiers pushed them into the back of the big transport and shut the door with a clang. The center contained pallets stacked with boxes. The three of them shuffled to bench seats around the outer edge of the windowless compartment. Quinn had barely sat when the transport lurched. After the initial jerk, the ride smoothed out.

"I can't believe they put us back here by ourselves," Sven said. "Who knows what mayhem we could get up to."

"I'm sure they're monitoring us," Quinn warned.

Sven winked at her. "No doubt. You been here before?'

"Tony and I met at Headquarters Strategic." Quinn purposely didn't mention Tenlos. If he was Andretti's exec, he had enough trouble already. "It was my last assignment."

"I thought you were at Sumpter."

"I was, but as a dependent. My husband—now ex-husband—was active duty, too."

Sven nodded. "I've never been here."

"What?" Tony sounded surprised. "I've seen you report from Strategic."

"When I report on things happening here, I do it remotely. Not that the viewers can tell. Our tech is that good." Sven stood to peer through the tiny window in the rear door. "I cut my teeth in the smaller markets. Then I was embedded with the Fifteenth Expeditionary Force. By the time I reached the top, they'd moved GNO to Robinson's. I'm too valuable in the studio to waste my time flying back and forth to Romara." He gave them a smug grin.

The transport stopped, and the rear door opened. "Get 'em out," Partens barked at the soldiers. Tenlos stood back, watching. Quinn wondered if he was feeling conflicted. She hoped so.

The vehicle had stopped close to a loading dock at the back of a large stone building. The soldiers formed up around them again and marched them down a ramp to a heavy metal door. Another set of soldiers waited there.

"These men will take the prisoners." Tenlos strolled closer. He took a tablet from the sergeant waiting inside and perused it before handing it to Partens.

She looked mutinous, but she took the tablet. With a scowl, she pressed her hand against the screen and handed it back. "Enjoy," she said sourly. "Mission complete, team." She led her crew back to the transport.

"They're all yours, Wilson." Tenlos nodded at the new squad. Without another word, he turned and strode away.

The soldiers hustled them inside. A narrow corridor, painted a sickening shade of mustard, stretched away in front of them. Wires and conduits hung from the ceiling, and the whole thing was lit by unshaded bulbs in rusty fixtures. A musty scent overwhelmed the sea tang.

"This looks like it came out of a horror vid," Sven joked. "Ought to be a guy with a saw jumping out of one of these doors."

"Shut up," Wilson barked, his words echoing down the long hallway. "Move."

They walked single file, with one soldier leading the way and the others interspersed between the prisoners. The route turned several times. Quinn had only been in the basement of Headquarters Strategic once. No one went down here if they could avoid it—the labyrinth of dismal passages was legendary in military circles. Several civilians had reported ghost sightings. Military personnel scoffed publicly, but none of them volunteered to enter "the dungeon."

Finally, they reached a heavy metal door. Wilson opened it and gestured for the soldiers to take them through. Inside, two old-fashioned cells, with metal bars and bare bunks, filled the space. The soldiers pushed them into a cell, Sven on one side, Quinn and Tony across from him. The doors clanged shut. The soldiers turned off the lights and left.

Black pressed against their eyes. Water dripped in the distance. Quinn felt her way to the bunk and sat. "How medieval. Dark, dank cells and dripping water. The legends are true."

"I've heard about this place," Tony said. "Andretti uses it to intimidate. He has a real, state-of-the-art cell block, but he uses this for fun. He nailed the ambience. Only missing a pile of bones in the corner and a deep pit." His voice was close.

"How do you know there aren't?" Quinn stuck her hand out until she hit something solid. It moved, and warm fingers closed around her cold digits.

"I didn't see 'em before they turned off the lights," Tony said. "So, I'm gonna assume they aren't there. You're icy."

"Just my hands and feet." Quinn laughed. "Pretty normal for me, actually. How long do you think he'll leave us down here?"

"Forever, if he gets his way."

"My manager is surely raising hell," Sven said from across the aisle. "I don't know if that will get us anything except another cellmate."

"He might get you out," Tony said, "if he promises positive coverage of the new administration. Andretti needs the media on his side if he's going to ride the dragon that is the Federation. Better men than him have been crushed by it. And by 'better,' I mean just as bad."

"Byral isn't going to promise positive reports. He might threaten negative coverage if Andretti doesn't let me go. I'll insist he release you as well. Dictators respond well to threats, right?"

Tony chuckled. "We can hope. But don't hold your breath. Andretti hates me and Quinn."

"Why is that?" Sven asked. "I heard the Sumpter story, and I didn't believe it. I mean, *you* being a Krimson spy, sure, I believe that, but not Quinn's part. Why did he target you two? Does this have something to do with that Tenlos guy?"

"No," Tony said. "Andretti hates Quinn. Always has. I'm sure that's why she was one of the lucky ones to get left behind."

"I figured it was Reggie's idea," Quinn said.

"Reggie's complicity made it easier, I'm sure. But his hatred of you is probably what sparked the idea in his nasty little mind." Tony's fingers tightened on her hand.

"Yeah, I suppose it was too good a deal to pass up." Quinn squeezed back.

"I'll bite," Sven said. "Why does he hate you?"

"Old story," Quinn said. "Dating back to…here, actually. I was friends with his first wife."

"Say no more," Sven said when she hesitated. "He's currently working on wife number five, so friends of number one are no doubt undesirable."

"Is that what you call someone you abandon on an asteroid scheduled to be purged, and then sentence to death?" Quin asked. "Undesirable?"

The lights flicked on, blinding them. Quinn pulled her hand away, not wanting to give their captors any ideas.

"Harvard," a voice said. "Come with us."

As Quinn's eyes adjusted to the light, she heard the clang of Sven's cell door opening. "I won't leave without my friends," Sven said.

Quinn blinked rapidly, clearing her eyes. Sven sat on the bunk in his cell, arms crossed. Two guards stood in the open cell door. "Out, now," one of them said.

Sven didn't move.

"Fine." The taller of the guards strode into the cell and grabbed

Sven by one arm. He hauled the other man to his feet, then sank his fist into Sven's gut. Sven doubled over, groaning. The guard dragged him out of the cell. Sven staggered against their cell, clutching the bars to keep from collapsing.

"I'll get you out," Sven croaked as they dragged him away. "Somehow."

CHAPTER 30

THE GUARDS LEFT, and the lights went out again. Quinn thrust her hand out, groping blindly for Tony. He scooted close and put an arm around her. "We'll be okay," he whispered.

"Are they listening to us?"

"Of course," Tony said. "Always assume that."

"So, we shouldn't talk about our super-secret escape plans."

Tony laughed. "Exactly. We wouldn't want them to know we're plotting."

He finger-traced designs on her palm. Quinn relaxed against him, soaking up his warmth. Then she sat up in surprise. He wasn't playing romantic games, tracing random designs on her palm. He was using Fendral code. She'd had to learn it in the academy, so it wasn't secret. But even if they had cameras in here, no one could see his fingers moving in the pitch-black. Federation night vision wasn't that good. She relaxed against him.

W. H. E. R. E. S. Pause. S. A. S. H. E. L

Crap! She'd forgotten about the caat!

Sashelle, where are you? She concentrated on the message, repeating it in her head.

I was wondering when you'd ask. Sashelle sounded bored. *I'm here.*

In the cell? Quinn squeezed Tony's fingers to stop him from distracting her.

No, then I'd be locked in too. The caat projected a mental eyeroll. *I'm outside the building.*

I can reach you outside the building? Quinn asked in astonishment. *I'm getting good at caat talking!*

No, Sashelle responded dryly. *I'm getting really good at listening.*

Whatever. Can you help us get out?

How do you propose I do that?

Why do I have to think of everything? Can you hear Tony?

He isn't as clear as you, Sashelle admitted. *Is he with you?*

Yes, right here.

I'll try again. There was a brief pause. *He can hear me now. It's almost as if you're a conduit.*

Is that a thing with your people? Quinn asked.

No.

Quinn waited for more, but the caat said nothing. She leaned against Tony, absorbing warmth from his body.

Tony sighed, then pulled her close and kissed her.

Quinn's brain spun into neutral, her whole being overtaken by feelings instead of thoughts. When he started to move away, she pulled him back.

After a few minutes, he released her and settled her back into his arm.

"Finally." Quinn laughed. "Took you long enough."

"What?" He leaned away as if to look at her, but the cell was completely dark. "You were married!'

"Francine told me ages ago you were in love with me," Quinn said. "And I haven't been married for months."

"If you knew, why didn't you make the first move?" He chuckled. "I was a sure thing."

"You're right, I should have moved in on you a long time ago."

She snuggled close. "But how are we going to get out of here? Much as I'd love to spend the rest of my life with you, I'm hoping it will be longer than a few hours in a cell."

He squeezed her hand warningly.

The Stealthy One says he thinks the Talker has done something with his tooth.

His tooth? Quinn asked. *Oh, the one with the chemicals!*

The caat didn't answer.

A glow caught Quinn's attention. A tiny spot, more a less-black place than light. She tried to look at it, but there wasn't enough to focus on. Then it grew. The darkness lifted little by little until the cell-locking mechanism glowed from within.

The tooth, Quinn thought at Sashelle. *He's melting the lock.*

She glanced at Tony, but the light didn't reach his face.

C.A.M.S. she wrote on his hand.

N.O.N.E. he wrote. S. T. A. Y. H. E. R. E. She squeezed his hand and let go, wondering how he knew about surveillance in this cell. The glow of the lock disappeared as he moved in front of it, then something groaned.

Quinn coughed, hard and loud, hoping to cover the sound if anyone was listening. "Tony?" she whimpered. "Will we ever get out of here? I'm scared." She sobbed into her hands, hoping it sounded real. She was cold and tired and scared, and that made crying too easy. "Tony?"

"I don't know," Tony said softly. "Try not to worry."

She hiccupped and whimpered to hide the grating sound from the door. Then it stopped. She sniffed a few times. "Maybe we should get some sleep."

"Good idea," Tony said from across the room. "See you in the morning. Whenever that is."

The Stealthy One is checking the door lock, Sashelle said.

To provide cover as Tony fiddled with the lock, Quinn rolled around on her bunk, muttering nonsense under her breath.

The rustling stopped. Quinn waited until Tony's soft steps returned, then she muttered a little more.

Something clicked.

She heaved a sigh, then breathed heavily for a few seconds, trailing off as if falling asleep. At least she hoped that was what it sounded like.

Moving as quietly as possible, she tiptoed across the cell to where she remembered the door being. She smacked into Tony's chest. He caught her elbows, holding her until she regained her balance, then he tugged her gently away from the bars.

They stopped at the door. At least Quinn assumed it was the door. She coughed and muttered to cover more scraping noises. Tony put a hand on her arm, and she stopped. He drew another message on her palm. R. E. A. D. Y.

R. U. N.

THE *MILLENNIUM PEREGRINE* soared through Romara's atmosphere on a direct course to Milana Field.

"The Executive Palace is in Romara," Francine objected. "That's where he'll have taken Quinn and Tony."

"We can't land at Romara Field," Lou said. "That place is huge, and they slot flights in tight. Everything is landed via AI. You have to release control of your ship to land." She shuddered. "There's no way we can slip in between flights. Even if we weren't cloaked, I wouldn't use that field."

She paused to check the screens and instruments. "And remember, not only do we have to land safely, we have to have a place to move the stealth gear to the Pulsar. We'd be spotted the instant we turned that thing off at Romara."

"But Milana is tiny." Francine pointed at the map she'd thrown on the screen. "They'll see us the instant we de-cloak there, too."

"Ah, that's what you might think." Lou pulled the map bigger and pointed. "I've used Milana before. It's remote. It hasn't been maintained in decades, not officially. My contacts make sure it looks worse than it is. The beacons don't work—unless you have the activation codes. Which I do. We'll land and park in this hangar. Then we can wake up the *soldaty* and move the stealth tech. Romara is close enough for the Pulsar, even fully loaded."

"I hate to be a downer, but my Pulsar only seats four," Fyo said.

"Kert's been working on that." Lou grinned at the young man lounging in the communications seat.

"Working on—I didn't give anyone permission to mess with my ship!" Fyo wailed. "What's he done to my baby?" He bolted out the door.

"I'd better go calm him down." Francine hurried after her brother.

In the cargo hold, the Pulsar had been pulled out of the special transport box Dusica's craftsmen had built. A pile of scrap metal lay in the corner, some of it suspiciously shiny. Fyo stood by the rear of the ship, staring. The sleek lines of the craft ended with the front seats. The rear end had been torn open like a tin can, and a huge box had been welded on behind the rear seats.

"Look what they did!" Fyo whispered, collapsing against the *soldaty* cube. "She'll never be the same."

"You can buy a new one," Francine said. "If we're successful, Sarterian Systems will probably *give* you a new one. They'll love the publicity this will create. Using one of their craft to rescue heroes of the revolution!" She hoped she wasn't laying it on too thick.

Fyo finally dragged his eyes away from the mutilated craft and looked hopefully at his sister. "You think?"

Dareen hurried into the cargo hold. "We're landing in ten minutes. Time to—" She glanced at the Pulsar, and her eyes and mouth went round. "Holy crap, what happened to her?"

"Your grandmother happened to her," Fyo muttered.

"Kert modified it for troop transport." Francine wondered why she felt she must apologize for that.

"He cut up a Sarterian Systems Pulsar Three coupe and glued on a box?!" Dareen cried. "That's criminal! She was such a beauty and now—"

"Get a grip, Dareen," Francine said. "It's a piece of machinery. We will use it to save our friends. That's a noble cause. Stop being so melodramatic."

The girl sighed. "She was so beautiful to fly."

"She was, wasn't she," Fyo commiserated.

"You two are ridiculous," Francine said. "I'm going to strap in."

CHAPTER 31

W. A. I. T. Quinn drew the message on Tony's forearm. S. A. S. S. Y.

I heard that, Sashelle said. *You know I don't like that name.*

Sorry, Quinn replied. *It's shorter when we're spelling things out. Is there anyone in the hallway?*

Do I look like a surveillance system?

Come on, Sashelle. You checked for us before.

That was different, Sashelle said. *There are too many people in this building. Too many human muddlings. I don't think any of them are near you, but I can't promise that.*

Oh. Quinn started to write on Tony's arm but gave up. *Sashelle, will you tell Tony?*

Yes. The long-suffering tone made Quinn's lips quirk. *He says get ready to run.*

Tony opened the door just far enough to peek through the crack. The light burned bright against the darkness of the cell block. He pulled the door wide and darted his head out. "Let's go."

The long, narrow hall was deserted. Strange that Andretti hadn't posted a guard. She and Tony were considered high-profile prisoners with a history of escape. Maybe the building's haunted history was working in their favor.

They trotted down the hall to the first cross-corridor. The overhead lights flickered. Tony checked both directions, then pulled her to the right.

"They have to be monitoring these halls, right?" Quinn whispered. "Why would they leave us unguarded?"

Tony glanced back at her and laid a finger against his lips.

They moved through the dismal hallways, turning, checking, running. It was an awkward tiptoe kind of running, trying to minimize the noise of their feet. Quinn had no idea where they were in relation to the cells or the exit, but Tony seemed to have a destination in mind.

At the next corner, a shadow lay across the intersecting halls.

Tony stopped. He held up a hand, telling her to stay back, then crept forward. At the intersection, he ducked low and poked his head around the corner. Then he straightened up and walked out of sight.

Quinn stood frozen in place. Was she supposed to follow? There was no sound of an altercation, no talking. Two shadows now lay across the intersection: Tony's and the other. Neither of them moved.

Quinn crept closer.

The other shadow twisted and fell, becoming that of a large feline.

What are you waiting for? Sashelle asked.

He told me to stay.

That's dog behavior. Be a caat.

"Sometimes you have to follow directions." Quinn peered around the corner.

Tony and the caat stood in the corridor. Quinn assumed they were speaking to each other, but she couldn't hear either side of the discussion. "Shouldn't we be running? They have to be watching these halls."

Sashelle loped away, heading for the next corner.

Tony nodded and followed the caat. "Always assume they're watching. But if that were the case, they should have grabbed us by now. Maybe they're understaffed? Andretti probably eliminated anyone he doesn't trust. That doesn't leave a lot of people."

"That cell block was empty," Quinn mused. "If he got rid of people, it was permanently. Yeesh."

"That wasn't the regular cell block. That was his 'intimidation' cell, remember? Which is probably why there were no cameras. He doesn't want anyone monitoring what goes on in there."

"He only took over the government a week ago," Quinn said.

"Headquarters Strategic has been his home base for twelve years. And he's been here full time since Sumpter. He owns this place and has for a long time."

They reached another corner, but this time, they didn't stop.

There's no one down here, Sashelle said.

I thought you said you couldn't be sure? Quinn breathed deep, trying to keep her rhythm. She was in much better shape than before, but living on a spaceship didn't allow much practice in running.

When I was outside, I couldn't tell.

That reminds me, Quinn said. *How did you get in?*

Found an open window. And I'm getting better at doorknobs.

Quinn suppressed the image of the caat scrabbling unsuccessfully at a door.

I saw that.

Are we going out through the window? Quinn asked. *Surely, they'll have the doors guarded.*

Too small. Sashelle sat waiting by a door at the end of the hall.

You're too small? But you're huge. When you were standing on your hind legs, you were as tall as Tony.

The window is too small for you. Humans are not as size-flexible as caats. She raised a paw and turned the doorknob. *This is the way out.*

You are *getting good at doors.* Quinn tried to imagine how the caat had gripped the knob and failed.

"We need weapons." Tony stopped in the doorway.

Quinn looked around. The maze-like hallways had been clear—

surprisingly bare for a basement—but this was a military facility. "You got a key to the armory? Speaking of which, what did you use to open the door down there?"

Tony held up a pair of bent wires.

"Where did you get those?" Quinn asked.

Tony smiled. "Paperclips. In the desk drawer by the cells. These idiots have no idea what a real Krimson spy can do. Do you remember where the armory is? We finance guys didn't get issued weapons."

"And you didn't know it's on the first floor, back of wing C?" Quinn frowned. "Try pulling the other leg. I'm sure you knew where everything was. I only knew because the head of supply was a friend of mine. She worked there when she needed a place with few interruptions. Not a lot of activity in the armory here, except the security guys."

"That is probably no longer the case. We'll have to try for it."

"You're going to steal weapons from the armory using a paperclip?"

"*You* have no idea what a real Krimson spy can do." He winked. "Besides, I have *two* paperclips."

They crept up the steps, stopping at the top to listen.

Sashelle? Quinn asked.

The caat's head turned and her golden eyes blinked in the dark stairwell. *There are people.*

Can you use your mind control magic to convince them we're not here? Quinn asked. *Or maybe make them think we're in uniform? We can walk out the door.* As she spoke, she twisted her hair up onto her head. She patted down her pockets, but there was nothing to hold the knot on her head.

Wordlessly, Tony held out one of the wires.

She shook her head and tucked her hair into her collar. *Can you?* she asked the caat again.

I don't know, Sashelle said. *I can try.*

Tony held up a hand. He pointed to the right and the signal for walk. Then he opened the door.

THE *PEREGRINE* BACKED into the dilapidated hangar, barely clearing the edges of the massive door. Francine hurried to pull the sliding panels across the building-wide opening. Marielle dragged the opposite door toward her, and they met in the middle. She smiled at the darker woman. They linked arms and hiked to the rear of the massive ship.

"What did they build this huge thing for?" Francine asked.

"Probably Veta-class ships," Marielle said. "That's what the premier rides on. They're a little smaller than the *Peregrine*. They used to have two stationed here, back in the day. When I was in the Secret Service, getting stationed out here was punishment."

"There was a whole base?"

"If you can call a barracks and one admin building a base. It's been turned over to the civilians." Marielle pulled Francine to a stop before they reached the cargo ramp. "They were not impressed."

The nose of the Pulsar slid out of the back of the larger ship. Gleaming ceramic paint covered the sleek cockpit. Then the rough, metal box came into view. The ship eased quietly down the ramp and parked.

Dareen climbed out. "That thing moves like a brick now," she called to Kert, who had followed the craft down the ramp.

"You don't know that," Kert replied. "You drove it twenty meters at low speed."

"It'll still do zero to two-eighty in two-point-three seconds?" The girl gave him a skeptical look.

"Ah, no." Kert started up a ladder built into the side of the *Peregrine*. "But it will get you where you're going."

Dareen came up to the other women.

"Don't even start." Francine held up a hand before Dareen could say anything.

"What?" Dareen pouted. "I wasn't going to complain. It's not my ship. I gotta help Kert." She walked away, muttering under her breath.

"Time to wake up the *soldaty*," Francine said.

Marielle shuddered. "Doesn't it bother you? I'm with Dareen on that. It's creepy."

"I grew up with it," Francine said. "We always took a cube on long trips. A smaller one—my dad only needed a couple of protection agents."

"You couldn't let them ride in the front, like normal people?" Marielle asked. "Like me and Aleksei? You aren't going to expect us to ride in a box, are you?"

"I would never make you ride in a box." Francine wrapped her arm around the other woman and hugged her. "Well, except when we do this rescue thing. But you'll be standing up."

"Ha-ha, very funny. And I got dibs on the back seat. Someone else can ride in the box."

They climbed the ramp into the cargo bay. Fyo and Aleksei stood by the *soldaty* cube.

"What do you mean you've never done this before?" Fyo asked. "You're *soldaty*. You ride in these things all the time!"

"Exactly." Aleksei poked a thumb at himself. "I ride inside. I've never been the guy out here pushing the buttons." He looked at Francine. "Have you, *Ledi* Faina?"

"Aleksei, I've asked you before," Francine said. "Please don't call me that."

"I'm sorry, *Ledi* Francine."

"Don't call me that either. Just Francine. Dusica isn't here to chew you out. And no, I've never started the waking process either. The squad leader always stayed awake when we traveled. It can't be that hard, though, right?" She pushed her brother out of the way and looked at the panel. "They wrote it in Old Russoskeni? Idiots."

She read through the directions, sounding out a couple of words. "I think it says press the green button. Or maybe it says never press the green button. But it's green, so..." She tapped the green rectangle on the screen.

Nothing happened.

She pressed it again, harder and longer. The screen flashed. "Now it says the process will take...either ten years or ten yams. No wait, I think that's ten minutes. I guess we'll see."

The cube rumbled and clicked loudly. The door on the end popped open, and a small cloud of vapor poofed out.

They all took a few steps back.

"IT'S BEEN FIFTEEN MINUTES," Fyo said. "Maybe we should call Dusica."

"We can't call anyone." Francine stared at the huge, white Russosken transport cube. "That would give away our position. These things are supposed to be fool-proof. They drop them out of transports with automatic timers! I'm going inside." She started forward.

Marielle blocked her way. "No. You stay here. I will go. Aleksei, back me up." She disappeared into the box. Aleksi stepped through the hatch to cover her.

"Clear!" Marielle's voice rang out. A few seconds later, she returned. "They're awake. They're putting on their armor. That takes time." She stepped over the high threshold.

A few minutes later, the *soldaty* filed out. They marched into the cargo bay and formed up into a neat array, four wide and five deep. The one on the corner stepped forward. "I am *Karpral* Vladimir Jones, leader of this platoon." He thumped his hand to his chest and bowed to Fyo and Francine. "At your service, *Voz'y Nachal'nik*."

CHAPTER 32

TONY STRODE out of the stairway and turned right, keeping his eyes straight ahead. If Sashelle's strange mind-bending skills were going to work, he needed to move as if he belonged here. The caat padded along at his side, with Quinn a couple of steps behind.

The corridors here were wider with high ceilings and thick rugs. Ornamental tables stood against the wall here and there, holding vases and sculptures. Tony had worked in Headquarters Strategic for four years, and he didn't remember it being this opulent.

A man approached from the opposite direction. Tony tucked his head, eyes on an invisible comtab. Sashelle had said the key to her illusion was not breaking the observers' expectations. Tony marched on, as if he had a meeting to attend and was running late.

It seemed to be working. No one tried to stop them, despite their grungy beige prison coveralls and soft slippers. Every second, Tony expected to hear someone yell "halt," but it didn't happen. They turned a corner down a slightly narrower corridor. This one had no carpet, no side tables. In fact, it looked more like the building he remembered. And at the end of the hallway was a blank metal door and an exit sign.

He forced himself to maintain an even pace, even though every fiber in his body longed to break into a run. He glanced over his shoulder to check on Quinn, making eye contact for a brief second. Her lips twitched into a tiny smile. They were going to make it.

"Hey! Who— Stop them!" a voice behind yelled.

"*Futz*. Run!" Tony sprinted for the door. He flung it open and turned to make sure Quinn was with him. She crashed into him, her body seizing as a stunner hit her. Tony caught her in his arms, trying to cushion her fall. Then his shackles locked up, and she slipped away. A stunner zinged, and he went out.

QUINN WINCED as Tony thudded to the floor. His face was slack, eyes wide and staring. She bit back a cry—he couldn't be dead. She tried to move, but the shackles held her in place. When his chest rose, she closed her eyes in relief. She tried to open her mouth, but her jaw wouldn't move.

"The boss wants that one out," a voice said from behind. "Hit him again if you need to."

"Yes, sir." A soldier stepped over her, leaning over Tony.

Someone grabbed her arms, wrenching her shoulders painfully as they dragged her away, backward, her feet bouncing along the floor behind. She watched Tony as long as she could, but her head bobbed uncontrollably, making it difficult to focus. Then they rounded a corner.

A door opened, and she was dragged through a large room with marble floors and thick drapes. Two men and a woman sat at desks near the door, working on screens and talking on comtabs. As she passed, one of the men glanced up. Tenlos. She pinned him with a pleading look, but he looked away.

Another door opened, and she was dropped on a thick, patterned carpet. The two men who had been dragging her turned and left.

"How nice to see you, Mrs. LaRaine." She knew that voice, and it curdled her blood. Andretti.

The man came into view, looming over her. She ground her teeth. Her lip quirked a bit as she realized she could move her jaw, but she didn't reply. This snake didn't deserve so much as a swear word. She let her eyes drift toward the ceiling, blurring his face as he leaned over her. Focus on the horizon, just like in the academy. She almost laughed, remembering the ritual exchange.

What color is the horizon?

It's blue! Space Force blue!

But this man was Space Force, too. She shuddered. Andretti tainted everything.

Andretti's leg moved, and his foot slammed into her ribs, pain spiking through her body. She gritted her teeth, not willing to cry out.

"Why must you keep showing up?" Andretti kicked her again.

She gasped this time, and he grinned. "Don't you know when to die?" He leaned over and something smacked her across the face. Her cheek and jaw exploded with pain, and the coppery taste of blood hit her tongue. Her eyes blurred with tears.

Andretti straightened, slapping something against his palm. "Not so fierce now, are you?"

As her eyes cleared, she recognized the small ceremonial club in his hands. Decades before, when he'd been a cadet, there had been a secret society at the academy. It had been shut down due to violent hazing. Andretti had always displayed the Zeretti Plain Drifters baton on his office wall, proud of his membership in that disreputable group.

At least, she'd always assumed it was pride. Now she knew he used the thing for torture, too.

Andretti grinned, and she realized she'd let her eyes follow his movement. She'd heard stories of people surviving torture, but she'd had little training in how to do it. Luckily, it didn't matter what she said. She had no secret information he could beat out of her. She focused on the horizon again.

I can help you, Sashelle said.

How? Can you get me out?

I don't think so. I'm still in the building. She sent an image of a small, enclosed space.

Are you under a desk?

Supply closet. I'm on a high shelf. I wasn't able to follow you. Too many alert people looking for unusual activity, so I hid.

How can you help me with torture? Quinn asked.

I just did, the caat said smugly.

An ache spread through Quinn's cheek and eye, but muted, overlaying the pain from the first hit. She wasn't sure, but she thought Andretti had hit her again. Somehow, Sashelle had dulled the pain.

"Premier," Tenlos's voice said from the doorway. "I have those reports you wanted."

"This is pointless anyway." Andretti stomped away. "She's useless. I don't know why she won't die and leave me in peace."

I guess I've been haunting him, Quinn thought.

That's what happens when you obsess over someone. They control you.

Andretti kept muttering, his voice getting lower as he moved across the huge room. *Is he mad that I didn't yell?*

He enjoys others' pain, Sashelle said. *I can feel it coming off him in waves. The desire to prove his superiority by hurting others. You aren't responding as he expected, and that makes him angry.*

Doesn't that make him more violent?

The man is distracting him, Sashelle said. *I'm working on him, too.*

Quinn lay on the floor, staring at the ceiling, letting the pain wash through her. She used the breathing techniques she'd learned in childbirth classes to push the burning ache through and away, tuning out Andretti's muttering argument with Tenlos.

A door opened, snapping Quinn out of her semi-trance.

"Take her to the cells." Andretti sounded defeated and a bit confused.

Quinn smiled a little, wincing as her lip split a little more. *Sashelle, you are amazing.*

I know.

DAREEN FLEW the Pulsar across the sand. The ocean crashed and hissed off to their right. On the left, high dunes blocked their view of a highway.

"This is boring," Fyo muttered.

"Believe me, little boy, in combat, boring is the good part," Marielle said from the rear seat.

"Don't call me little boy!" Fyo cried, sounding even more childish.

"Why don't you fly?" Dareen offered him the controls.

"Even flying is boring here." Fyo crossed his arms. "It's straight and flat. I'll fly when we get to the base."

"I don't think so." Francine sat beside Marielle in the rear-facing seat. Beyond them, the cobbled-together metal box held *Karpral* Jones and his nineteen *soldaty*. Lou, End, Kert, and Stene had stayed with the ship so they could swoop to the rescue when needed. "This thing might have stealth tech, but that doesn't keep us from running into things."

"Are you saying I'm a bad pilot?" Fyo demanded.

"I'm saying the base is very busy and will require a lot of skill to keep from hitting anything."

"I thought that's why we're going in at night," Fyo protested.

"I'm not sure it makes a lot of difference," Marielle said. "My contacts here tell me the base has been busy at all hours."

Three heads snapped her direction. "You've been in contact with people on the base?!" Francine asked.

"Watch where you're driving," Marielle said over her shoulder at Dareen. She turned back to Francine. "I have contacts in the Secret Service. I contacted them when we jumped into the system, through triple-routed and encrypted message. They're the ones who told us Andretti would be at Florenz instead of Romara. How did you think I knew that?"

"I dunno," Francine answered. "I guess I thought Lou— Never mind. What else did they tell you."

"Not a lot." Marielle glanced at the *soldaty*. "Many of them have been arrested. Anyone who tried to protect Premier Li or Admiral Corvair-Addison was killed or jailed. Those who remain are either loyal to Andretti or in hiding, waiting for a chance to take back the Federation."

"Will they help us?" Francine asked.

"Shouldn't we have discussed all this before we left the ship?" Dareen muttered.

"I don't know if any of them are in a position to help us," Marielle said. "If we start something big enough, they'll jump in. But our mission is not to overthrow the government, it's to rescue Tony and Quinn."

"You don't know Tony very well," Dareen said. "If you rescue him, he's not going to come home with us. He's been working toward revolution for too long. He'll grab this opportunity and exploit it as far as he can. At a minimum, he's going to want to take down Andretti."

CHAPTER 33

HARD SURFACE. Cold. Tony lay on a floor or bench or hard bunk. Soft voices murmured somewhere beyond his feet. Scents of citrus and floral tickled his nose. He cracked his eyelids a bare slit, hoping no one would notice.

He lay on the marble floor in one of the huge executive offices of the Headquarters Strategic building. He wasn't sure which one, but probably the commander's. If he remembered correctly, there was a bank of windows to his left. Outside, a ten-meter drop to the ground. Even if he could make it out the windows, the fall would likely kill him in this state.

Sashelle, he thought. *Did they get you too? Where's Quinn?*

The caat didn't answer. That was not good.

His eyes slid to the left and widened involuntarily. A line of soldiers stood in front of the windows, silent and unmoving, with every eye trained on him. Figuring escape was out of the question, for now, he sat up.

"So nice of you to join us, Mr. Bergen."

He rolled to his feet and turned to face Admiral Andretti. "Do you practice your evil villain clichés in front of a mirror?"

Andretti looked blank for a second—his puffy face going slack—and then he glared. "How did you get out of your cell?"

"One of your guys must have left a key. Where's Quinn?" Tony glanced at the huge crystal chandelier hanging from the center of the room, then at the soldiers by the wall. "What's with the audience?"

"Obviously leaving you unsupervised was a very bad idea," Andretti said. "I wanted to talk to you before the execution, so I had them bring you here."

"Your office?" He looked at the enormous desk, the plush leather furniture grouped around an empty fireplace, and the thick drapes behind the soldiers. "Not bad, but hardly the Executive Palace."

"It's better than the palace." Andretti spread his arms wide. "I'm a smart man, a very smart man. I'm staying here, in my power base. Taking over a government can make some people a little unhappy."

"And others a little bit dead. Where's Quinn?"

"Templeton is locked in a cell where she belongs. Where you belong too, but only until you're both in the ground. Or maybe I'll put your heads on pikes. Isn't that what they used to do in the good old days? Heads on pikes. Very intimidating. I would have made a very good dictator."

"Would have?" Tony crossed his arms. "What do you want? I don't have all day."

"You have exactly as much time as I give you." Andretti moved to his desk. "I have a signed execution order right here." He lifted a thick sheet of paper and dropped it back onto the desk.

Tony could barely make out his name in the swirling calligraphy. "Very pretty, but I don't think it's mine."

"It's yours if I say it's yours. I'm a busy man, so stop wasting my time, Berger."

"There you go again. You've got the wrong guy. My name isn't Berger."

"Of course it isn't. You're a spy. That's your cover. It doesn't matter, because that's the name you used here in the Federation. I have you here. I can do anything I want to you."

"Do you want to know my real name?" Tony asked.

"Why would I care? I told you, your name doesn't matter."

"You might care, if you knew what it was." Tony faked a lazy smile. Maybe if he stalled long enough, Sashelle could give him a hand. *Sashelle? Are you there?*

Nothing.

"I don't care." Andretti slid a hand over his terrible haircut. "What is it?"

"Never mind," Tony said. "What did you want? You said you needed my help?"

"I didn't say that."

"Yes, you did. You had them bring me here because you wanted to speak to me."

"I am a very busy man," Andretti said. "I don't have time to talk to every spy who gets arrested."

"Fine, I'll go back to my cell." Tony headed for the door. "Let me know when you're ready to talk." He reached out to grab the doorknob when one of the more alert soldiers stepped in the way. Tony's hand banged into the man's armor. "Sorry, didn't see you there."

The soldier stared impassively at Tony.

"Bring him back here!" Andretti yelled. "You can't walk out! You're a prisoner. This is my building, my planet, my nation. You have to do what I say."

"No, I don't." Tony sat on the couch by the fireplace. Toying with Andretti was fun, but a bit of a tightrope walk. The man might have him shot.

"Bring him over here!" Andretti said again.

The soldier yanked Tony off the couch, nearly dislocating his shoulder. Tony bit his tongue, drawing blood, but swallowed the yelp. He wouldn't give this bully the satisfaction of knowing the soldier had hurt him.

"I can have you flogged, you know." Andretti licked his thick lips. "I have the best floggers."

"I'm not a Federation soldier, so you can't," Tony said. "The

Athenos Convention has rules for prisoners of war, and you can't have them flogged."

"You aren't a prisoner of war." Spittle flew from Andretti's mouth. "You're a spy. The Athenos Convention doesn't apply to you. I had my lawyers check. They're very good at what they do. I pay a lot of credits for the best."

"Fine, you're right." Tony glanced at the soldier. "I'm not in uniform, so I'm not an enemy combatant. But the Commonwealth will be unhappy with you if you torture one of their citizens. That would look bad. Not a great way to start out if you want to be taken seriously on the galactic stage." He glanced at the soldier who had returned to his post by the window. Something caught his eye beyond them. *Sashelle, is that you?*

Still no answer.

"You'd be better off to trade me back to the Commonwealth." Tony smiled at the premier. "You could probably get two or three spies in exchange for me. Even more, if you throw in Quinn. They love her there."

Andretti's eyes narrowed. "That is not going to happen. She should have died on Sumpter. I'm going to make sure it happens this time." He slammed his hand on the desk. "Take him to the high-security cells."

The soldier hurried across the room and grabbed Tony's arm again.

Tony resisted his pull. "I thought you wanted to talk to me?"

"I've had enough of you," Andretti said. "I'm a very busy man. Very powerful. I don't have time for you."

Tony followed the soldier out. "He's a very busy man," he muttered to the soldier.

"Very powerful," the soldier said.

Tony's head snapped around. A potential ally? Or a sycophant?

The other man ignored him.

They left the opulent office and went through a door at the end of the hallway. It looked like every other door on this floor—thick, polished wood with scrollwork around the edges. The other side was solid metal, black and scarred. They entered a stark cement stairwell, with open tread-steps leading up and down. The soldier pushed Tony down the steps. He flailed at the railing, barely grabbing it in time to arrest his fall. Definitely not an ally.

They went down two flights and out another scarred black door. This part of the basement bore little resemblance to the narrow, dingy hallways they'd traversed earlier. The soldier pushed him along the wide, white hallway, stopping at another black door. It opened, revealing a modern cell with a clear front and a high-tech lock. And a woman drooping the bench inside.

"Quinn!" Tony yanked his arm out of the soldier's grasp and ran across the room to the cell. Quinn sat inside, nursing a swollen lip and black eye. "What happened?"

"It's nothing," Quinn winced as she jumped up. "Are you okay?"

"I'm fine." Tony pressed his hands against the glass. "It doesn't look like nothing."

"Stay away from the window." The man who'd brought him in pushed him to the back of the room.

Beside the door, an armed guard sat behind a tall desk. "Where's this one going? I'm outta blocks."

The soldier who'd brought him down nodded at the guard. "Put him in with her. Open it up."

"We need more cells," the guard muttered. "It's not smart to put them together. Who knows depravity they'll get up to?" He waggled his eyebrows in a sickening way. "Keep an eye on her while I open the glass."

Tony caught Quinn's eye. He glanced at the soldier standing near the transparent panel and nodded slightly. Quinn's lips turned up on the uninjured side, and she returned his nod. Tony eased closer to the man by the controls.

The guard swiped his card through a reader and slapped his hand on the access panel. The cell's clear front whooshed up into the ceiling. Tony launched himself at the guard controlling the door. He slammed the man's head against the wall and gave him a couple of swift jabs to the gut. The guard doubled over. Tony yanked his weapon from the holster on the guard's belt.

"Bio-lock!" Quinn screeched.

Tony tossed the useless weapon aside and pressed his forearm against the man's neck, shoving him into the wall. The guard's hands scrabbled at Tony's face. Tony pushed harder, turning his head away from the man's reaching fingers. They tangled in his hair and yanked. Using his free hand, Tony pinned the man's dominant arm to the wall and kneed him in the groin.

The man grabbed Tony's arm, trying to push it away. Tony grinned and waited. The man slumped, his legs collapsing beneath him. Tony let him slide to the floor, then grabbed a pair of restraints and slapped them onto the man's wrists.

It felt like it had taken forever, but Tony knew from experience that very little time had passed. He spun around to help Quinn.

She clung to the soldier's back, her arm wrapped around his neck in a chokehold. As Tony watched, the man collapsed on the floor, out cold. Quinn released her choke hold and dug in the man's belt pouches for restraints. She locked them on and rolled the man farther into the cell. Her swollen lip had split, and her hair stuck to her sweaty face. Tony thought she'd never looked more beautiful.

Quinn pushed her hair out of her eyes, wincing when her hand brushed against her bruised face. "What are you staring at?"

"You." He took her hand. "You're amazing."

"You're not so bad yourself."

"I am going to kiss you now," Tony said. "Very carefully, so I don't hurt your lip, but don't take that for a lack of passion." He pulled her close.

Quinn laughed and winced again. "I appreciate your concern."

He kissed her gently, reveling in the feel of her body against his. She pressed herself closer, and he lost track of time. Then he heard her soft whimper and pulled away. "Are you okay? Did Andretti do this?"

"Of course. It could have been worse." She kissed him again, quickly. "Much as I would love to spend the rest of my life kissing you, I think we have work to do."

"The rest of your life?" Tony grinned. "That's the second time you've said that. I'm going to hold you to it."

CHAPTER 34

TONY LIFTED the guard's shoulders to wrestle him into the cell.

"Don't." Quinn touched his arm. "We need him to get the others out."

"Good call. Wait. Others?"

"There are a bunch of people in here." She slid behind the guard's desk. "Grab his card. I'll show you."

Tony tossed her the card, and she swiped it through the reader. Tony heaved the man up and pressed his hand against the access panel. A menu appeared. Quinn stared down at it, then started swiping.

"How did you know the weapons were bio-locked?" Tony crossed the room to the weapon he'd tossed away.

"I worked on the final prototype contract when I was at DRiP," Quinn said, referring to the Defense Research Program. "They have a distinctive shape." She pointed at the bulge on the stock where the user's thumb rested.

"Is there any way we can use these?" Tony picked up the two weapons.

"I don't know. But one of these folks might." She pressed a button and made a flourishing gesture toward the cell.

With a grinding noise, the clear-fronted cell holding Tony's soldier slid into a wall. Another cell slid forward into the place the first had vacated. Two men dressed in suits looked up in surprise when the door opened.

"Name, rank, and serial number," Tony said.

"What?" The men exchanged a confused look.

"This is Jorgen Adeyemi and Payam Tuati," Quinn read off the access screen. "They're Secret Service."

"Who are you?" The taller man stepped warily out of the cell. His companion moved behind him, sliding toward the door.

"Stop right there." Tony pointed the useless weapon at him. "Which side are you on?"

"We were locked up in Andretti's dissident storage facility," the tall one said. "Which side do you think we're on? And that gun is useless."

"Fair enough. Do you know how to make them work?" Tony held out the weapon, handle first, to the shorter man trying to flank him.

The guy grunted. "I'm Adeyemi. This is Tuati. We were security for Premier Li. Fairly far down the ranks. Everyone above us was executed."

"I'm sorry to hear that," Quinn said. "I'm Quinn Templeton."

"The traitor?" Confusion then understanding crossed over Adeyemi's face. "Wait. Andretti's the one who had you convicted." He glanced at his partner.

Tuati nodded. "That changes things. What'd you do, serve his coffee wrong?"

Quinn crossed her arms over her chest. "I don't serve coffee. We escaped from Fort Sumpter after he left us there to die, and we brought a bunch of people with us. Including his most recent ex-wife."

Tuati snapped his fingers. "It's making sense now. What's the plan?"

Quinn glanced at Tony. "We're going to get the rest of the prisoners out. And then we're going to raid the armory, and we're going to take Andretti down." She tapped the display and rotated the cell block again.

"I thought we were going to escape." Tony chuckled.

"We have friends now." Quinn waved at the two men.

"Do you know who's in here?" Tuati asked. "Are you sure they'll be any help?"

"We'll take anyone we can get," Tony said.

When they'd finished emptying the cells, twenty-three men and six women stood before them. Most of them were Secret Service, with a few scientists and military personnel thrown in. All bore bruises and two had broken bones.

"Wend!" Tony cried as Tuati helped a woman with a broken leg out of a cell. "I'm amazed you're alive."

"You and me both," Wend said.

"We need to find a medical station," Quinn said. "Those two will be a liability."

"Agreed," Tony said a little sadly. "Wend would be a real asset if she were healthy." He nodded at a shorter man loitering near the back of the room. "That one makes me a little twitchy."

"Twitchy?" Quinn asked.

"I trust my instincts. Ninety-five percent of the time, they're right. He's going to be a problem." He caught Adeyemi's eye and beckoned him over. "What do you know about our short friend near the back?"

Adeyemi looked the man over. His eyes widened a fraction. "That's Carson Zuniga. He needs to go back into a cell. He was in here before Andretti took over. Krimson spy."

Quinn glanced at Tony, and he shook his head.

Adeyemi noticed the movement. "You think I'm wrong?"

"About locking him up?" Tony asked. "No. About him being a Krimson spy? I'm not convinced on that one."

"Because *you* are one," Adeyemi said, his tone wondering. "You really are a Krimson spy. That wasn't a ploy of Andretti's."

Tony gripped Adeyemi's arm. "Do you want to get rid of

Andretti? Because I can do that. But if you're going to throw around accusations and turn this group against me instead of him, we'll all end up locked in those cells again. Focus on the mission. Discussions of my past can wait."

Adeyemi looked Tony up and down. After a few seconds, he nodded. "You're right. First priority is Andretti. Everything after that can wait. I'll put Zuniga where he belongs." He nodded again, then caught Tuati's eye and jerked his head. They circled through the crowd, closing in on the short man.

"Maybe we should put Adeyemi back into a box," Quinn whispered. "As soon as we take down Andretti, he's going to be all over you."

"Then I won't be where he can reach me." Tony shrugged. "Don't worry, I've outwitted smarter agents than him before."

"You owe me forever." Quinn propped her fists on her hips. "You'd better not get yourself locked up or killed, because I expect you to come through."

Tony leaned in and kissed the undamaged side of her mouth, hard and quick. "Don't worry, I always come through."

DAREEN TURNED THE PULSAR INLAND, weaving through the dunes. "We're coming within sight of the base in a few minutes. Fyo, hit the stealth."

Fyo opened the case bolted to the once-sleek dash and pressed the activation button.

Buzzing vibrated through Dareen's jaw. "Just like last time. I thought the shielding would stop that."

"You mean the sound?" Fyo rubbed behind his ear. "Is that normal?"

"That's what it did when we tried it this morning," Marielle said. "I thought that was part of the deal."

"It is," Dareen said. "I mean, that's what it did before. But I never noticed it when the *Peregrine* was flying in stealth mode."

"We were a lot farther from the generator," Francine said. "And the ship's systems might have dampened it or shielded whatever is causing that."

"Yeah, but that's the problem," Dareen said. "The ship protected us from the device. How do we know those weird neurological effects aren't going to happen?"

"I guess we don't," Francine said. "Keep an eye on each other, and if anyone does something stupid, we'll try to stop them."

"If we're not too stupid ourselves," Dareen muttered. "What about the *soldaty*?"

Francine looked back at the twenty men standing in the box bolted to the back of the pulsar. "They're probably protected by their helmets. Maybe we should put tinfoil on our heads."

Dareen laughed. "That would look excellent. We're approaching Florenz now. I guess we'll see if this thing works."

She increased altitude as they approached the base. The wide sand dunes had given way to scrubby grass and marshy meadows. Ahead a four-meter-high fence surrounded an airfield. Bright lights illuminated everything inside the fence. In the distance, buildings crouched alongside the tarmac, and a huge, castle-like structure stood beyond them.

"That's Headquarters Strategic." Marielle had loosened her seat restraints and was kneeling on the seat to face forward.

"You should buckle up," Dareen said. "If the stealth tech doesn't work, it's going to get bumpy."

"If the stealth tech doesn't work, we'll be fried to a crisp before we can crash," Marielle said. "Base security includes a pulse field around the perimeter. If it's triggered, we're toast. Literally."

"*Futz!*" Dareen slowed the craft.

"What are you doing?" Francine demanded. "Keep going."

"I didn't do that!" Dareen lifted both hands. "Fyo?"

"I don't want to be toast!" Fyo cried.

"Don't worry," Francine said. "This tech will work. It's been tested extensively. It was made to work against Federation equipment."

"I thought it was made *by* the Federation," Fyo said. "Didn't Dareen bring it out of Lunesco for the Commonwealth?"

"Yes, exactly," Francine said. "It's Federation tech, so it'll work against their stuff. They don't want their secret agents getting fried when they come home."

Fyo thought for a moment, then the craft increased speed.

"And stop messing with the ship!" Dareen slapped at his hand. "You said you didn't want to drive!"

Marielle turned around and tightened her restraints. "It was made to work against Federation equipment? Who told you that?"

"No one." Francine shrugged. "It should work."

"On a spaceship, not a sports car. Spaceships don't have to fly through base perimeter defenses; they fly over."

"Good idea!' Francine said. "How high do the defenses go?"

"Too high for this ship with all that weight back there." Marielle sighed. "Keep your fingers crossed."

CHAPTER 35

TONY AND ADEYEMI stood in the middle of the room, with the freed prisoners ranged along one wall. Quinn stood behind the two men, near the cell controls, while Tuati guarded the door.

"We're going to divide into teams," Tony said. The released prisoners stood quietly, listening to him speak. Much better than the group on Varitas. "We'll send a small advance force to invade the armory. A second group is going to hit supply and get us some communications gear. The rest of us will hang back, watching the rear, until we get the equipment we need. Then we'll split into three groups. Adeyemi will take a team up the south stairwell. I'll bring another team up the north. The third group will climb up from the outside. That's the riskiest mission, and we'll only take it on if we can find stealth and climbing or lifting gear."

He looked at the group. "Anyone with climbing experience?" Several hands went up. "Great. You five will be the external assault team, following agent Tuati. Assuming we have gear, you'll climb up the outside and wait until we give a signal to come in. If we don't find the comms gear, we'll come up with a lower tech signal."

"Peters and Wend, you stay here," Adeyemi said. "There's a medical station behind the last cell. You can get patched up and we'll extract you if the mission fails. Make sure you're as mobile as possible."

"Keep an eye on Zuniga," Tony muttered to Wend, pointing toward the occupied cell at the front of the rotating bank. He glanced at Quinn. "I don't suppose you'd like to stay and help them?"

"Because I'm a woman?" she bristled.

"Because I've finally let you know how I feel, and I don't want you to get killed before…" He shrugged. "It's not fair to ask you that, but I don't want to lose you."

"That's sweet." Her tone clearly belied her words. "Maybe you should stay here, and I'll go beat the bad guys."

He held up his hands. "Forget I said anything. I knew it was stupid before the words left my mouth."

"And yet you said them anyway." She patted his cheek. "You're going to need all the help you can get."

"Fair enough," Tony agreed. "And you've become a formidable foe. The way you took down that guard…"

Tuati broke in. "You two lovebirds ready?"

"Let's go." Tony led the way. They crept out of the detention section and up the south stairs. At the top, they stopped. Tuati took a group of three specially trained operatives and ghosted into wing C. A few muffled thuds and grunts reached their ears inside the stairwell, and then the door opened again. Tuati and his crew dumped a pair of unconscious men on the floor and removed their weapons as well as their camouflage pants and jackets. Two men wearing prisoner coveralls hurriedly donned the uniforms.

"These are standard issue—no bio-locks." Tuati handed a blaster to Tony. "We generally save those for the folks guarding the highest-level politicians. That guard in the detention cell having one was a change in protocol. I guess Andretti is a bit paranoid." He laughed as he straightened his suit, pulling his jacket down over the pistol he'd removed from one soldier's belt. "If you can pick up a few more, they'll come in handy."

The four disappeared into the building.

Tony handed the blaster to Quinn. "Watch the stairs. I'm not too worried about the basement, but we could get traffic from above." He and Adeyemi moved into the hallway. Tony signaled for Adeyemi to check offices closer to the armory. He moved toward the lobby.

It was late. Most of the doors Tony checked were locked. One swung open when he turned the knob, but the lights were off. He pushed the door ajar, checking for occupants. Inside, he found a long overcoat hanging on a hook. He pulled it over his prison coverall and moved to the desk.

Ah. A small, pink pistol holstered to the underside of the desk. This one had no bio-lock—obviously a civilian model. He slid it into the coat pocket. A drawer netted a box of ammo.

He froze. Someone was moving quietly in the next room. He tiptoed over and pressed his ear to the door. Soft voices, then a moan and a grunt. He smothered a laugh. They were too busy to notice the outer office being ransacked. He wedged a doorstop under the door to keep them inside and let himself out of the office.

He checked a few more doors but didn't find any additional weapons.

"Halt!" Quinn stood just inside the door, blaster pointed at him.

"It's me," Tony said. "Where's the rest of the team?"

Quinn pointed. They sat on the steps leading to the basement. "We only have the one weapon, so I'm watching the upper levels and the door."

Tony showed her his pistol.

She grinned. "That looks deadly. Take the door, will you?"

A few minutes later, the door opened again. Quinn swung around, weapon aimed.

"It's me," Tuati said, staying out of view.

Tony leaned out far enough to see the other man, then waved him inside.

"We took the armory and supply. Got everything we need." Tuati grinned. "Come on, let's get you folks armed. Quinn, stay here and guard the rear." He handed a package to Tony. "Earbuds."

Tony took one and handed the package to Quinn. "Take one and pass them along."

Tuati peeked through the door, then whispered instructions. "Get your earbud in. Make sure you can hear Rahman. If you can, reply with your name and ten-by-ten. We'll get you a weapon."

Quinn stood in the doorway, watching, while Tuati checked each person's comm gear. Tony watched the stairwell. They sent small groups to the armory. "Walk as if you belong here," Tony told them. "If anyone questions you, take them out."

The armory groups came back, each person loaded with multiple weapons. A tall, thin man handed Tony a blast rifle and a stunner. "Tuati said you wanted these."

"Any problems?"

"Nope. Took out a pair of nosy parkers, but no problems."

Tony nodded. He hated killing innocents, but anyone working in this building under Andretti was part of the problem. He turned to the group. "Are we ready?"

CHAPTER 36

THE PULSAR SLID over the high fence onto Florenz Base. Nothing happened. No sirens, no lights, no death rays. Dareen sucked in a deep breath. "That was easy."

"Just the first step." Marielle leaned over her shoulder, pointing at a large, dark building sitting along the airstrip. "Take us down behind that hangar."

"That's a long way from the HQ," Fyo said.

"We can't risk getting any closer," Marielle said. "Have you seen this vehicle? It has 'low-rent revolution' written all over it."

"It's invisible," Dareen reminded her.

Marielle slapped her forehead. "With all that worry about setting off the pulse field, I forgot we're stealthed. I can't wrap my head around what it means. This is a gamechanger. I wonder if they can make individual units? This would be terrifying for the Service. Enemies we can't see?" She shuddered. "Get us as close to the building as you can without running into anyone."

Dareen bristled. "Hey, I'm a good pilot."

"Yeah, but if the other idiots can't see you, they could run into you," Marielle said.

Dareen nodded reluctantly.

"Luckily, there don't appear to be many people out and about." Fyo squinted through the front window.

"That's why we picked late night. Andretti enacted a curfew, even on base. Essential personnel only after seven," Marielle reminded him. "Pull right up to that back door. We'll be visible for a few seconds as we exit the vehicle and enter the building, but it's the best we can do. Francine." She turned around again. "How quickly can you hack into their security?"

Francine had been working quietly in the back seat. "I've connected and gotten through the first firewall, but I haven't found the surveillance system yet. I wish we had Quinn. This was her job when she worked here."

"If we had Quinn, we wouldn't need to rescue her," Marielle said. "And besides, she worked here ten years ago. Tech changes fast."

"I'm not sure this has changed much," Francine said. "That's one of the reasons I'm having trouble. This is old stuff. Before my time."

"Do your best," Marielle said. "We can physically disable any cams we see, but that will alert them. And newer cams are too small to find."

"I don't think you have to worry about newer," Francine said. "This stuff is ancient. Anything more current than my grandmother wouldn't work on this system."

Dareen snapped her fingers to get their attention. "We're coming up to the door. Do you want to talk to the guys in back?"

"Thanks for keeping us on task." Marielle bumped the back of Darren's shoulder. "*Karpral* Jones, we're almost there. Are your men ready?"

Dareen couldn't hear the response. Then Marielle said, "Excellent. We might need someone to open the door. We're working on security, but we're not there, yet." She gripped Dareen's shoulder again then pointed. "Once we're all out, take the ship behind that building. Wait for my signal."

"I don't want to wait with the ship," Dareen protested. "I want to come with you. I can shoot a blaster as well as anyone else."

"I've seen you in action," Marielle said. "You're getting better, but we have a squad of trained Russosken. Civilians will get in the way."

"What about Fyo and Francine?" Dareen demanded. "Why do they get to help?"

"Oh, they don't."

"What?" Francine cried.

"This is no job for a civilian. Did you really think Jones would let you come along?" Marielle asked. "You'd be a huge liability. All three of you will stay here. Aleksei and a pair of *soldaty* will stay with you. We need you to keep working on the security system. That's better done from somewhere relatively safe."

Francine growled. Fyo didn't say anything. Dareen glanced at him, and he didn't seem unhappy to be left behind.

"I'm the *nachal'nik*. I never thought they'd let me go inside. I'm thrilled they let me come this far. Aleksei wanted me to stay on the *Peregrine*."

"And you're okay with that?" Dareen had been developing a little crush on Fyo, but the warm fuzzies all turned to cold, wet cement. "You'll let other people do the hard work?"

"They've trained for this. I haven't. I have degrees in accounting and management, not stuff-breaking and people-killing." He shivered. "I know my shortcomings."

Dareen grimaced. "I've been going into dangerous situations my whole life. I don't see why I should stop now."

"Dangerous, yes." Marielle opened the back door. "But not combat. Leave this to us."

⊏⊐

END SAT at the comm station of the *Peregrine*, waiting to hear from his sister. It felt like hours, but a quick glance at the chrono indicated barely thirty minutes had passed. "They should be there by now."

Lou dozed in the command chair. When the comms pinged, she sat up with a grunt. "What is it?" Maybe she hadn't been asleep.

"It's Dareen." End swiped an icon and his sister's voice came through.

"I've delivered the package, and now I'm waiting."

"She doesn't sound happy," Lou commented.

"I'm not," Dareen said. "They're making me and Fyo and Francine wait in the car."

"You're the getaway driver," End said. "Of course you have to wait in the car."

"I suppose." She didn't sound any happier.

"Did Francine get the security system jammed?" End scrolled through the plan again.

"I dunno," Dareen said. "Francine, did you?"

Francine's voice sounded far away. "I've got it fritzing. Intermittent glitches everywhere—especially where our people are. But if anyone tries to fix it... Wait. No, it's okay. I have to stay on this."

"She's busy, but it's working," Dareen said. "Fyo is playing solitaire. Aleksei and a couple of the box *soldaty* are standing guard outside. I'm going to turn the cloak off because we're hidden, and I don't trust that thing."

"If anyone scans you with a heat sensor, they'll see you," Lou warned. "And the stealth tech is safe. The lab guys said so."

"It was safe on the ship," Dareen said flatly. "I don't trust Uncle Kert's cobbled-together temp installation."

"Leave it on," Lou said. "You're clearly not behaving irrationally."

"Fine," Dareen grumbled. "We need to keep the chatter down. Dareen out."

The signal cut before they could respond.

"She's taking that better than I'd hoped. Let me know when Amanda calls." Lou closed her eyes and tilted her chair back.

"Amanda?" End said. "She's calling us? Why?"

"She's running this whole revolution. Remember? This rescue will be a perfect distraction."

"You're using Tony as a distraction?" End's voice cracked a little. "That's pretty cold."

"I'm not doing anything that will put Tony in danger," Lou snapped, her eyes popping open. "At least, not any more danger than he's already in. But as soon as Andretti's folks notice the rescue attempt, Amanda's people will attack. Andretti will have to split his forces. That will help both of us."

"What if they don't notice?"

"Marielle will take care of that." Lou smiled a little. "She'll leave a couple of surprises behind."

"Do the rest of them know?"

"Why should they?" Lou sat up. "They'll get in the way. Marielle's a pro, and she's commanding the *soldaty*. She'll tell people what they need to know."

End rubbed his eyes. All this scheming made his head hurt. When this rescue was done, it was time to go back to Mom and Dad.

The comm system pinged. End checked the screen. "That's Amanda. At least, I think it is. The system doesn't recognize her."

"Put her on."

The dark-haired beauty appeared on screen. Today, she looked all business. Military business. She wore high-grade body armor, and her hair was pulled back in a thick braid. End grinned. She looked hot. Even hotter than usual.

"Lou, End. Nice to see you."

Lou grunted. "What's your status?"

"Right to business." Amanda jerked her chin down in approval. "Excellent. We're poised to attack at the first indication of disruption. So far, I haven't seen or heard anything. Are your assets in position?"

"Of course," Lou said. "And if you see a Pulsar with a big-ass chunk of metal glued to the back, don't shoot. That's Dareen."

"I hope she's staying out of the way," Amanda said. "If she gets between my troops and their objective, I can't promise her safety."

"She's stationed beyond this building." Lou flicked an image up on the screen. It showed a satellite image of the base with an arrow pointing to a small outbuilding. "They're tucked in behind."

"Roger, we see that building on our system," Amanda confirmed. "But there's no craft there."

"They're there," Lou said. "You can't see them."

"You got it?" Amanda's eyes grew wide. "The stealth tech?"

"I did." Lou grinned. "But you can't have it."

"Yeah, I know. Commonwealth property. Pretty hypocritical, if you ask me. You stole it from the Feds." Amanda shook her head.

"Steal your own," Lou replied. "Besides, our people fixed it."

Amanda held up a finger. "Hang on." She turned away, listening. "I gotta go. We've got activity." The screen went blank.

"Call your sister and tell her to keep her head down," Lou said. "Things are going to get loud."

CHAPTER 37

QUINN STOOD on the landing between the second and third floor. Tony and the rest of their team waited on the steps above. They had the shortest distance to cover of the three teams, so now they had to wait. If anyone came into the stairwell, they would be neutralized. Quinn hoped that was non-lethal, but she wasn't going to get in the way. Sometimes war required killing.

Sashelle, she called again. There was no answer. She'd been trying to locate the caat since Andretti had her thrown into that cell. The shielding in the newer detention facility might have blocked her thoughts, but the caat should be able to hear her from here.

"We're in position," Adeyemi said over the comms.

"We're in front of the building." Tuati's voice was clipped. "Damn spotlights. Lot of activity out here. Looks like they recalled some security people."

"How many?" Tony asked.

"I'd guess a couple units," Tuati said. "We can't lift as long as there are people out front. We'd be sitting ducks."

"Can you take out the lights?" Adeyemi asked.

"Of course, if you want to give away the surprise."

"We'll move in," Adeyemi said. "As soon as you hear fighting, kill the lights and come on up."

"Roger."

"On my mark," Tony said. "Three. Two. One. Mark."

He flung the door open, and the team surged through. Weapons fired. Quinn raced up the steps, pausing at the door. She peeked around the corner. Bodies sprawled in the hall, most of them enemy soldiers. The rest of her team crouched over the prone men and women, removing weapons and checking vitals.

"This one's still alive."

"Kill him."

"No." Tony tossed cuffs at the first speaker. "Restrain him. We'll lock them in this office." He pointed through an open door.

One of the younger men in their group looked at Quinn. "I haven't been in combat before." Sweat beaded his upper lip. "Not up close like this. I'm a scientist."

"You have to think of them as targets, not people," Quinn said. "You can't remember they're people until later. What's your name?"

"Rivers. Have you done this a lot?"

"I've been in a couple sticky situations lately. It's us or them. They won't hesitate to kill you, so you have to take them out first."

He nodded but looked uncertain.

"Look, if you're not sure about this, you shouldn't come," Quinn said. "We can't have a liability. And I don't want to drag you into something you aren't ready for. You could stand guard on the wounded."

"No," he said. "This is my future. I want to make it better. And having Andretti in command won't do that."

Quinn nodded. "Then let's go."

They made their way up the hallway, stepping around the casualties. As they passed the room Tony had indicated, Quinn looked in. Two injured men lay on the floor. Mo Aziz, a rotund scientist who'd insisted on coming along, sat on a desk chair, weapon pointed at an injured enemy. He clutched his other hand to his chest, his breath coming hard and fast.

Quinn checked his pulse. "Are you okay?"

"I'll be fine," Aziz said. "But better I stay here than get in the way." He jerked his head in the direction of Andretti's office.

"Go back and guard the prisoners." She hurried on.

They caught up with the rest of the team at a cross-corridor. Tony directed two men to take positions near the corner, one high and the other low. He counted down on his fingers, and they ducked out into the hall. Weapons whined, cries and thuds echoing weirdly in the wide space.

"Go!"

They raced across the hallway, bent low. Weapons sang out, and Rivers grunted. He sagged against the wall.

"Where are you hit?" Quinn asked.

"Just singed." He straightened and brushed at the burnt fabric of his sleeve. "The heat surprised me. I'm good."

They moved on. Around another corner. More firing. Two of their team went down. Quinn pressed her fingers against one man's neck. "He's dead." She picked up his weapon and handed it to Rivers, and they moved on again.

Run. Fire. Duck. Stop. Fire. Run. Check the wounded. It went on for what felt like hours. When they reached the door to Andretti's office, Quinn was shocked to see their numbers had dwindled to six. Four from their team and two from Adeyemi's.

"Can we take him out with only six?" Quinn asked.

"We've got Tuati's group outside," Tony said. "It's enough."

"We're in position," Adeyemi told Tuati.

"We've got more combatants incoming," Tuati replied. "I think they might be on our side, though. They shot the guards at the door."

"Amanda came through," Tony said. "Can we loop her into our comm?"

"How do you know it's Amanda?" Quinn squashed a stupid twinge of jealousy.

"Who else would it be?" Tony replied. "She's been prepping for this for months. We're creating a perfect distraction."

"Stop chatting, ladies," Adeyemi said. "On my mark. Three. Two—"

The door burst open. Tony, Quinn, Rivers, Adeyemi and the other two all fired. A man collapsed to the floor, jamming the door open.

"Now!" Adeyemi roared, lunging over the prone man.

They burst into the room.

The inner door snapped shut. Over her thudding heart, Quinn heard something heavy being dragged. "They're blocking the door!"

Adeyemi ran across the room. Beyond the heavy couch, a sheet of blue sparkles flared like a divider across the room. His body seized, and he fell to the floor.

"Force shield!" Tony said. "Herinton, Valiyev, watch the hall. We don't want him sneaking out another door."

"There isn't another door to the hall," Rivers said. "I've been in that office. There's no other exit."

"Watch the hall anyway," Tony said. "They could break through the wall."

"You've been in the director's office?" Quinn asked over her shoulder as she ran to Adeyemi. He lay on the floor, eyes open, breathing. "He's stunned." She grabbed his shoulders.

"I dated one of his executive officers for a while." Rivers grabbed Adeyemi's legs to help her move him. "You could say I got a private tour. While Andretti was gone, of course."

Tony tapped his earbud. "Tuati, Adeyemi is down. Where are you?"

"We just launched," Tuati said. "These are the slowest damn anti-grav lifters. We'll be at altitude in about three seconds."

"Hold," Tony said. "We can't get into the inner room. They've got a force shield, so if you go in, you'll be on your own."

"Roger." A flicker of movement drew their eyes to the windows.

Tuati waved from beyond the glass. "We can hover for about ten minutes, but if they get the spotlights back on, we're dead."

"Are they likely to get the spots on?" Tony ran to the windows.

"It would require replacing certain fragile parts, so probably not."

Tony opened a window, and the external assault team climbed in.

"You need another access to that office." Tuati jumped from the windowsill and hurried to check on Adeyemi. "We'll go back out if you can find another door. Pincer move."

"Can we break down a wall in the hallway?" Quinn asked. "They can't have force shields all around, can they?"

"Maybe, but it's worth a try," Tony said. "Tuati, you and your team wait here. Watch the door. When I signal, get your butts out that window and come in hot. We'll need the distraction. Quinn, Rivers, you're with me."

Tuati looked up from his former cellmate and gave a thumbs-up. "We'll keep them in."

Quinn followed Tony to the hallway, Rivers hot on their heels. The tall young man sprinted a few meters down the hall and tapped the wall. "Should be right here."

Tony eyed the wall, tapping in a couple places. "I haven't done a lot of demolition. I assume a shaped charge would do. Do we have any?"

Quinn shook her head. "We can burn through it with the blaster. Like we did at Dusica's house." She elbowed him aside and drew a rectangle on the wall with her finger. "They'll see us coming, though."

"They already know we're out here, so don't worry about that." Tony caressed her shoulder. "You get burning. We'll set up a perimeter." He sent Rivers and Herinton to the next cross-corridor, while he and Valiyev retraced their steps.

Quinn nodded and set to work.

CHAPTER 38

AMBASSADOR, a voice said inside Francine's head.

"Sashelle!" Francine cried.

"Sashelle?" Dareen chimed in. "Where is she?"

I'm inside the facility, Sashelle said. *The Purveyor and the Stealthy One are on the third floor, attacking a thug.*

"Are they okay?" Francine asked.

They are not dead; they are fighting, Sashelle said matter-of-factly. *It is the way. However, they may require your help.*

"What can I do?" Francine asked.

There is a blue fizzing wall, as at your litter-mate's den.

Sometimes translating the caat's comments required a little thought. "Oh, there's a force shield? Tell Quinn I'm in the security system. I'll see if I can turn it off."

The caat's presence faded from Francine's mind.

⸻

MARIELLE LED her *soldaty* assault team into the headquarters building. Amanda had teams attacking other targets tonight, and they'd dialed into her comm system. They'd gotten pinned down at the rear door but had eventually won through. Her team methodically cleared the ground floor, rounding up anyone who wasn't dead.

"Clear!" Jones yelled.

"Next floor!" Marielle called. "Kalisowsky, protect our six!"

"Yes, ma'am!"

She sent her squad to the next story while she dragged a prisoner to the door. Amanda's teams had set up a temporary holding pen in the parking lot behind the building. The force shield ran on an independent power supply, so no one inside the building could free the prisoners. Auntie B on Lunesco, also known as General Beatrix LaGama, had given Amanda some pointers on that.

Marielle handed the last prisoner over to Kalisowsky. "Get someone to take him out to the pen, then come back to guard this door." She headed for the stairs to rejoin her team

---

THE AMBASSADOR IS SHUTTING *down the fizzy blue.*

Sashelle's voice intruded on Quinn's mind. She shook her head to clear it, and the weapon in her hand joggled, marring her otherwise straight cut. "When?"

Predictably, the caat didn't answer.

"Tuati! Stay sharp," she called. "The force shield is going down! Not sure when."

"Roger." Nothing seemed to faze Tuati.

"Tony, Sashelle's getting into the mix," Quinn called through the comm. "Keep a sharp eye."

"We won't see her if she doesn't want to be seen," Tony said. "And I trust her to take care of herself."

"You'd better fall back." She shifted to the final cut. "Twenty more centimeters and I'll be in!"

"We're coming." Tony clattered down the hall, recalling the others as he went. "Tuati, you ready?"

"How sure are we this force shield is going down?" Tuati asked. "I can send my guys through the window."

"Sashelle, what's the timing on the blue fizzy?" Quinn yelled. Rivers, Valiyev, and Herinton gave her confused looks, but she ignored them. She juggled her quickly heating weapon from hand to hand, trying to keep the beam steady. "This thing is getting hot. Ten centimeters, Tuati."

Tony gestured for Valiyev and Herinton to take up places on each side of the cuts.

"Damn it, I need to know if I go around or through?" Tuati' voice finally took on an edge of frustration.

"Sashelle?" Quinn's beam burned steadily through the remaining wall, almost to her starting point.

Now.

"Now!" Quinn yelled.

"It's down!" Tuati called. At the same instant, Tony kicked the wall Quinn had been burning. A ripping, splintering crackled through the air, and the section fell inward.

Valiyev and Herinton leaned in from each side, peppering the room with pulses from their blasters. The door inside the room slammed open.

"Watch for friendlies!" Tony cried.

Bolts of energy sailed through the hole. Quinn dropped to her stomach, her blaster unwilling to fire after the abuse of cutting through the wall. She rolled away from the opening, coming to rest under a side table.

A vase above her head crashed to the ground mere centimeters from her nose. She grabbed the table and tipped it forward to provide cover.

The noise stopped.

"Come out with your hands on your heads!" Tony shouted.

Nothing happened.

"They're toast, boss," Tuati said. "Come on in."

Quinn straightened slowly, dust and debris falling from her

head and shoulders. She climbed over the table, her arms aching from holding the blaster steady. Her face began to throb, as if finally realizing she'd been beaten earlier today. She shuffled to the hole.

"Stop right there," an annoyingly familiar voice said behind her.

Quinn stopped, sighed, then slowly turned. "What do you want?"

Reggie stood in the hallway, backed by half-a-dozen Federation soldiers with weapons drawn.

"It's over, Reggie." Quinn started forward, but the soldiers lifted their weapons, pointing them at her head. She stopped. "Andretti is dead."

"No, he isn't," Tony said. "Quinn, come here."

Quinn gestured toward the hole in the wall.

Curiosity seemed to overcome revenge. "Go on," Reggie said. "Watch her, boys."

The soldiers at Reggie's back exchanged looks. Quinn nearly laughed at their expressions. She made eye contact with a soldier standing behind Reggie—a grizzled man with chief chevrons and a name badge that read Horgan. When he nodded, she climbed through the hole. Reggie and the soldiers followed.

Inside, smoke obscured much of the room. Blaster fire had damaged the walls and furnishings. Shards of glass hung from the window frames, and the wind licked into the room, swirling dust and smoke together. A section of the inner wall had been pulled away, revealing a narrow stairway.

"He's escaped." Tony knelt on the floor by the windows beside a body. "We should have known the coward had an escape route. Tuati and his men are on it."

Quinn crossed the room to Tony's side. Sven Harvard lay on the floor, his dark face pale, eyes closed. His chest rose slowly, and Tony held a bloody wad of fabric against his side. "See if you can find a first aid kit."

Someone handed her a box before she could move. She knelt on

Sven's other side and opened it. A moan drew her attention away. A man in uniform lay nearby, his breathing ragged. "That's Tenlos!"

"He's one of theirs, Quinn," Tony said. "He could have helped us, but he didn't."

"He's injured." Quinn pulled a device out of the med kit. "I won't leave him to suffer. I'll take care of Sven, too. Go get Andretti."

Tony looked at his friend. Quinn pulled Tony's hand away and placed the pressure healer against Sven's side. The device sealed over the wound.

"Go," she said. "Someone has to make sure he doesn't get away."

"I don't think Tuati would let that happen." Tony wiped his hands on his coveralls, leaving bloody smears. "But I'm sure he could use help."

"I got this," Quinn said. "Go."

Tony went.

MARIELLE HURRIED through the deserted ground floor. As she rounded a corner, the creaking of rusty hinges caught her attention. She turned, stepping behind an open door to peer down the wide hallway.

A section of the wall had pushed away. How had her team missed that hidden door? It swung toward her enough to let someone peek through the crack, but she couldn't see who. Or how many.

"Kalisowsky," she whispered into her comm. "Movement on the south corridor. I've got a concealed exit being opened. Sending coordinates." She swiped at the comtab strapped to her forearm.

"Sidorov and Vasiliev are near you," Kalisowsky said. "I've looped them in."

"Someone is trying to sneak out," Marielle said. "Door opens toward you."

"We're moving into place," Vasiliev said.

She caught a flicker of movement through the glass door at the far end of the hall. The hidden door beside her clicked shut. "*Futz*, they saw you. They've pulled back. Where are they going? Someone get a schematic with that passage on it!"

The exit at the end of the hall opened, and Sidorov and Vasiliev hurried in ducking to find cover. One turned over a table, while the other dashed behind another open door.

"Blueprints for this facility are classified," another voice said. "We knew the copies we got weren't reliable."

"Kalisowsky, to me." Marielle said. "Sidorov, Vasiliev, let's go." She switched channels and called the rest of her team upstairs. "Jones, stake out this corridor up there, too. This passage probably has a staircase and several exits. And we need something to detect hidden doorways!"

The door eased ajar again. The muzzle of a weapon stuck out. Sidorov and Vasiliev froze.

Marielle leapt forward, ramming into the door, catching the muzzle between it and the frame.

"Hey!" a voice yelled.

Marielle grabbed the muzzle and shoved it up. Vasiliev and Sidorov raced forward, positioning themselves around the door. "Hands up!" Marielle yelled.

The door slammed open, catching Marielle in the face and knocking her across the hall. Blaster fire rained out of the doorway. Vasiliev and Sidorov scrambled for cover.

A head peeked out. Marielle squinted through the smoke, ignoring her throbbing nose. The man wasn't wearing a helmet. In fact, he wore a creased suit and a stained shirt. "Identify yourself," she barked.

The man turned, weapon pointed at Marielle. "You are Russosken," he said in surprise.

"Yes and no." Marielle cleared the mirror setting on her helmet. "Working with Free Fed Revolutionaries. Who are you?"

"Tuati. Secret Service. Well, former Secret Service. Did Andretti come this way?"

"Is he kneeling here begging for his life?" Marielle asked. "No, he didn't."

"*Futz*, we lost him!" Tuati said.

"There's another stairway here!" a familiar voice called.

"Tony?" Marielle yelled.

"Marielle, is that you?" Tony stuck his head out. "Come on, he must have come this way." He disappeared into the dark.

CHAPTER 39

TONY LED the team down another stairway. This one ended in a scratched black door, similar to the doors they'd seen near Andretti's dungeon. Tony mentally slapped his forehead. Of course, Andretti had a secret passage to his dungeon. The man was a villain stereotype.

Tuati pushed past Tony. "Let us go first. We're trained for this."

"Don't be stupid." Marielle grabbed Tuati's shoulder. "We've got armor."

"I want Andretti alive," Tuati growled.

"So do a lot of people," Marielle said. "I'll take him however I can get him. Unless he has a tunnel out of this place, we've got him cornered. Amanda has people all over this base. Vasiliev, take point."

"A tunnel wouldn't surprise me at this point," Tuati muttered.

Marielle's team pushed forward, shuffling the rest of the group back up the steps. Tony was stuck on the landing where he couldn't see any action. Fair enough. His forte was spying, not running an assault team.

"Go!" Marielle cried. Light streamed into the stairwell as the door burst open, slamming against the wall. People shuffled forward, and Tony gained a few steps. Now he could see over the others' heads as Marielle's team cleared the basement corridor.

They fanned out, and Tuati's team filtered behind, moving both directions along the hallway. Tony followed at a slight distance, scanning the walls for additional hidden doors. He rubbed his ear, feeling a tickle inside.

Stealthy One.

Sashelle! Tony replied. *Where have you been?*

Helping. The caat sent a confusing sequence of images showing a blue force field, a run through a gray landscape, and a sleek racing craft that had been melted at the back.

Where are you now? Tony asked.

I am in the building, not far from you. I have something you might want.

What would that be?

Come and see.

"There's a cat down here," someone said.

"What's it doing?" Tony sprinted toward the voice. One of Tuati's men stopped him at a corner, checked both ways, then waved him on.

"Nothing." Tuati stood in the middle of the hall. Sashelle sat in a doorway. "But it won't let us clear this room. It's huge."

"That's Sashelle," Tony said. "She's a Hadriana caat. Their size is flexible."

Tuati gave him a funny look.

"I know where we are." Tony stuck his hand in his pocket and jungled the straightened paper clips. "This is Andretti's private dungeon. What did you want to show me, Sashelle?"

The caat dropped its jaw in a feline grin. *Look inside.*

Tony nodded to Tuati. "Let's see what she caught."

"What she caught?" Tuati said, disbelief written on his face. "Just get it out of the way. I don't want to shoot a dumb animal."

Sashelle's fur stood on end, and she arched her back, spitting.

"He doesn't know, Sashelle," Tony said. "Don't worry, we'll

educate him. Let them in." He grinned at Tuati as Sashelle paced away from the door, glaring. "She's probably smarter than you are. And she has something we want. At least that's what she said."

"She said?" Tuati shook his head. "Did anyone check you for head injuries?" Without waiting for a reply, he called in his team. "Clear this room. Use one of those toss-n-stuns our new friends gave us."

Tony and Sashelle moved back a few paces. "It's Andretti, right?" He tried to picture the man's face.

Of course.

"How'd you do it?"

The caat lifted a paw to groom herself. *I am a predator. I hunted. He was running, so I chased.*

Tuati yanked open the door, tossed in a canister, and slammed it shut.

Whoomp.

A few wisps of smoke filtered around the door. They waited, counting, then Tuati opened the door. Haze shimmered in the dim hallway lights.

"Lights are on the right." Tony had noted the switch location when the guards dumped them earlier.

Light spilled out into the dim corridor, changing the haze to fog. "Stay low," Tony reminded Tuati.

Tuati shot him a glare and bent double, leading his team inside with weapons drawn. A cheer went up. "We got him!"

QUINN CHECKED the screen on the pressure healer. It showed Sven's vital signs slowly moving toward green. She draped the thin trauma blanket over him and moved back to Tenlos. The air reeked of singed fabric and burning carpet.

"Quinn!" Reggie called.

"I'm busy, Reggie. Go away."

"Quinn Templeton, I arrest you in the name of the Federation under the authority of Premier Andretti."

"You and what army, Reggie?"

After ten seconds of blessed silence, she turned. Reggie stood near the hole in the wall. His squad of soldiers had deserted him. Most of them had ripped off their Federation unit patches and run. The remaining two—the grizzled chief and a master sergeant—had blasters trained on Reggie.

"It's over," Quinn said. "You lost. These men are smart enough to see the writing on the wall. Maybe you should follow their lead."

"You traitors!" Reggie howled at the men.

"Sir, you're gonna want to modulate your voice," the chief said. "The lady is right. Andretti's rule is over."

"Thank you, Chief Horgan," she said. "It's good to see you. I'm kind of surprised you're still alive."

"That makes two of us, ma'am."

"Horgan?" Reggie asked. "You know him? That name sounds familiar."

Quinn sighed. "Maybe because he was assigned to Sumpter with you. His wife, Cyn, was left behind with me. She helped us get the shuttle running. We couldn't have escaped without her." She turned back to the wounded.

"She's said the same of you, Ms. Templeton."

"How is it that everyone is on your side?" Reggie raved. "Everyone loves Quinn! What a great leader! Too bad she left the force! We wish she was back!"

"Sir, I'm gonna have to ask you again to modulate your voice," Horgan said. "I'm not gonna ask you a third time."

"What—" Reggie's voice cut off mid-rant.

Quinn looked up.

The muzzle of Horgan's weapon pressed against Reggie's throat. "I'll take him to another location."

"If anyone questions you, tell them I sent you. Or Tony Bergen," Quinn said. "And thanks."

"Quinn?" The whisper barely reached her ears.

She turned back to Sven, already forgetting Reggie's existence. "You'll be okay, Sven. I've got a pressure healer on you. Your vitals are going up."

"The kid," Sven whispered. "Tenlos."

Her eyes narrowed. "He could have helped us."

"He did," Sven said. "He saved my life. Dove in front of a blaster. He saved yours, too. He 'forgot' to set a guard when we arrived. Andretti was reaming him a new one when you attacked. And before that. He stopped Andretti from beating you to death."

She'd wondered at the time if Tenlos was trying to help. "How do you know?"

"I was in the anteroom when they dragged you in," Sven said. "Didn't you see me? In the corner?"

Quinn shook her head.

"After you went in, he told me he owed you. He was going to get you out. Poor kid was conflicted. 'I swore an oath,' he kept saying." Sven took a ragged breath.

Quinn's eyes moved to Tenlos. "I can respect that. It took me long enough to get over my own oath."

"Can you help him?"

"I'm going to try." She dragged the med kit closer to Tenlos and went to work.

TUATI DRAGGED Andretti's limp body out of the dungeon.

"Good place for him," Tony said. "I kind of love the idea of him cowering in that pit."

Tuati grimaced. "I've never seen a detention cell like that, except in the movies."

"It was his own personal sadist's paradise," Tony said. "I expect a lot of off-the-books prisoners have ended up in there over the last twelve years. He's treated StratCom as his own personal kingdom for a long time."

"Yeah, that secret stairway didn't get built in the last few days," Tuati agreed.

Amanda arrived, surrounded by FFR soldiers. "You got him! Is he dead?"

"No," Tuati said. "Although if you want to look the other way for a minute…"

"No," Amanda said. "Let's not start our new country using the old ways. We'll hold him and try him and execute him fairly."

"Sounds like you've already decided on his guilt." Tony hid a grin.

"Duh," Amanda said. "I said fair, not idiotic. Erickson, find somewhere to lock him up."

"I'll show you to the high-security cells," Tuati said. "I'm intimately familiar with them."

"Perfect." Amanda smiled. "We have medical personnel on the way. Either of you need a check?"

"I'm good," Tony said. "But Sven needs help. He's up in the commander's office. I'm going there now."

"I'll send them up as soon as they arrive." Amanda gestured to her soldiers. Two of them grabbed Andretti by the arms and dragged him down the hall.

CHAPTER 40

SEVERAL DAYS LATER, the *Swan of the Night* landed at Milana Field. It taxied off the runway and parked near the large hangar where the *Peregrine* lay hidden. Liz worked through the shutdown sequence and climbed out of her seat, stretching.

Maerk met her in the lounge. "Your mother is here."

They popped both ends of the airlock, letting the cool ocean breeze flow into the ship.

"What's that smell?" Ellianne's face wrinkled in disgust.

"That's the sea," Maerk said.

"Don't you remember?" Lucas said. "You were born here."

"I was two when we left," Ellianne said. "Do you remember being two?"

"If you don't stop arguing right now, I will lock you both in the cargo hold and you won't get off the ship." The tactic had worked on Maerk's own kids, why not someone else's?

"We'll behave." Ellianne made a zipping motion across her lips.

"Space scouts' honor." Lucas performed a jaunty salute.

"You two are too cute." Liz ruffled Lucas's hair. "Let's go see what kind of mayhem Tony's been up to."

Lucas grunted and smoothed his hair.

They jumped down the steps and started across the tarmac toward Fyo's shiny new Pulsar. Fyo and End leaned against the gleaming hood, grinning. Fyo said something to the woman who climbed out.

"Lucas! Ellianne!" Quinn raced to her children, throwing her arms around them. "I've missed you so much!"

While the little family greeted each other, Maerk and Liz joined End and Fyo.

"Good to see you, son." Maerk hugged End, slapping him on the back.

"You missed all the fun!" Fyo exclaimed.

Maerk gave the young Russosken a superior smirk. "So did you."

"Who told you that?"

"Dareen," they all said in chorus.

"We didn't miss *all* the fun," Fyo said. "At least we were here to watch. You were stuck babysitting."

"I'll be honest with you." Maerk clapped the younger man on the shoulder. "I've had enough fighting to last a lifetime. I prefer to 'miss the fun.' I'll live longer."

"I kind of miss it," Liz said. At the look on her ex-husband's face, she held up a hand. "I'm not looking for trouble. But a little excitement every now and then is a good thing."

"Maybe we can find some non-lethal excitement now that things have cooled down a bit," Maerk allowed. "I heard Amanda is running the show."

"True," Fyo said. "She's got people setting up elections, writing constitutions, all kinds of crazy stuff. She keeps saying she's 'only the interim president,' but Pete has started a campaign for her. And she hasn't told him to stop."

Quinn straightened up, keeping one arm around each child. "Let's go back to the HQ. You won't believe how much they've accomplished in the last five days."

"We only have room for four in this little beauty." Fyo ran a loving hand over the front fender of his new craft.

"That's why I asked Dareen to bring the other one," Quinn said.

The modified Pulsar zipped around the hangar and pulled to a stop. The door opened. "All aboard the Romara express!" Dareen sang as she climbed out. "First stop, Provisional Republic Headquarters."

"Dareen!" Ellianne screamed, throwing herself at the older girl.

Lucas gave a casual wave and climbed into the newer craft with Fyo and End.

"I guess that leaves you with us," Liz told Quinn.

Dareen released Ellianne and hugged her parents.

"I'm so proud of you!" Liz said.

"We both are." Maerk wrapped his arms around both of them.

"I didn't do anything," Dareen protested. "I sat in the getaway car."

"You got the team where they needed to go," Liz said. "There's no shame in providing support."

"And it's a heck of a lot safer," Quinn said. "Most of the time."

"Can we ride in the back?" Ellianne cried.

Quinn laughed. "Sure." She lifted her daughter over the side and deposited her in the troop box. Then she gave Dareen a look. "Keep the speed down."

Dareen winked. "Yes, ma'am."

THE TEAM GATHERED in Amanda's new office. The blood-stained carpet and furnishings destroyed in Andretti's capture had been replaced with simpler items from around the building. A huge conference table sat in the empty space where the last battle had burned. Amanda sat at the head of the table, with Pete and Sebi Maarteen on either side. Sven Harvard sat at the other end, with Adrian Tenlos on one side and Lou Marconi on the other.

As Quinn paused in the doorway, Tony came up behind her.

She turned and smiled. "There you are!" She threw her arms around him and kissed him soundly.

The room erupted in hoots, catcalls, and cheers.

Tony released her. "What are you people, five years old?"

"Finally," Francine said. "I'm so glad you two finally figured it out. Took you long enough."

"I had to wait a respectable period after her divorce."

Quinn laughed. "Is that what you were waiting for?"

"You could have made the first move," Tony reminded her.

"Next time." Quinn slapped his rear end. They all laughed.

"Before this degenerates into a free-for-all," Amanda said, "let's eat."

I hope it doesn't taste of SwifKlens, Sashelle said.

Francine met Quinn's eyes, and they both smiled at the caat's complaint.

Everyone took their seats, digging into the meal and talking about plans for the future.

"I'm going to apply to the academy," Dareen declared. "The Commonwealth Academy." She glanced at Amanda. "No offense."

Amanda's lips twisted wryly. "None taken. How about you, End? Are you academy-bound, too?"

"Hell, no," End declared. "With Dareen gone, Gramma's gonna need me."

"Don't flatter yourself," Lou growled. "I can find a new pilot."

"Adrian here is a pilot." Sven clapped Tenlos on the shoulder.

"You aren't staying with the Space Force?" Disappointment tinged Amanda's voice.

Tenlos cleared his throat. "I've thought about it. I'm halfway to retirement. If those years at the Federation even count?" He raised his eyebrows.

"That has yet to be decided." Sebi flourished his hand like a magician. "The Republic will evaluate each officer on their merits and decisions will be made."

"How's that for a non-answer?" Tony said under his breath.

"Right." Tenlos turned to Lou. "If you're looking for another pilot, I'd be honored to be given an opportunity to—"

"You're going to have to cut the long-winded speeches," Lou said. "I'll give you a try, but only because Sven and Tony put in a good word for you."

"You did?" Tenlos looked from Sven to Tony in surprise.

Both men nodded.

"Speaking of good words, Sebi—" Tony changed the subject. "What happened with that Russosken kid on Varitas?"

"Gavrie?" Sebi grimaced. "You were right about Orin. She was feeding information to the Russosken all along. *And* to the Federation. She was a triple agent. Or maybe quadruple. Once Gavrie exposed her, we got amnesty for him and his sister. They're living with *Ledi* Semenova now."

Tony laughed. "They might have been better off in prison with their father."

Maarteen chuckled. "You may be right. That woman is a tyrant. Edwin and Bart are going to have their hands full keeping her out of their business."

Maarteen and Tony spent the next few minutes recounting their visit to Varitas.

"What about the Zielinskys?" Amanda asked when the conversation lulled. "What mayhem are you two planning?"

Fyo sat up straight, lifting his chin. "I am the *nachal'nik*. I will take care of my people."

"And Marielle and I will help him." Francine smiled at her partner.

"Your people will be members of the Republic," Amanda objected.

"There's no reason we can't be both citizens of the Republic and Russosken," Aleksei said.

"As long as the Russosken doesn't plan to intimidate and charge for protection, you're right." Pete lifted his hand, pointing two fingers at his eyes, then at Fyo.

Fyo smirked.

Amanda stood and lifted a glass. "I'd like to propose a toast. To the new Republic!"

As they raised their glasses, Sven and Tony snickered.

"What?" Amanda demanded.

"The force is strong with this one," Sven muttered.

The two men broke into loud cackles.

"Enough!" Amanda cried. "I'm trying to make a speech here!" She glared at them until they settled down.

Who makes a speech at a family gathering? Sashelle scoffed.

Be nice, Quinn replied.

Hadriana caats don't do "nice."

Quinn chuckled. *You know, Sashelle, we couldn't have done this without you.*

I know, said the caat. *Don't forget your promise to me. You will give my people a say in how Hadriana is ruled.*

I will talk to Amanda before we leave, Quinn promised. *It will be a pleasure to take Hadriana away from the LaRaines and hand it over to you.*

As Amanda launched into her prepared speech, Quinn gazed around the table at the people most dear to her. Tony, Ellianne, and Lucas. Francine, Marielle, Fyo, and Aleksei. Dareen, Liz, Maerk, End, even Kert and Stene. And Sashelle, curled up on the windowsill, pretending to ignore them. They all had a place in her heart.

"Amanda sure can talk," Tony whispered in her ear.

"Perfect for a politician," Quinn replied.

"What about you? What's next for you?"

"You mean what's next for us? You promised me forever. Several times, remember?"

"Of course." Under the table, he squeezed her hand. "What's next for us?"

"Something exciting, I'm sure."

The End

THANK you so much for reading! I've already started working a Krimson Empire/Space Janitor/Colonial Explorer Corps crossover, so if you like any of those series, you'll want to join my newsletter and find out when that will be coming out!

If you haven't read any of those series, check them out on my website, juliahuni.com.

Thank you so much to those who supported the relaunch of this series through Kickstarter. Supporting authors you love helps us write more books!

Turn the page to read more about that, and see my other series.

And thanks for coming along on the ride.

AUTHOR NOTES

September 14, 2023

Thank you for reading the *Krimson Empire* series!

Don't go away—as I said I've begun work on a book that will tie this series into the rest of the *Huniverse*. And I'm writing a short story about Tony and Quinn meeting Triana and O'Neill (from my most popular series: Space Janitor.) I promised that to my kickstarter backers but it will be shared with my newsletter subscribers next year, so sign up before you forget!

If you enjoyed my story and haven't read any of my other books, they're available now—there' an "also by Julia Huni" page at the end of this book, or you can visit my website juliahuni.com.

If you'd like to keep up to date on what's going on with my writing, sign up here. Plus, you can download a short story about Sashelle. And at some point, you'll also have access to the Krimson Empire prequel I wrote for the campaign.

Thanks to the team who originally beta read this series: James Caplan, Kelly O'Donnell, John Ashmore, and especially Mickey

AUTHOR NOTES

Cocker, who has taken the hyper jump to the great library in the sky. We miss you, Mickey!

Thanks to Craig Martelle, who believed in this series and published it back in 2020. He has a massive backlog of books, a bazillion of which he wrote, and another crazillion he published for authors he wanted to help, so check them out.

Thanks so much to my amazing Kickstarter backers. I've listed your names on the next page. Without you, this relaunch would have been so much harder!

Thanks to my sprint team who virtually cheered me on as I edited this series and ran the campaign: AM Scott, Hillary Avis, Paula Lester, Marcus Alexander Hart, Kate Pickford, and Lou Cadle. They all write awesome books, too. Look the up when you get a chance!

And, of course, thanks to my family who keep me sane when the work starts making me crazy.

If you know anyone who'd like a copy of these books, please send them to juliahuni.com. I make a little more selling direct, and they'll save a little. Win-win!

And if you enjoy hopeful science fiction with heart and humor, check out my other series.

You can find me all over the inter webs.

Email: julia@juliahuni.com
Amazon https://www.amazon.com/stores/author/B07FMNHLK3
Bookbub https://www.bookbub.com/authors/julia-huni
Facebook https://www.facebook.com/Julia.Huni.Author/
Instagram https://www.instagram.com/Julia.Huni.Author/

Thanks to my fabulous Kickstarter supporters:

Alice Hickcox

AUTHOR NOTES

AM Scott
Andy fytczyk
Angelica Quiggle
B. Plaga
Barb Collishaw
Brenton Held
Bridget Horn
Buzz
C. Gockel
Carl Blakemore
Carl Walter
Carol Van Natta
Cate Dean
Chicomedallas123
Christian Meyer
Clark 'the dragon' Willis
Clive Green
Craig Shapcott
Daniel Nicholls
Danielle Menon
Dave Arrington
David Haskins
Debbie Adler
Diana Dupre
Don Bartenstein
Donna J. Berkley
E. C. Eklund
Edgar Middel
Elizabeth Chaldekas
Erudessa Gentian
fred oelrich
Gary Olsen
GhostCat
Ginger Booth

AUTHOR NOTES

Giovanni Colina
Greg Levick
Heiko Koenig
Hope Terrell
Ian Bannon
Isaac 'Will It Work' Dansicker
Jack Green
Jacquelin Baumann
Jade Paterson
James Parks
James Vink
Jane
Jeff
Jim Gotaas
John Idlor
John Listorti
John Wollenbecker
K. R. Stone
Karl Hakimian
Kate Harvey
Kate Sheeran Swed
Katy Board
Kevin Black
Klint Demetrio
Laura Rainbow Dragon
Laura Waggoner
Laury Hutt
Liliana E.
Luke Italiano
M. E. Grauel
Mandy
Marc Sangalli
Marie Devey
Mark Parish

AUTHOR NOTES

Martin
Mel
Michael Carter
Michael Ditlefsen
Michael L. Whitt
Michelle Ackerman
Michelle Hughes
Mick Buckley
Mike W.
Moe Naguib
Niall Gordon
Nik W
Norm Coots
Patrick Dempsey
Patrick Hay
Paul
Pauline Baird Jones
Peggy Hall
Peter Foote
Peter J.
Peter Warnock
Ranel Stephenson Capron
Regina Dowling
Rich Trieu
Robert D. Stewart
Robert Parker
Rodney Johnson
Roger M
Rosheen Halstead
Ross Bernheim
Sarah Heile
Sheryl A Knowles
Stephen Ballentine
Steve Huth

AUTHOR NOTES

Steven Whysong
Susan Nakaba
Sven Lugar
Ted
(The other) Ted
Ted M. Young
Terry Twyford
The Creative Fund by BackerKit
Thomas Monaghan
Timothy Greenshields
Tom Kam
Trent
Tricia Babinski
Valerie Fetsch
Vic Tapscott
walshjk
wayne
werelord
Wesley Dawes
William Andrew Campbell (WAC)
Wolf Pack Entertainment
Yvette

ALSO BY JULIA HUNI

Colonial Explorer Corps
The Earth Concurrence
The Grissom Contention
The Saha Declination
The Darenti Paradox

Recycled World
Recycled World
Reduced World

Space Janitor
The Vacuum of Space
The Dust of Kaku
The Trouble with Tinsel
Glitter in the Stars
Sweeping S'Ride
Orbital Operations (a prequel)

Tales of a Former Space Janitor
The Rings of Grissom
Planetary Spin Cycle
Waxing the Moon of Lewei
Changing the Speed of Light Bulbs

Friends of a Former Space Janitor

Dark Quasar Rising

Krimson Empire
Krimson Run
Krimson Spark
Krimson Surge
Krimson Flare

Julia also writes sweet, Earth-bound romantic comedy that won't steam your glasses under the name Lia Huni.

Printed in Great Britain
by Amazon